A Gypsy's Life Struggles

REJEANNE COUPAL

A Gypsy's Life Struggles

Cover designed by Eddie Vega.

Rejeanne Coupal Publishing RCP

Plattsburgh, NY 12901

ISBN-10: 0-9969756-0-8
ISBN-13: 978-0-9969756-0-5

A Gypsy's Life Struggles

Quietly endure, silently suffer and patiently wait."

   –Martin Luther King, Jr., *Why We Can't Wait*

"… people with nothing to declare carry the most."

   –Jonathan Safran Foer, *Extremely Loud and*

   Incredibly Close

"Never judge the life of another man. You never know his struggles."

   –Lailah Gifty Akita, *Beautiful Quotes*

CHAPTER 1

The gypsy way of life wasn't as carefree as onlookers thought it was. It was a painful, restricted, and very narrow existence. Persecution followed them everywhere, and it took many forms. Discrimination was always in their path, and banishment for them was an ongoing threat. They had to use their wits and wiles if they were to continue to exist.

Chovinne was thinking about just how difficult life was for gypsies, how she and the others were ostracized from society. It hurt and angered her, not to be accepted or respected for who she was, a nomadic person trying to co-exist in a harsh environment.

Her horse was cantering at an easy gait. It was a nice day to be out riding. She bent down and put her arms around his neck. She loved this horse; she had raised him almost single-handedly since he was a colt. It was evident even then that Reliant possessed a superior intellect. Within a very short time, she had trained him to perform many tasks on command.

Suddenly Reliant's body stiffened and he raised his head, all the while nervously sniffing at the air. Shaking herself out of her reverie, she became aware of an ominous sight in the distance. It was the distinct form of a person hanging from a tree. A uniform pressure of both legs against the horse's flanks spurred him into a gallop. Men who had been assembled under the tree swiftly rode away when they saw her riding towards them. Arriving closer to the figure, she hurriedly dismounted. As she approached, she saw, with disbelief, that the figure was her father. Chovinne took a few steps back to her horse and reached into her leather bag for a knife.

The knife shook in her hand. She had never known fear like this before. Her breath came in short, rapid gasps. She willed her trembling hands to be still. Supporting her father's body with her own she tried to cut the rope that was squeezing the life from his body. Chovinne noticed the knot on the rope was behind her father's head. In their haste to hang him, they had placed the knot on the right side of his neck, throwing his neck forward, allowing him to live by hanging on the rope. He was struggling to breathe. The rope was too tight. Her mind was racing. She must think of something. The only option left to her was to cut the rope above his head, hoping her strength would last. She severed the rope, and let the knife fall from her hand. She placed her arms around his waist and, gently, eased her father's body to the ground. Kneeling beside him, she squeezed her fingers between the rope and his neck. With a great effort she freed him from his suffocating torture, slowly eased the rope over his head, and laid it on the ground.

She didn't know how much damage the strangulation had done. His neck was so swollen and discolored from the tightness of the rope that she couldn't find a pulse point. She placed her fingers in front of his ears, here, she thought she detected a very feeble pulse.

She put her arms around him and elevated him to a semi-sitting position so she could look more carefully at his back. It was a vicious attack. It was clear that he had been whipped. Only a whip could have cut into his flesh this way. Her tears fell upon her father's wounds creating indentations in his blood that splashed on her. His back was quivering uncontrollably, the welts crimson and elevated. The shirt he was wearing had been sliced into shreds by the forceful wielding of the cat. Pieces of cloth were embedded in his deep wounds, some overlapping from one deep welt into another. Sinews were exposed, white, ragged and very swollen. He was covered with blood and, by this time, so was she.

Attending to the task at hand, she hadn't noticed the whip, the implement of madness and fury, until that second. The whipstock, thrown on the ground by the perpetrators, was lying a short distance from her feet. It was a naval cat. The rope was as thick as, if not thicker than, a burly man's wrist. The twisted and knotted ends carelessly overlapped each other exhausted and spent.

"Papa, Papa, can you hear me? If you can hear me, move your fingers."

After what seemed like an eternity, they moved slightly. Her body swayed with relief at the acknowledgement.

"Papa, listen closely to what I have to say. You're hurt very badly. I can't help you here. I'm going to have to bring you home. It's going to hurt you when I move you but it's the only way. I don't have any medicine here to help you. We can't wait. You're losing blood."

She called to her horse to move in closer to her. A less obedient horse would have refused to remain so near this bloody scene.

She picked up her knife, the rope, and the cat from the ground and placed them in a leather bag that always accompanied her.

Upon her command, Reliant slowly lowered his body to the ground. This accomplished, she very carefully put her hands under her father's arms and gently pulled him to the horse. Securing herself on Reliant, she gave a gigantic effort and hoisted her father's limp body in front of her. Grabbing the horse's reins with her free hand, she gave the command for him to get up.

They slowly made their way back to the caravan. She didn't want to traumatize her father's condition any more than was necessary. The mile back to the gypsy encampment seemed endless.

Her dramatic entrance at the encampment was shocking; a hush fell over the entire group. Women, men, and children stopped whatever they were doing and stared in disbelief at what they were seeing.

Chovinne began giving directions to everyone within the sound of her voice.

"Dudras, take Papa inside the caravan. Remove what's left of his clothing. Be careful not to reopen his wounds."

"Subina, hurry, bring me my medicinal herbs, water and linens."

She motioned to the other women to come and help.

In no time, Subina returned with everything she had requested. Chovinne's hand reached for the comfrey. This was an excellent healing herb and would be best for his wounds. She added water to the comfrey flour and formed a paste. Subina had worked quickly and she had already cut the linens into pieces so that the paste could be spread on the cloth and then applied to the wounds. It was a slow process. Her father's body was severely cut. When she was finished, she covered him with a lightweight sheet. There wasn't anything more to do except to make him comfortable and wait.

Elderberry branches were placed at the entrance to the caravan. According to gypsy tradition, they provided an invincible barrier, preventing evil spirits from advancing within. A constant vigil had begun.

She felt a hand on her shoulder. Looking up she saw that it was Dudras, her cousin. He whispered in her ear that he wanted to talk to her. She nodded her head indicating that she would.

Getting to her feet, she whispered, "I don't want to talk here. Let's go to the far end of the caravan where it's more private."

"What does this all mean? I found this rope and cat in the bag that I took to your caravan. Who did this? Did you see who hung and whipped him?"

"They were still there around him, but fled when I interrupted them. You know that Reliant is faster than any horse. I would easily have overtaken them if I hadn't stopped to investigate. I believe I recognized someone. He's one of us."

"Chovinne," Dudras' voice was incredulous, "do you realize what you're saying? You're saying he is of our blood, a gypsy."

"I know," she said, heaving a great sigh, "we always worry about this kind of persecution perpetuated against us from outsiders. It's inconceivable that one of the family would turn against his own."

Papa must first confirm my suspicions. When he does, we'll talk. He'll decide how he wants to handle this matter. Then, I'll get in touch with you and Subina. Together we'll carry out his instructions."

"Exactly what is it that you want me to do?"

"For the moment keep in mind what I have said. Don't repeat our conversation to anyone. I must get back to Papa, now. Remember what I said. It's important. We'll talk again later."

Dudras watched her walking away. He couldn't remember ever having been so overwhelmed with grief as he was at this moment. He knew that he must heed her warning and not yet let anyone know what they suspected.

Once again at her father's bedside, she slowly sat down on the chair close to the bed. Taking her father's hand in hers, she held on tightly. She hoped some of her strength would enter his body. Looking at him lying there so helpless, so hurt, fueled her determination. Quiet, cold, steely anger consumed her.

She grew up that day; her carefree days were over. Her father's responsibilities were hers now. She alone was in control of her destiny, and the destinies of those whom she had to protect.

Motioning to Subina, who was at the entrance to the caravan, to follow her, Chovinne got up and went outside.

"Subina, tell the rest of the family that I've called a meeting for nine o'clock tonight. I want everyone there. We need this time together, to know that we are still a family."

"What are you going to tell them?"

"Only what I know."

"They will have a million questions for you."

"I'll tell them what I can."

"I'm sorry. It's a terrible tragedy for all of us, but especially for you."

"This is very frightening for us all, but I'll see to it that we all stay together."

"I know that you'll do everything you can for us. You'll find a way."

Subina knew her well enough to suspect that she knew something but wasn't prepared to share it with anyone yet.

"Would you please relay my instructions to the others? I have many things to attend to."

Subina watched Chovinne leave. Then she left to do as Chovinne had asked.

CHAPTER 2

Time passed so slowly; every second was an eternity. She was so tired. Chovinne felt a pressure on her arm. She had drifted into a semi-conscious state, not fully aware of her surroundings. This time the pressure on her arm was more insistent. She was wide awake now. Chovinne knew instinctively that it was her father trying to get her attention, to communicate with her.

"Papa, oh Papa, you are finally back with me. I've been so afraid." She took his hand in hers and kissed him on the forehead.

It was a few minutes before he spoke. It was a small whisper. She had to strain her ears to hear him. He gazed intently into her large, luminous, black eyes. His lips trembled, and his voice quivered from weakness and grief as he spoke.

"Chovinne, I won't survive this. It'll beat me. I've never hurt so much. My body is too broken to heal, and my heart, my heart can't be mended. There are no medicines to help me now."

"Papa, please don't talk that way. Things look bad right now, but I'll help you get well. Together we can fight this. Don't you know that?"

Her face was close to his. He weakly stroked her cheek with his fingertips. "You must listen and understand. I won't survive to see you much older. You'll have to go on without me. You must be strong. It's very important, because you will be taking my place as the head of the family. They will look to you for guidance."

He began to cough and gasp.

He lay still for a minute with his eyes closed. Regaining some strength, he opened his eyes and began speaking again.

"I don't have much time to tell you who did this to me and why. I must also get my final wishes in order, so pay close attention and hear me well."

She listened while he spoke. Her eyes were riveted on him. The enormity of her love and concern for her father was very evident on her tired face. She didn't move a muscle, engrossed only in what he was saying. She wasn't surprised by her father's revelations. When he had finished, she told him what she had seen.

"Papa, I've called a meeting for tonight, before I knew that I would be speaking with you. They are very frightened and confused."

"What were you planning to tell them?"

"I wasn't going to tell them the truth yet. I was going to tell them that I was in charge until you got better."

"That is exactly what you should do. I don't want you to tell them that you've talked to me. Tell them my condition hasn't changed. This will give us the time we need to formulate a plan of action."

Together they discussed, step by step, what they would do.

"He'll pay for what he did to you Papa, I guarantee it. He'll never get away from me, never!"

Reaching for her hand, he looked soberly at Chovinne and spoke grimly.

"I want to tell you this before I die, and I don't want you to forget it. Don't let this experience make you cold and

8

distant. But at the same time let it cause you to be ever on your guard. Don't judge anyone or anything at face value. Be skeptical and watchful. It'll save you from pain and heartache, and maybe even save your life. Hear beyond the words, see more than you see. Don't have blind trust. Life is survival and the animal instinct in people will surface when it comes down to staying alive and getting what they want."

"Chovinne, life experiences are like tailwinds in our backs, always pushing us forward. This collection of experiences gives us a frame of reference to adjust our lives accordingly to new situations. You are learning this younger than most. I'm sorry for that. You are now plunged into a situation you never anticipated. You are in the middle. It's unfair."

Chovinne listened to her father speak. Her eyes never leaving his face, she watched him intently. She had never seen such sadness before. He was a broken man, and she knew there wasn't anything she could do to repair his heart or his body.

"Papa, I love you and many others do also. Remember that. We are all with you; all the rest of us. You were betrayed by one. Betrayal is a terrible wound. But we'll begin to mend it tonight."

Taking his hand from hers, she placed it carefully by his side on the bed.

"Don't worry anymore. I'll take care of you now. It's important that you sleep. I'll start implementing our plan of action tonight. We'll catch him. Then, punishment will be imposed."

Soberly, she set about their plan. She had to be very careful, though. It wasn't long before each detail was formulated in her mind. She was happy about that. It meant it wouldn't be long before the cowardly assassin would be brought before the clan.

Chovinne looked outside. She noticed that the moon was

full. She could see the members of the clan gathering for the meeting. She watched them group in clusters to speak to one another. Women and men together, arms flailing, talking, it seemed, in each other's faces. They had been subdued earlier but now they were agitated. They were tired of not knowing what was going on inside the caravan. She knew it was more than time to go out and talk to them. Grabbing her shawl, she hastily placed it around her shoulders. Just before pushing back the door, she hesitated a moment to compose herself. After taking a deep breath, she stepped outside.

The coolness of the night air wove itself into the very fabric of her being. She clutched her shawl even closer to her body, her arms crisscrossed over her chest. She had it all together now, everything would fall into place as planned. Walking toward the clan, she spoke in a brisk tone.

"Everyone," she beckoned, "come. It's time to talk."

Quickly they all settled down close to the crackling fire. She stood in front of them. From the visible anguish in their faces, she could see that her father was dearly loved.

"I know you must have a lot of questions for me. Your hearts must be terribly saddened. The fright you feel surpasses anything you have ever encountered before."

Shouts arose from the crowd. "What happened Chovinne? Tell us. We want to know."

"Please calm down, I'll tell you what happened." And she did.

"Now more than at any other time we all need to be calm, it'll benefit no one to be hot-headed and hot-tempered. I'm investigating this matter. I have the unenviable task of bringing my father's assassin to justice. It'll take time to do what I must."

"One last thing I have to say to all of you before we disperse. Now that my father is incapacitated, all discussions and actions regarding the best interests of the family will be approved only by me."

CHAPTER 3

She watched them leave. She stood there for a long time looking at the sky. It was a beautiful moonlit night, a magical night. The stars sparkled. Suddenly, a shooting star streaking across the sky startled her, breaking her concentration. Turning on her heel she began walking rapidly back to her caravan. She had gone only a short distance when she heard the sound of the owl, the merimasko cerikclo, the portent of death. Her chest tightened, her knees became weak and her legs rubbery. The blood drained from her face. There was no mistaking the mournful cry; the harbinger of death had made itself heard.

Chovinne fell to her knees, her heart breaking. Great sobs racked her body. Torrents of tears blinded her vision. She had been hopeful until now, but this she couldn't deny. Death was imminent. A gypsy prophecy was close to realization.

She knelt there on the ground for a long time, rocking her body back and forth, unaware of the rest of the world. Eventually there were no tears left, just a great emptiness.

She heard footsteps behind her. She had thought she was alone. It wouldn't be good for the rest of the gypsies to know that she had broken down. They needed someone strong to guide them. Their confidence in her would be shaken. Getting up she turned to face the approaching person. She saw that it was Subina. Relieved she found her voice.

"I'm glad it's you."

There was concern in Subina's voice.

"You were gone a long time," she said.

Chovinne blurted out, "I heard it."

"What did you hear?"

"The death bird."

"Are you sure it wasn't something else?" she asked, "You could be mistaken, couldn't you?"

"No, there's no mistake," she said sadly.

"I'm so sorry." Subina handed her a handkerchief to wipe her eyes. She helped smooth Chovinne's hair and clothing which were in disarray.

"This is all so terrible. I'm sorry that I can't do anything to help you."

Together they walked silently to the caravan, where Dudras was waiting for them. Together they discussed at length the plans already outlined by her and her father.

"Dudras, do you have any questions? Are you sure you understand exactly what to do?"

"It's completely clear." There was a discernible edge in his voice. "I know exactly what to do," he replied.

She then turned her attention to Subina.

"You mustn't let anyone in the caravan, under any pretext. Papa isn't to be disturbed under any circumstances."

"You can depend on me."

"I will station two men outside the caravan to help you. We can't be too careful."

"Good, everything is settled. Tomorrow brings another day and we have much to do."

Taking their cue, Dudras and Subina left.

Going over to her father's bed, Chovinne whispered to him.

"You heard everything, didn't you?"

He nodded his head.

"We begin tomorrow."
She kissed his forehead.
He opened his eyes, looked at her and smiled.
"Get some rest now," she told him, "I love you."

CHAPTER 4

Chovinne awoke very early the next morning prepared for the day's eventualities. She washed and dressed quickly. Breakfast would be eaten on the way. She put some fruit and bread inside her leather bag. Next she walked back to her bed. Getting on her knees, she bent down and pulled out some paintings, four in all, from beneath her bed. She looked lovingly at them. They were her treasures. Her father had recognized her artistic talent from seeing her childhood sketches. When they had spent time at the Abbey, he had asked Abbot Paul if he would help develop her talents. She smiled, remembering how difficult it had been to persuade her father to sit for his portrait. His argument was that there were more interesting subjects to paint. She would have none of it. She was determined to have him pose, and, finally, he agreed to be her subject. Her fingers traced the silhouette on the canvas, wishing she could relive those carefree days. Although he tried to conceal it, she could tell that when he saw the portrait her father was pleased. He said that it was nice. He couldn't say more, because it would sound too egotistical. She told him how handsome he was. She had captured the true essence of her father, his goodness shone through. The kindness in his eyes, the impishness in his smile, the robust good health, all visible. She remembered how she would sit beside him and watch him grease his beard and black hair with a sweet-smelling walnut oil, smiling and talking to her as she watched. Many gypsies were metallurgists so he made jewelry for himself and for her. He would wear earrings made from old gold, silver or copper. His necklaces of coral and colored glass captured the colors of a rainbow. He wore wide braided trousers and waistcoats embroidered in silver and gold with a pilgrim's cloak across his shoulders. Attached to his broad leather belt was a knife whose handle glittered. He was an impressive sight.

She stared at the paintings remembering every detail, because her memories were all that she would have left. She would have to sell them in order to have money to buy her mourning clothes. She also needed funds to hire an undertaker and to purchase an extra large coffin. Gypsies traditionally left something in the coffin as they viewed the body, paying their last respects. She also needed to purchase the services of a jobmaster, who would supply her family with horses and carriages for a distinguished funeral procession.

She had so much to do. She wrapped a blanket around her paintings to protect them. She knotted two corners of the blanket together, then the other two corners, overlapping them, creating a handle. She walked over to her father, kissed him goodbye, and left the caravan.

Reliant was always happy to see his friend. With his head held high and his eyes bright, his feet always did a little dance whenever he saw her. He always nuzzled her hand to be petted. It was his way of greeting her. He had already been fed and saddled. After hugging and talking softly to him, she quickly mounted him and set off for London.

CHAPTER 5

Moving frequently from place to place, she had traversed over many roads of different construction. Her father had taken the time to explain the different kinds to her.

Looking down she could see the makeup of this road. It consisted of a series of stones that had been shaped to form a continuous surface. This flat surface insured smooth traffic and an easy flow. This kind of road had been built by the Romans at the height of their empire.

Much to her dismay, though, most other constructed roads were not of this caliber. Some were paved with huge granite blocks or setts, which provided a reasonably firm surface for heavy traffic until they began to wear. After a few years of use, they gave off huge clouds of thick, choking dust.

The macadamized roads weren't better. They consisted of little stones, no more than one inch in diameter. These loose stones were a danger to horses and pedestrians alike. These roads were also dusty in dry weather and extremely muddy when wet.

No road surfaces were worse than wooden blocks. They were more quiet than any other kind of roads but extremely dangerous when wet. Vehicles and pedestrians alike had no control on such a surface. Accidents were commonplace. It wasn't unusual to see downed horses and overturned vehicles.

She could now see London as well as smell it. She considered herself fortunate that she did not have to live in the city. Although the gypsy life was difficult, she could at least breathe the fresher air outside its perimeter.

Londoners lived with perpetual smoke, dust, garbage, and dung. No amount of wind could ever blow away the smoke and smells that surrounded them. London was a soiled city. Cathedral spires were almost obscured by the brown, rusty smoke that was emitted from the city's continuous chimneys.

Choking, suffocating dust was a fact of life here, enveloping and encircling each person in this city. It was much like an insect caught in a spider's web, knowing full well that no matter what it tried to do to extricate itself, it was an exercise in futility. The city's pollution was like the spider with its victims; it would likewise make them sick and, eventually, take their lives.

Trying to cope with the problem, parishes farmed out to contractors the task of toning down the dust. These men were seen working from 5 a.m. to 7 p.m., spreading water from their iron tanks on the ground to lay the dust.

She had seen paupers employed to sweep up the city streets. The garbage that was created by the enormous traffic was carted to dumps outside the city. Dung, hay and straw was taken to depots and sold to farmers.

Making her way through the city streets, she saw many sights. The shopkeepers were already preparing for the day, displaying vegetables and fruit by the bushels. Shopkeepers placed as much of their merchandise as possible outside, to attract the attention of passers-by. They absentmindedly looked up at her, acknowledging her presence with a nod of their heads.

The Fancy Ware dealer was setting up his display in his cart. The sham jewelry he sold was cheap and pretty. Even the poorest people would buy a glittering brooch, earrings or necklace to have one pretty possession in their otherwise meaningless, tortured existence.

Bootblacks were setting up between stores. They were a vast army of unskilled poor whose only source of income was blacking people's boots and shoes. They were seen everywhere.

Cheap Fish Sellers were hawking each side of the street, their barrows filled to capacity with perch, roach, dace, gudgeon, and small jack.

The Mush-fakers were already busy mending umbrellas.

The basket shopkeeper was arranging his baskets in front of his shop. He had a large array of them, from small baskets to very large ones.

A Buy-a-broom girl was selling at a crossing. Her face was totally blank. She wore a blue coat fastened close to her neck. She stood motionless with her arms crossed in front of her.

Further down the street Chovinne could hear the melodic singing of the birds in the bird shops. The activity at bird shops in London never ceased. Shoppers bought the birds because hearing them sing brought joy to their lives. Others purchased the birds to supply food for the dinner table.

A bird catcher, outside one of the bird shops, was carefully removing the bird cages from his cart. Birds in confinement were easily agitated. These birds were all the more agitated, because their confinement was so recent. He did not want to stress them any more than was necessary. She remembered seeing the bird-catchers in the fields, plains, heaths, and woods that surrounded the city. From the onset of daylight and during the intense heat of the day, often during the night and even in the winter's excruciatingly cold chill, the bird-catchers were constantly in pursuit of the birds.

She was very knowledgeable about birds since she herself

caught them for bird shops and street sale. She, often, out of necessity to sell her catch, had gone into bird shops. The bird shops all were very crowded and stifling. White rats, hedgehogs and guinea pigs were also sold at these shops. The smell in the bird shops was often repugnant. Small birds of every description were available for purchase in cages that were displayed from hooks in the ceiling. The birds that interested her the most were the nightingales.

Only the hand-reared nightingales that had successfully weathered incarceration and survived were sold. Nightingales were migratory birds, and their mortality rate was higher than that of any other birds. When the time for migration approached, many of them became uneasy, flailing themselves against the wires of their cages. Many of them died within a few days. The paradox is that, while many of them died, many of them also become reconciled to their cages and didn't seem to notice the passing seasons.

Paper coverings were placed on the nightingale cages to give the appearance of twilight or night time. This paper covering induced the birds to sing during the daytime. The paper covering was gradually withdrawn until no longer needed.

Thrushes were hand-reared for the London bird-shop market. The bird catchers robbed the nests of their young whenever they found them. The tiny, infant thrushes were placed in wicker-work cages. They were fed grubs, worms and snails. They must have grown sufficiently before they could be sold to the shopkeepers.

Thrushes were also caught by netting. These fresh-caught thrushes didn't command as high a price as a seasoned throstle in high song.

Larks always sold welll, sky-larks, wood-larks, tit-larks and mud-larks. They adapted well to the confines of their cages. Some shoppers bought larks for their singing quality. Others bought them for pies, while others roasted them. She remembered hearing that sixty thousand larks were caught yearly in London.

She could sell redbreasts, but, shoppers had difficulty dealing with robins being confined. Blackbirds were less in demand because they did not sing freely in captivity.

Linnets were in great supply and were the cheapest birds sold in London.

Bullfinches were highly prized by the rich, as only they could afford them. Bullfinches began to whistle when they were a little more than two months old. At this stage, Chovinne brought them to professional bullfinch trainers. The birds were taught by degrees to become good pipers. Light was gradually admitted and a suitable amount of food was given to them. A bird-organ imitating notes that resembled that of a bullfinch was introduced. Rewarded by light and food, the birds would practice the notes they heard continuously. They would pipe for as long as they lived.

The goldfinch was also in demand because of its beauty, liveliness and longevity.

Choffinches and greenfinches were less requested. Their songs were only fair.

The demand for canaries had greatly diminished.

As she looked about, she saw that the costermongers had already arrived. Everyone was moving about; passing, crossing and crowding each other in every direction.

On both sides of the street, crowded with customers, were stationed the refreshment barrows. Each person shouted their different cries. The milk stalls, coffee stalls and pea-soup stalls were doing a brisk sale.

She had to direct her horse to dodge and sidestep conveyances of all kinds that crisscrossed in her way. Many pony and donkey carts dotted the street. The carts were constructed to facilitate displaying their goods. Some square carts were constructed so that the sides as well as the front and back could be put down to advantage.

The oblong carts that she saw were constructed with rails behind them. A tray was placed on the rails. This tray as well as the cart beds were filled with produce.

Passing by other carts, she noticed the very plain pony carts. They had neither sides, front nor hind parts. Only the beds could be used for display. This type was usually manufactured at home.

Her attention was distracted from stalls by the sight of a small, tattered boy holding a willow handbasket selling lucifer matches. There were so many like him in London. Each child trying to exist from day to day in any way he could.

Next to him stood his mother who made the lucifer matches. She worked in an unventilated building where white phosphorus was used to make them. Breathing the vapors emitted from this white phosphorus caused her to develop a disease known as "phossy jaw", a type of bone cancer, a necrotic breakdown of the jawbone. She had lost many of her teeth, and excess saliva created a constant drool from her mouth. Chovinne also observed lighter patches of skin on her face and hands. This was due to the matches spontaneously igniting and burning her while at work.

The different sights and people were what made London such an interesting place.

CHAPTER 6

Even at this early hour, the street commerce was already bustling.

Having arrived early, she would insure a prominent place for herself. One that could easily be seen by all passersby, whether they were walking, on horseback or in a carriage.

A short distance from where she was a "writer without hands" was displaying his work before him. This man was an enigma. Despite terribly overwhelming odds, he was able to care for himself. She watched him while he worked. Using one stump, he held his pen or tools on the other stump. In this fashion he could move the two together, thereby, making it possible for him to write and work. He made his living by making ornaments, decorative flower vases, hand-racks, and hand-screens and selling them on the streets. The hand-screens he made bore religious inscriptions.

A "penny profile-cutter" was setting up a canvas booth next to hers. She watched him as he displayed his black paper and white cards. A person's profile was sketched and cut on black paper and then mounted on a white card. If the person wanted his profile bronzed and framed, it cost more than the advertised penny.

The sky was overcast as it almost always was in London. It looked threatening. She hoped that it was just a lingering black cloud, and that it wouldn't pour its contents on her that day. Pushing thoughts of the weather aside, she set about the task of displaying her art. It wasn't long before shoppers began milling around the street vendors.

Mothers had their small children by the hand dragging them from place to place. Soon the children, who became overtired, began to whine, kick each other and pull each other's hair. This behavior upset their mothers who in turn resorted to slapping their children to make them behave. Shoppers were gesticulating while discussing the prices of goods with the merchants. Some of them strolled over to look at her paintings, quibbled with her over the price, but found the price she was asking for her paintings to be too prohibitive and walked away. A few hours had passed. She scanned the faces. No one was looking in her direction. There was no sign of an imminent sale.

Chovinne then focused her attention upon the street traffic. People were scurrying everywhere. She noticed that a beautiful ebony Brougham carriage was inching its way down the street. The carriage was drawn by a satin-skinned chestnut displaying a silver-plated harness on its back. The coachman atop the box was screaming profanities at the pedestrians and at the occupants of other carriages who were blocking his way, thereby, impeding his movement.

As the carriage approached her, one of its wheels hit a large hole in the street. This jolted the carriage which caused a back wheel to fall off, awkwardly tilting the carriage. The occupant of the carriage swiftly scrambled out of his enclosure on his hands and knees. She noticed that he was visibly shaken. He quickly got up and rushed to help his coachman who was having difficulty controlling the horse. He was striking the animal with his whip cutting into its flesh with each brutal stroke. This hurt and frightened the horse and exacerbated an already tense situation.

She could see they needed help. In a loud and

authoritative voice, she told them to move away from the horse.

"You'll get nowhere with that animal, treating him like that," she shouted at the coachman.

Startled, they both looked at her and stepped back. As she walked toward the horse, she began speaking soothingly to it. Her movements were slow and deliberate. When she was close enough, she slowly and carefully reached for the nose piece. With her other hand, she stroked the horse's neck whispering softly to him all the while. Almost immediately, he became calm.

The two men were amazed at her skill and self-confidence.

"You," she said, as she spun to face the coachmen, her wrath evident on her face, "were abusive to this animal whipping him as you did."

"He deserved it. He must obey me. I must have absolute control over him. I'll employ any means at my disposal to make sure that he knows that I control him," he answered defiantly.

"Love and patience are essential if you ever expect the best from horses. You must be firm with them, but you must never strike them in anger or otherwise. In the final analysis, a firm and kindly nature will produce horses of excellence. They will be willing to go to any length to protect and please their master," she stated emphatically.

The passenger, who up to this point, she had virtually unnoticed, walked up to her and began speaking.

"This situation would have turned out very badly if you hadn't been here to help us. I'm totally in your debt. How can I repay you?"

Looking at the coachmen, she replied, "You can hire someone more sensitive, caring and understanding to care for this beautiful animal."

"Consider it done, but, you haven't answered my

question. How can I repay you personally?"

"There's no need for that. You needed help and I'm glad I was here to help you."

"You are very gracious. Again, thank you."

She looked at him. She hadn't previously noticed how young and handsome he was. He had dark hair and the bluest eyes she had ever seen. Her thoughts were interrupted when he again spoke.

"Please forgive my coachman. My name is Andrew," he said, extending his hand to her.

While he was talking to her, he couldn't help noticing how incredibly beautiful she was. She had a dark complexion, and long black hair that glistened and curled slightly at the ends. Her eyes were dark, large, brilliant and striking. The outer corners of her eyes were triangulated which greatly accentuated them. Her eyebrows were strongly marked. Golden earrings adorned her ears. He liked what he saw.

"I must return to my paintings now."

Instead of leaving, he followed her. He picked up one of her paintings and looked at it closely. The painting was of her father.

"This is very good."

Then, he looked at the others. The other paintings were of the gypsy clan sitting around a campfire, gypsy fortune tellers at work, the Abbey and it's surrounding landscapes, and Reliant, her horse.

"These are beautiful paintings," he exclaimed, "I hope that you don't mind my asking why you would want to part with them."

"It's very simple. I need the money right now."

He was again surprised by her candor.

"How much are they?"

"Why do you want to know?"

"Because I'm interested in buying them."

"You are? I told you, you don't owe me anything. I was glad to be able to help you."

"I'm an art lover and collector. I recognize beautiful paintings when I see them. Now name your price!"

She told him how much she wanted.

"Sold," Andrew replied without hesitation.

She was surprised.

"I hope that you enjoy them," she said as she turned around to begin collecting them. Her hand and eyes lingered on her father's portrait, taking in every detail for the last time, knowing that the memory would have to last a lifetime. Although she was an artist, she knew she couldn't duplicate it. A tear came to her eye, and she hurriedly wiped it away.

It didn't go unnoticed by Andrew. He didn't understand her sadness, but he knew it was inappropriate to ask.

He had just met her but, for some unknown reason, seeing her distressed disturbed him. He wanted to help her, but after seeing how she had handled herself, he knew she was a very capable person in her own right.

"Here are the paintings, I hope you enjoy them."

"I know I will, This has been an extraordinary day. One, I'm not going to forget. You saved me from what could have become a catastrophic situation. I don't even know your name."

"Chovinne."

"When can I see you again, under more pleasant conditions?"

She didn't answer immediately. Finally, she said, "You're aware that I'm a gypsy?"

"Of course I am."

"Well, don't you know about gypsies? We aren't ordinary people. Our lives are different. Why on earth would you want to see me again?"

"As a matter of fact, I have heard many stories about gypsies. I'm sure they were all exaggerated," responded

Andrew.

She didn't answer.

"Well," he said, smiling at her, "when can I see you again?"

"It'll be some time before I'll be free for leisure activities."

"Why?" he asked, openly dismayed.

"There are matters that need my immediate and long range attention. These matters will consume all my time for an indefinite period. I really must leave now."

She turned from him and began walking toward her horse. Andrew followed her. He gave her his hand to help her as she got astride her horse. He noticed that it was a thoroughbred, a magnificent animal. He thought to himself, a regal horse for a regal lady.

"Chovinne, I want to thank you again for your kindness. I hope that your efforts to reconcile, whatever it is that you must reconcile, will be rewarded to your advantage."

In the short time he was with her, she had captivated him like no other. He knew in his heart that they were destined to be together.

CHAPTER 7

The downtown shopping district had a myriad of shops. She looked around her and decided upon a shop which she had always found particularly charming, but had never dared to venture within. Above the door was a large signboard with painted letters. The store's outside masonry was constructed of bricks. The shop front had a large glass door and long glass windows. The blue shutters had been opened to allow the light to enter the shop. The name of the shop was written on the glass in connecting golden characters. A large flat surface was built into the windows where goods were displayed. The windows of this shop were beautifully decorated.

There was a compendium of cameos, pendants, broaches and rings. Hair camlets, combs, brushes, complexion creams and bath salts were abundant. There were silk handkerchiefs, paisley shawls, black kid gloves, snuff boxes, parasol and mother-of-pearl buttons. All were displayed to advantage on the flat surfaces for optimum viewing by the shoppers passing by the shop. Iron and wooden rods were suspended from the ceiling to the top of the windows. They were used to display dresses and crinolines. A particularly stunning red silk dress with a matching crinoline caught Chovinne's eye. This was the one she wanted.

She opened the door and stood in the doorway. It was a

magnificent shop. The effect on her was profound. It took her breath away. Blue velvet draperies hung majestically in the windows and dark heavily patterned wallpaper covered the walls. An imported Turkish carpet with soft colorful hues lay on the floor. Horsehair sofas were advantageously placed facing each other in the center of the shop to facilitate conversation among the shoppers. Occasional tables, with horsehair chairs placed on either side of them, were dispersed at various places in the shop. More expensive jewelry was displayed at eye level behind a glass enclosure built into the wall.

Gas lamps provided the lighting for the shop's interior.

Fashionably dressed women and men were engrossed in conversation.

She closed the door and began to walk toward the shopkeeper who was standing behind a glass enclosed display case.

"I would like to purchase the red silk dress and matching crinoline you have displayed in your window."

He lifted his head slowly. With a glance that quickly swept over her body, he noticed that she wasn't one of his regular clients. She wasn't even a person of good standing. In fact, she was just a common gypsy.

He didn't even hide the look of disdain he felt as he looked her squarely in the face.

It was suddenly very quiet. It was an incredibly deafening silence.

She turned and looked around her, aware that the cliques of shoppers had stopped talking and were staring at her with contempt, like she was vermin that had crawled in from the street.

She remained outwardly calm, but inside she was seething. She stared back at them. She wouldn't let them intimidate her. She was determined to stay and make her purchase.

The atmosphere was very tense.

The shopkeeper hurriedly left the security behind the display case to confront her.

She turned to face him.

"I assume you have the money to pay for these items," he stated, in a loud voice.

She opened her mouth to respond, but closed it again when he continued to speak, without waiting for an answer.

"We don't want your kind frequenting this establishment. It denigrates us and is bad for business. Our more affluent clientele won't want to come here if the likes of you are permitted to shop here."

She was incensed at this cruel man but kept her self-control. He wanted to humiliate her in front of these people while exaggerating his own importance. Some gypsies did questionable things, but the same was true of the Gorgio population. It still wasn't an excuse for his behavior.

He was still in a tirade when he suddenly began to choke. He tried in vain to get his breath. He began to gasp. He clutched his throat with his hands to indicate the source of his distress. With a barely audible whisper, he begged her to help him. He was terrified of dying.

Chovinne remained motionless.

He sank to his knees, looked up at her, grabbing her hand, imploring her one last time with his eyes to assist him.

She looked down at him, her eyes riveted on his face.

Suddenly the man before her began to get some air in his lungs. The grip on his throat visibly loosened. He was breathing normally again.

He was truly shaken. Minutes passed before he was able to stand. He had been truly humiliated.

"I hope you can forgive me. I would like to make amends for my inexcusable behavior. I would like you to please accept the dress you admired as a token of my deepest regret for the demeaning and mortifying position that I inflicted upon you. My only excuse is that over the years I have lost my capacity for compassion for people such as yourself, people who are trying to survive as best they can in these wretched times. Instead of feeling superior to you and others, I should be grateful for my quite comfortable life in this inhospitable world."

She didn't say anything. She just continued to look at him trying to judge his sincerity.

Finally, after what seemed like an eternity, she was convinced that he was being sincere.

"I do accept your apology, but would you hurry? I'm in a rush and I would appreciate it if you could wrap my package so that I can be on my way."

The shopkeeper's face broke out in a broad smile, showing his teeth, and the laugh lines on each side of his mouth.

"Yes, yes, right away."

Hurriedly he walked to the window, retrieved the dress and brought it to the counter. There he produced a box from beneath the counter and neatly folded the dress within it.

"Would you also permit me to package some other items for you with my compliments?"

"If it would make you feel better, you may."

In another large box, he carefully inserted some personal hygiene items, some jewelry and some silk handkerchiefs. He also included red kid gloves, a red silk shawl and a parasol.

When he finished with the boxes, he handed them to her. "I know I'm being repetitious, but I do want you to know that I'm sorry, and that I would like you to feel free to come back here anytime. I'll be happy to help you in any way that I can."

"Thank you," she said as she turned around and faced all the shoppers who were still staring at her. She walked towards the door, opened it and quietly left.

All the people in the shop were aware that they had witnessed something strange and mystifying, but were at a loss to explain it.

Once outside, she only had to walk to the shop next door to purchase a hat.

The Operative Hat Factory was another experience for her. She had never entered any shops like this before either, because she simply could not afford to buy anything. Within its confines was an array of the most beautiful decorative hats any women could ever hope to own.

She saw black and white satin bonnets trimmed with ribbons and flowers. Silk bonnets decorated with red silk ribbons and red silk flowers. Straw bonnets trimmed with red velvet and red flowers and cotton velvet bonnets.

Chovinne selected a red silk bonnet with red silk ribbons and red silk flowers.

The shopkeeper who had been keeping a watchful eye on his customers immediately noticed when she had made a decision. He was by her side in an instant.

"This hat pleases you? You wish to try it on?"

"Yes, I could be interested in it, if it suits me," she responded.

"Then follow me please. I'll show you where you can best judge whether you will want to purchase it or not."

The shopkeeper led her to the center of the shop where a vanity with a looking-glass and a chair was placed for women and men to view themselves while trying on their hats.

She placed the hat on her head. She was pleased to see that it looked so pretty on her. She wanted everything to be perfect.

The shopkeeper was standing behind her and was showering upon her a profusion of superfluous compliments.

"You will be the envy of every woman who sees you. No

one could look finer in that hat than you do. Your black hair blends beautifully with red. It is extremely flattering."

She smiled at him. Her smile was her most captivating feature. She was amused by his compliments, but she wasn't the type of person who was won over by them.

She removed the hat from her head and handed it to him.

The shopkeeper looked at her quizzically, asking, "Will you be purchasing it then?"

"Yes, I'm quite satisfied with it."

"Very well. I'll wrap it for you. I won't be but a moment." He hurriedly walked away and quickly returned with her purchase.

She paid him and left.

Across the street was The Boot and Shoe Shop. She needed to purchase a pair of boots. The shop displayed much of its merchandise outside for all to see. She carefully selected a pair of black leather boots. Bringing them inside, she tried them on for fit. She stood up and wiggled her toes in them. They did not pinch her feet. In fact, they fit perfectly.

The boots were the last of her purchases. The task at hand, the most important on her agenda, was now uppermost in her mind. She would have to make arrangements for her father's funeral.

She secured all of her purchases together with leather straps. After giving them a final inspection to reassure herself that they wouldn't become undone, she got astride her horse.

Chovinne now embarked on the most psychologically strenuous part of her journey. She was weary. The pain she felt in her heart was excruciating. This was the first in a sequence of final preparations that she would need to confront and complete.

CHAPTER 8

She was within viewing distance of the Abbey. Her hands gently applied pressure on the reins, causing her horse to come to a stop. She wanted time to gaze at a sight that was dear to her before she continued. The magnificent, venerable, oak trees had grown even more majestic. Sheep grazed in the pastures. Pheasants were perched, in a row, on an old stone wall. Everything was as it was, when she first came here. This place had always had a calming effect on her. Life was so tranquil here. Love was everywhere. There was no meanness; kindness and serenity prevailed. No one's voice was ever raised in anger and no one's hand was ever raised against another person. These monks lived as close to peace with one another and with nature as anyone would ever find anywhere.

She had first come here as a small child. Her father and the rest of the gypsies had been in dire straits. No matter how often or how hard they had tried, they hadn't been able to find employment. In desperation her father had swallowed his pride and had come to this Abbey. He had asked the Abbot if, in exchange for food, he and the others could work on restoring the buildings. This could not have pleased the Abbot more. He proceeded to tell her father how sorely he was needed. The Abbot knew that gypsies were austere goldsmiths, silversmiths, blacksmiths, and masons.

Her father's help would be greatly appreciated. Abbeys were still rebuilding and restoring after centuries of pilfering and destruction. The shrines in the abbeys had been robbed of their jewels. The gold and silver plate had been stolen from their altars. Their stained glass windows, vestments and furniture had also been taken away. The abbeys had been brazenly stripped of their floors. Lead was removed from their roofs and had been melted down. The wanton seizures of brass from their belfries left them barren. All grain and livestock had capriciously been disposed of to wealthy landowners. Slowly, with hard work, the Abbey was again habitable. The bell tower was the only thing that had not been touched.

Her familiarity with the structure of the Abbey and the grounds facilitated her movement within. She crossed one of the many little footbridges that spanned the large swannery pond. She had often sat on the grassy bank, just to watch the graceful swans cruise the placid water.

She adeptly made her way to the cloister which was situated on the southern side of the Abbey, protecting it from the cold winds. The cloister was an enclosed rectangular space surrounded on all four sides by a grass court. The four walls were roofed over. On the east and two remaining sides were the other buildings which were necessary for the monks' daily life here.

The outer wall of the cloister was divided into small carrels. In these small enclosed spaces, the monks would sit at their desks and pursue their studies. Many also used the cloisters to meditate and to quietly discuss religious matters.

The cloister was one of Abbot Paul's favorite places. She knew she would find him here. She could visualize him, a rotund man who was much too hard on himself, constantly saying that he ate too much and was forever atoning for his perceived sin of gluttony. On his forehead was a large raised strawberry birthmark. She remembered that as a little girl that birthmark had proved rather distracting for her. It would at times break her concentration as she spoke to him. She wanted to ask him about it, but couldn't ever find the courage to do so. She instinctively felt this would hurt him and she definitely wouldn't do that. As she became more familiar with him, she rarely, if ever, noticed the birthmark and it ceased to be a problem.

Abbot Paul's back was to her as she walked toward the carrel. He was, as he always was, ever since she had known him, sitting there in the carrel, his head bowed, silent and contemplative. During this period, he was oblivious to time and the world around him. His primary purpose in life was prayer and solitude, daily devotional readings and meditation.

She tapped his shoulder and waited. It was a few minutes before the Abbot blessed himself. He stood up and turned around to face the intruder of his spiritual solitude. Seeing Chovinne standing there before him, the solemnness left his face. He took a step forward, put his arms around her, and embraced her.

"My Little One," he exclaimed happily.

This was the same term of endearment he had used for her ever since she was a child.

Abbot Paul noticed that she was very quiet, not her usual exuberant self. Something was wrong. Her arms were very tight around his neck and her body was tense and rigid. He relaxed his arms around her, gently prying her arms from him. He took both of her hands in his and stepped back to face her.

Her face said it all. Something was dreadfully wrong.

"There is much to this visit, isn't there little one?"

"Whatever it is, it's very important to you."

"Tell me what it is. What is making you so sad? How can I help you?"

"Come, let us sit down over there."

He indicated the stone carved benches lining the walls. He noticed that she continued to hold on tightly to his hands as they both slowly walked over to the bench. Her fingernails were digging into his flesh, hurting him, but he said nothing.

The trauma she was facing was overwhelming for her. He would have to be patient. She would tell him in her own time. Several minutes elapsed before she spoke.

"Papa asked me to come and talk to you, to ask you ...," her voice trailed off. She couldn't continue.

Whatever she had to say was far more serious than he had first thought. A feeling of dread consumed his body.

"Tell me, Chovinne, I'll do whatever I can to help your father and you."

"It's very serious. Papa is dying. He doesn't have much time left. He has sent me to ask you if you will say his requiem mass and allow him to be buried in your cemetery."

Abbot Paul closed his eyes. This couldn't be happening. He was totally unprepared for what he was hearing. A very dear friend was dying. This revelation made him feel ill. He had difficulty calming his turbulent stomach.

Concealing his own feelings of distraughtness from her, he questioned her to elicit more information.

"Has your father been ill? Did he have an accident? What happened?"

"It's much more serious than that. He was the victim of very unscrupulous men, without conscience, who whipped and hanged him."

Stunned, he could only stare at her as she continued to speak. She proceeded to tell him every detail of the events that had occurred from the time she had found her father until that very moment.

"Now you know it all."

"What will you do now?"

"I have yet to deal with these people. It'll be done when I

return, I promise you that."

Her face was furious.

"I will do what Papa and I have carefully planned. Make no mistake, justice will be done!"

He looked at her face. Her jaw was firmly set. This was now a person with whom to be reckoned.

"Papa asked me to give this letter to you. I held the paper and steadied his trembling hands while he wrote it."

She took a letter from her pocket and handed it to him.

Extending his hand, he took the letter. It would be the last communication with his trusted and dear friend.

"Tell your father to ease his mind. I'll say his requiem mass, and I would be honored to have him buried here in our cemetery."

"He will be so relieved to know that. He is very frightened. Although people think the practice no longer exists, it's still done. He fears that resurrectionists and body snatchers will disturb his grave if he is buried elsewhere. He knows that these resurrectionists are always looking for gypsy bodies to dig up, for medical purposes, before they have had a chance to decay. This terrifies him. The bodies of our dead are especially in demand, since body snatchers associate gypsies with magic."

"All the more reason for him to be buried with us. I, too, don't want harm to come to his body after death," he replied.

"Time is getting short. I must be on my way now. Papa will be anxious. I have been gone all day. He will find much comfort knowing you will fulfill his requests. Thank you from the bottom of our hearts."

"Until the next time we meet, little one, remember that I love you. You'll always have a haven from the world here."

They again embraced. Silently, she left.

He watched her leave until he could no longer see her in the distance.

The time had now come for him to read the letter. His

hands trembled as he broke the dried paste wafers that bound the folded sheet of paper. A small cross of pure gold was enclosed inside. It read,

> *My Dearest Friend,*
>
> *I couldn't die without letting you know how much your friendship has meant to me all these years. Your kindness to me, my little daughter, and to my family in times of need was appreciated more than my words can express to you now.*
>
> *The Abbey allowed me, for a time, to escape from the harsh realities of life. Being there with you allowed me to mend a tired mind. Those times were the happiest of my life. I thank you for that.*
>
> *The cross enclosed with this letter is my gift to you. I wanted you to have something that I made especially for you. I give it to you with much love. Goodbye, dear friend.*
>
> *Miset*

It had been a very long time since Abbot Paul had cried. His tears fell unabashedly upon his cloak. He raised his arms to his shoulders, and, with both hands, he raised his cowl above his head. He didn't want the other monks to see him cry. He wanted to be alone in his grief.

CHAPTER 9

It had been a very long day. Chovinne was glad to be within eyesight of the gypsy encampment. She was almost home. She realized how dear these gypsies were to her. They were her life.

Small cooking fires lit up the area and the flickering lights gave a decided glow of warmth and family.

Their caravans were always set up on the city peripheries. It provided the gypsies with only temporary accommodations. During this brief period, they were able to rest, recreate, and find temporary employment in either the country or the city.

They could not remain in any one location for very long before the authorities made them move on to different sites. These displacements forced them into almost perpetual motion. This nomadicity took them to the northern, southern, eastern and western boundaries of the city.

She breathed in deeply, relieved to be back home. She inhaled the delicious aroma of roasting larks. It made her empty stomach growl in anticipation.

Subina was the first to notice her as she came riding in.

When she had dismounted, Subina took the horse's reins from her.

As they walked together, she said.

"It's important that you should eat first and then speak to

the others. They are frightened. This hanging has shaken everyone very badly. Being kept in the dark is making them restless. They won't be able to control themselves much longer. I will see to your horse so that you can attend to them. We will talk later in the caravan."

Chovinne sat down before the campfire. Her head was bent downward with her elbows resting on her knees. She massaged her forehead and temples with her fingers, trying to relieve the stress and fatigue that had become her constant companions during this time. The massage didn't help.

It wasn't long before the rest of the family joined her. One of the women had prepared a plate and a cup of peppermint tea. She handed it to her.

Chovinne took it gratefully, thanked her, and began eating voraciously.

The family watched her eat, waiting patiently for her to finish. She had hardly finished her meal when the barrage of questions began.

"Where have you been all this time?"

"What have you been doing?"

"What could take you so long?"

"Are you keeping information from us?"

"Why all the secrets?"

She took a deep breath before answering them.

"First, let me tell you that I'm grateful for the way you have conducted yourselves. You've shown much strength and self-restraint. I know it's very difficult for all of you. I appreciate the time you have given me. I had to do this my way."

"I'm asking you to grant me a little more time, until tomorrow at mid-morning. We'll all assemble then, and you'll know what I know."

Members of the clan looked at each other and began speaking collectively. All of them had the same pressing thought. When the clatter died down, one of the elders spoke for himself and the clan.

"This is it, Chovinne. We'll give you only until tomorrow. This not knowing and waiting is killing us."

"All will be settled tomorrow. I promise."

"Now, I'm going to see Papa. I don't want to keep him waiting for me any longer."

Her father was propped up on pillows. He saw her as she entered the caravan. There was a smile on his face as she walked over to him.

"I'm so relieved that you are back home. I've missed you. First, how are you?"

"I'm tired, Papa, very, very tired. It has been a very long day, but I'm not too tired to give you a hug and a kiss."

She put her arms around him, but not too tightly. She was afraid that she might hurt him if she did. There was such little precious time left for them to be together. Finally, reluctantly, she relaxed her grip on him and straightened her body to a seating position. She took his hand in her own and held it. In the past, as now, holding her father's hand gave her comfort.

Her father was the first to speak.

"Chovinne, we can't avoid it any longer. We must talk about the future, the near and distant. Were you able to make all the arrangements?"

"Yes, I have. You can rest easily now. All the final arrangements for your funeral have been made. Abbot Paul will do as you have asked."

"The money that I gave you, it was enough then?"

"No, it wasn't. I had to sell my paintings."

Her father looked at her for a long moment. There were tears in his eyes. Then, solemnly, he said to her.

"You loved those paintings so much. They have been part of you for so long. You shouldn't have sold them. It must have been so difficult for you to part with them."

"Papa, listen to me."

She lowered her head and looked into her father's sad eyes.

"I loved my paintings. Yes, they did mean a lot to me, but you mean so much more. I want you to have the best that money can buy, and now you will have what you wanted so much."

Tears welled in her father's eyes. He squeezed her hand. He asked her to bend down a little closer so that he could kiss her cheek.

"You have made such a sacrifice for me. Thank you for making my last wishes possible. It's so comforting to know that I'll have a proper funeral and that my burial will be in consecrated ground."

"There is more that we have to discuss. I want you to prepare my body. I don't want Gorgios touching me. I only want your tender loving hands to wash and to dress me for exposition in my coffin. You already know what clothes I want to wear. The same clothing I wore for the portrait you painted. Place a lock of your hair on the pillow beside my cheek. It will be comforting for me to have it there. I want your loving preparations to be my remembrance in the next world, not those of a stranger. This will make me happy."

She opened her mouth to interrupt.

Her father gently placed a finger on her lips to stop her from speaking.

"Let me continue, I have a need to say these things while I can. I know that what I have asked is contrary to gypsy tradition, but that is the way it has to be for me. It's important to me to use what little time there is left to tell you these things."

"I also want you to be able to speak about me after I am dead. It won't make me restless or vengeful nor cause me discomfort or disturbances."

"Papa, are you sure?" Gypsies don't talk of such things. It's not our custom."

"No, no. You should talk about me. I want you to remember me. Someday you will find someone you will want to share your life with and have children. I want you to tell them about their grandfather. I want you to tell them about our times together, our adventures, places we saw, and people we met."

"Most of all, I don't want you to be sad. We must all die. I didn't choose to die so soon or with such violence inflicted upon my body."

"Chovinne, remember the values I have taught you. Let them be a guide to live by. Put a premium on them. But, at the same time, don't let anyone stand in the way of your goals. Be ruthless for something you believe in. Will you do these things for me?"

"It will be easy to remember you. What would have been difficult would have been not to."

"As my successor, you must not lean on anyone. Dependence on others will diminish your substance as a leader. Dependence minimizes the esteem others have of you and slowly erodes any respect they have. It's seen as a sign of weakness."

"When all this is done, I want you to live your life, to enjoy it. I'll always be at your side. I'll never die as long as you don't let me. You can do this by keeping me alive in your mind and in your heart."

"Now I want to discuss with you what I want done with my possessions. I want you to keep all the jewelry and silver. Sell them as you need the money. I don't want you to torch either caravan as is our custom. You'll need them also. No animals are to be destroyed. When you sell them, sell only to Gorgios, not to other gypsies. With the fear of spirits among us, it is not wise. Put only those things in my coffin that I'll need in the next world. It's important that all my clothing, tools, eating utensils be deposited with me. I have discussed everything that was pressing on my mind with you. I feel much better now."

"Those packages you brought with you," his eyes wandered over to the place where she had put them down when she had come into the caravan, "are they the clothes you will be wearing for my funeral?"

"Yes," Chovinne said, "I found the dress in an exclusive shop, and everything else in adjoining shops. I was very fortunate that they had everything I needed."

"What I would really like would be for you to put those clothes on for me."

She looked at him quizzically. She couldn't imagine why he would subject himself to seeing her in the dress she had bought specifically for his funeral.

Seeing the questioning expression on her face, he said to her.

"I know you must find this a strange request, but it's important that my eyes see you as you will look on that final day they put me to rest. I'll bring this last vision of you into the next world. It will be the one that will remain with me forever."

Without a word, she walked over to where her packages lay. She picked them up, then, walked over to change behind a dressing screen.

It wasn't long before she emerged.

Her father looked at her for a long moment before he spoke.

"You are everything I hoped you would be. An intelligent, strong, wise and capable gypsy woman. I love you Chovinne, forever."

CHAPTER 10

The incessant pounding awakened her from a sound sleep. Slowly she straightened herself to a sitting position on the chair where she had been half-sitting and half-lying all night. Her body ached terribly and her head throbbed. Sitting there, the cobwebs began to slowly filter from her mind. This was the day she and her father would have their revenge. A window, which was at eye level in the caravan, provided her with a good vantage location from which to view what was happening outside. The scaffold was nearly completed. She saw that the dimensions were conventional, just as she had specified. The gruesome wooden structure stood ten feet high, twenty feet long and fifteen feet wide. The gallows was situated in the center of the platform. Suspended from the crossbar was a rope made from strong hemp. The slip noose of the rope was formed by nine twists and a knot. The scaffold was nestled under large trees providing the concealment necessary for their purposes.

She saw Dudras talking with the other gypsy men. She was fortunate that he was such a responsible man.

As she watched, he left the men and started walking toward her caravan.

She greeted him at the door.

"Come in and sit down, I am going to make myself a cup of tea. Would you like one?"

46

"I would love some. I could really use a cup."

He sat down heavily on the chair next to the table.

"Are you prepared for all of this?" he asked.

"I'm more than prepared. The anticipation is difficult to cope with. I'm glad that I don't have to wait much longer."

She poured the water into the tea leaves and carried the steaming cups to the table.

Placing his cup before him, she asked, "Have you attended to every detail we discussed? It is very important that everything goes according to Papa's and my plans.

"Nothing has been left to chance. The clan members we took into our confidence are fulfilling their obligations to the family. They're waiting until they receive word that the scaffold is completed. Then, they'll do what they must. We gypsies will have our justice our way."

"Yes," she agreed, "our day has come."

"Now I have to return to the men. Thank you for the tea. I'll see you later. Soon everything will be ready."

She watched as he walked away.

"Chovinne, what time is it?" Her father's voice startled her. She didn't think he was awake.

"It's half-past eight, Papa. We have one and one-half hours before we all meet outside."

"Come and sit beside me, Chovinne. I don't want to be alone."

She hurriedly went to his bedside. As she sat down beside him, she looked at him. She could only manage a weak smile for him.

"It has come to this Papa. Who would have ever thought that an assembly with such far reaching consequences would take place today and be with us forever? The aftermath will be a constant reminder for me. You'll have paid with your life. I'll have lost a father and the rest of the family will have lost a loving friend."

There was such sadness in his eyes that the pain she felt

for him crushed her heart.

Totally lost in her thoughts, she didn't see or hear Subina enter the caravan. It wasn't until she shook her arm vigorously that she got her attention.

"It's time to go out there and face the families. They're all anxiously waiting for you."

She nodded her head in agreement, then turned to her father.

"Papa it's time. Are you ready to go?"

"Yes. I'm ready."

She went to the door, opened it, and motioned to four, strong men waiting there to come inside the caravan.

"He's ready for you. Handle him very carefully."

Obediently and with precision, he was removed from his bed and placed on a palanquin. The men handled their task with extreme adeptness. They exited the caravan without any difficulty.

She followed closely behind the somber procession. The clan watched as they slowly walked to the newly constructed scaffold. Once they reached the top, the men carefully placed Miset on a bed that had been brought there to accommodate him. Pillows were placed under his head and his upper torso to enable him to see the clan below him.

There wasn't a sound anywhere. Time was standing still for him. The leaves on the trees didn't rustle, birds ceased chirping, the dogs and other animals were subdued. The babies weren't crying, and the children were noticeably quiet and withdrawn. Nothing and no one wanted to intrude. All seemed aware that something without precedent was imminent.

"I want to thank you all for your patience since this dreadful incident happened to me."

The clan was startled to hear him speak. They had been told that Miset was unconscious when Chovinne had found him, and that he had not regained consciousness.

A dull roar arose from the clan.

Miset raised his arm to signal for silence.

"Please, my dearest loved ones, listen to me. Calm yourselves. I didn't like lying to you. I'll now tell you the reasons why I decided to do this. I needed time to formulate a plan. I, along with my daughter, felt that if all of you thought I was incapacitated, it would give us time to do what we had to do, to get on with the task of bringing my assassins to justice."

"My daughter and I will finally put an end to all the inquiries, speculation and waiting that you have endured."

"Chovinne and I have agreed on the right punishment that should be doled out to my attackers."

"Hanging would be appropriate for the person who did this to me," he said, in a voice dripping with contempt.

"Don't you agree, Linuet?"

The clan had been so engrossed in the events unfolding on the scaffold that they were oblivious to the sound of horses' hooves in the background. It wasn't until Miset addressed one particular person, looking beyond them, that they turned around, their faces aghast.

Linuet, Miset's brother, along with four other men sat astride their horses awaiting their fate. They were being closely guarded by family members.

"Linuet, I don't want you to go through life without knowing what it is like to have a rope tightened around your neck, turning you off. You, too, should have the chance to experience this. We are waiting for you... come up here on the scaffold. We have a rope for you."

Linuet's face had turned an ashen gray pallor.

Dudras walked toward Linuet, unmistakable fury etched upon his face. With a determined hand, he pulled Linuet from his horse. Gripping his arm with a viselike grip, he escorted him to the top of the scaffold. Linuet paused briefly to look at his brother, opened his mouth to speak, but decided against it. There was nothing he could say. He had committed an abominable crime. He wouldn't find forgiveness here.

Both of them continued walking to where Chovinne was standing and waiting.

She waited a few minutes before speaking. She looked at the family and then at Linuet.

Her steely black eyes were fixed upon his face. This woman, his niece, facing him was now a stranger to him. There wasn't a hint of compassion on her face. A shiver of dread went down his spine; his body was goosefleshed. He prepared himself for the worst.

She began to speak.

"You've committed many criminal acts. You thought one more wouldn't matter. You would get away with it. No one would suspect you. What you didn't count on was the fact that I would find Papa, and that I would find him alive, after you and the others left him for dead."

"The swill I drank, the rum and the beer...I lost my head," interrupted Linuet.

"What you did, you did to your own brother!"

"Chovinne, please be merciful. I am family. I am of your blood, please," he cried.

"I don't want to be reminded of that. It doesn't make any difference to me now. You ceased to be of my blood when you let your greed envelop you, body and soul."

"You ask for my mercy. Mercy is just a word to you, just like brother is just a word which holds no particular meaning for you."

"Where was your mercy when you, along with the other men, whipped and hanged my father? You left him there, thinking you had completed your demonic deed."

"You had nothing to fear. Dead men don't speak, do they Linuet?"

Cries of anguish arose from the clan. Up until that

moment, the clan had been too stunned to react. They now took menacing steps toward the scaffold.

"Stop!" she admonished, "I'm dealing with this."

The acidic tone in her voice made them stop. They accepted and respected the authority of their new voivode.

She looked at them. Their faces were so concerned. The pain they felt was etched on each and every one. She had to show them she was capable, even though it broke her heart to have to speak harshly to them. Their future and hers depended upon her capability to be an insightful and forceful leader.

"Now that you are all calm again, I'll continue.'

She focused her attention upon Linuet once again.

"I had my suspicions about you even before Papa was able to speak to me. I recognized you at the tree. Your lifestyle has always been chaotic. You are a man driven to self destruction. You have always cheated and lied. Anything was permissible as long as you profited from it. That is why Dudras and the other appointed men were alerted from the start. You were to be always watched and followed, day and night. It turned out that Papa and I were right. You were seen with these men in a saloon, night after night, using blood money to drink yourself senseless. There was only one way you could buy that swill. That was with the money you stole from Papa by substituting your own coins."

She paused here, catching her breath. She looked at the clan. Their faces were incredulous, dumbfounded. Some knew about the process of coining, others did not.

"I will explain to those of you who do not know, what coining is and how it is done."

"Linuet took a shilling piece and other coins and scoured them using soap and water. He then allowed them to dry. He greased them with suet or tallow, later, partially wiping off some of it. He prepared the coins in this way and then impressed them in plaster of Paris to make an accurate cast of the two sides. The two casts were then fitted together as the mold, and then dried out. He poured cheap molten metal through a small hole made on one side. When this dried and solidified, the "gat" was then carefully trimmed with scissors. At this stage, the coins were ready to be coated. His next step was to get a galvanic battery with nitric acid and sulphuric acid, diluting each in water to a certain strength. After this was done, he used some cyanide and attached a copper wire to a screw of the battery. Then he immersed this in the cyanide of silver. It is this way that the process of electroplating begins. When this was done, he took some oil and lampback and formed a composition. He slummed the coins with it, taking away their bright color. This made the coins fit for circulation. All the coins were wrapped separately in paper to prevent them from rubbing together. Just before he paid this man, he rubbed each piece separately again so that his counterfeit coins would resemble genuine coins. It was these coins that Linuet used to pay for the four horses my father bought."

"Papa didn't feel well, so he asked Linuet to go to the Piccadilly Horse Auction to buy four harness horses for our caravans."

"Linuet paid for the horses with the counterfeit coins, keeping the real money Papa gave him for himself. He used Papa's money to buy beer, gin and rum in the saloons. The rest of the money he gambled away. Dudras got this information by going to the saloons and asking questions."

She now turned her body so she could look at Linuet, but not completely away from the clan.

"Those men told Dudras that they saw you talking to a man they knew who sold horses at Piccadilly. They said that the man was very angry. They heard him accuse you of giving him counterfeit coins. They also heard him demand that you pay the money you owed him or else return the horses. They saw you and four other men leave with him. They don't know what happened after that."

"We know Linuet, because Papa lived to tell us."

It was a moment before she could continue.

"You knew Papa was going into the city on business two days ago. You planned to trap him. You convinced this man that Papa had agreed to do the honest thing and pay him the money he owed. This man agreed to go with you believing what you said."

"Lies, all lies. You staged it very well Linuet."

"You and your accomplices jumped off your horses and threw my father to the ground. Papa was stunned. He didn't understand what you were saying. He had given you the money to pay for the horses. He asked you to explain. You told this man that Papa was pretending, and that you would teach him a lesson. One of the men brought you a cat and you whipped my father mercilessly. The man tried to intervene, telling you to stop, but you wouldn't. The next thing my father knew you had a rope around his neck. This man again interceded on my father's behalf. This time you shoved him to the ground, telling him not to interfere, or else you would hang him also. You hung my father to make sure the man, as well as no one else, would know the truth. Also, by hanging my father, you erased the debt and ended any questions."

"Imagine this man's astonishment when Dudras found him at Piccadilly and gave him the money that I had given him to pay for the horses."

She took a few steps toward him, and faced him squarely, looking at him contemptuously.

"You have always charmed your way through life. Your fast talk and smooth manner captivate people, throwing them off guard. They believe you to be sincere and that is their first mistake."

"This is where your betrayal has brought us all."

She swung her arm out in a wide circular motion emphasizing their circumstances.

She took the rope, which was hanging only a few inches away from her, in her hands and placed it around Linuet's neck.

Turning around, she looked at Dudras. "I'm finished. It's now up to you."

She left Linuet and went to her father's side taking his hand in hers. Together they watched as Dudras worked at the gallows. Upon his signal, two men who had been standing next to the uprights knocked them away. The clicking sound of the drop broke the silence. The clan gasped as the body fell beneath the rough planks to the hard ground below. The hard fall stunned Linuet's body. He lay there quietly. Minutes passed before he slowly and deliberately turned his head back and forth. There weren't any ruptured vertebrae. He wasn't hurt. Why had they let him live? The question burned inside his mind.

Brusquely, he was jerked to his feet. The rapid movement made his head spin, he almost fell and had to be supported. He was quickly ushered up the steps, onto the scaffold once again.

He was brought before Chovinne and her father.

Looking at them, he spoke. "I don't understand. Why are you letting me live? What more do you have planned for me?"

"We could have handed you and the others over to the magistrates. They would have decided your fate. We felt that for the first time in your life, Linuet, you should experience the magnitude of your transgressions. You'll have a lot of time to dwell upon all of us who have been affected by your actions. I'll have lost a father, your wife will have lost a husband, and your children their father. The family will always have doubts as to whether one of them could be similarly betrayed. They will always be looking over their shoulders."

"We have booked passage for you on a ship that will be sailing for America tomorrow. You will be taken aboard ship and guarded by Dudras' friends for the duration of the voyage. What you do when you disembark in America is up to you. You are totally ostracized by the gypsy community. Word of your betrayal has traveled great distances. You won't be welcome anywhere among our people."

"It would have been much better for me if you had let me die. Have you no heart sending me to a strange land? What will I do? How will I live? What will become of me?"

"I don't know or care. I do recommend though that you not lie, steal, or cheat to accomplish your goals. You have seen where that kind of behavior has brought you."

"Your accomplices have papers that have been issued and processed by some friends who work at the court house. They will board ship for a penal colony in Australia. Irons will be provided for them. They will be placed with the convicts already there."

"Will I be allowed to say goodbye to my wife and children before I leave?" he questioned.

"You will see them for one half hour, no longer."

"Is there anything I can say that will change Miset's and your mind?"

"No, it's final!"

She turned her attention to her father.

"Papa, we are finished here."

Miset looked at all the faces below him. It would be very difficult to speak with a heart as full of sorrow as his was. Nevertheless, he would try.

"My loved ones, this is the last time that I will see you all gathered before me. The final time that I will speak to you as your voivode and friend."

"Our lives have been hard, but we had each other. The hard times were endured, because we could depend on one another. I want this to continue. It is vital for your survival."

He looked at Chovinne as he spoke.

"I want you to love and trust Chovinne as you have loved and trusted me. When I die, she will become your voivode. This was discussed earlier and you all agreed to it, and now you must live by your words. My daughter is a very capable woman. She has foresight and determination, qualities that will preserve the unity of the gypsies."

"There is more that I would like to say but I cannot. I'm too weak and tired."

He closed his eyes, but not before perceptible tears were observed by everyone.

Chovinne squeezed his hand tightly. He opened his tear-filled eyes.

"Remember, I love you and I will always be with you."

"And I love you Papa, forever."

The clan had climbed the steps leading to the scaffold. They formed a single line, each waiting until his or her turn to place a farewell kiss upon the forehead of their beloved voivode.

Death came quietly, serenely. A death befitting someone of his dignity.

It was done. It was now over. His sorrow and pain erased by death.

She had to put aside her tears and concentrate on the tasks that lay ahead of her. She looked at the family; she didn't have to speak.

Dudras immediately whisked Linuet away from the scaffold. Emotions were high and grief rampant, and he believed the slightest provocation would make the clan lose control. He was sure he and the others wouldn't be able to suppress their outrage if this happened.

CHAPTER 11

Gypsies love their deceased, but are frightened by the mystifying aspects of death. They fear the spirit of their deceased has changed them into highly powerful and dangerous forces to be reckoned with. They especially fear the dead person's power for revenge.

They believe the dead are very unhappy with their circumstances. Any member of the community who feels that they might have done the dying person any wrong asks for forgiveness during this time for fear of repercussions after their death.

Gypsies view death with horror. Death is a mystery and a crisis. The separation and pain associated with the death of a loved one is alleviated by having a family vigil before death, a proper period of mourning, and a proper funeral after death.

This social function with the large group in attendance gives them continuing solidarity. A reassurance that although there is a break in their unity, their continuity will prevail.

The vigil assured the dying person that he or she still remained a part of the community.

In attendance, within the confines of the encampment, were many gypsies who had traveled very far to be there, after being notified by word of mouth of Miset's impending death. Everything else that was important in their lives paled in comparison to the call they received for family solidarity.

Gypsies have an aversion to touching dead bodies, or even entering a caravan that had been occupied by the dead person, nor would they mention his name ever again.

Subina left the entourage adjacent to the scaffold. She anticipated Chovinne would need help, but wouldn't request it during this time. She quickly walked to her caravan, and began gathering everything she had taken from Chovinne's caravan the previous day. In a basket she placed some soap, a comb, walnut oil, lavender water, and linens. With her right hand, she placed Miset's clothes on her left arm. She hurried because she knew Chovinne would be along any minute, and she wanted to intercept her to give her these items she would need. It caused her great sorrow to see her in such pain.

She didn't have to wait long. She saw her making her way to her caravan, her head down, lost in her thoughts.

She called out to her, "Chovinne, stop, wait, I have some things for you."

Startled, Chovinne stopped and looked at her.

Subina noticed the fatigue etched on her face. Her black eyes had lost some of their luster.

"I removed these things from your caravan yesterday before ...," she didn't finish. She couldn't bring herself to mention Miset's name, fearing to bring him discomfort, and force him to enter the realm of the living.

"I can't do anymore for you than this, you understand don't you?" she asked.

"Subina, thank you, it's more than enough. I'm very grateful, and I do understand your fears."

They stood there for a moment looking at one another through tear-brimmed eyes.

"They are waiting for me in the tent. I must go."

CHAPTER 12

The coffin had already been delivered and had been placed in the center of the huge tent. She had purchased a shell, a lead coffin and the outside case. She honored her father by purchasing only the best coffin money could buy.

Her father's body had been placed on a bed by the Gorgio undertaker and his assistants. They had remained to help her.

She immediately went about the task of preparing her father's body in compliance with his wishes.

Her arms felt heavy as she washed his face and body with lavender water. She wanted him to smell good.. She looked at him. Pain and death had altered his appearance. This once vital man was now a pale, lifeless form before her. She would do all in her power to make him look as handsome as he once was.

She motioned to the assistants standing in front of her to hold her father while she dressed him in the same clothes he had worn for his portrait. When she finished, they carefully laid him back down. She took the walnut oil and comb from the table. She combed the oil through her father's hair to make it glisten. When she was finished, she took a long look at him to make sure he looked fine. Reassured that he did, she called to the Gorgios.

"You may lift him now and place him in the coffin."

The men were adept at this familiar line of work. The strongest man positioned himself next to her father's head, the second placed himself near the center of his torso, and the other at his feet. With one singular, swift motion, they transferred the body to the lead coffin.

She had brought her paints with her. When she opened one of the containers, her thoughts strayed to another time and another place. The days when, as a child, she was permitted to stay in the Abbey's hostelry. She had stayed behind to receive an education, which she ardently pursued, learning everything she could.

She and Abbot Paul often went into the countryside, into the many open fields and mysterious wooded areas to capture insects they would need for their artist's paints. Once the insects dried, they ground their bodies into a fine powder which produced many different hues. The one she selected today would give her a red pigment when water was added to it. As she thought of these things a slight smile crossed her face. She remembered herself as she was then. A little snip of a girl, surrounded by waist high grasses, the wind blowing her hair about, with not a care in the world.

Harsh reality brought her back from her reverie. The red pigment that she artfully applied to her father's face gave it a rosy color that she wanted. She worked until she was satisfied that he looked like his former self. Her final labor of love was to wind a linen cloth bandage tightly around her father's chin and head so that his mouth remained closed.

She stood by her father's coffin, her fingers gripping the side. She wondered if there was something better beyond this existence on earth, an existence that was for the most part sorrowful, painful, and tragic for all its inhabitants. No one was left unscathed from one kind of tribulation or another.

She raised her arms and with her hands removed her favorite coral necklace from around her neck. She wound the necklace around her father's fingers. She wanted the necklace to bring him good luck in the next world.

She cut a lock of her hair and placed it on the pillow beside him, close to his cheek, as he had requested. She cut a lock of her father's hair to place inside a charm which would remain with her always.

She placed some candles, lucifer matches, eating utensils, his knife, and his violin next to him in the coffin. He would need these in the next world.

The final article that she placed in the coffin, above her father's head, was the horseshoe which had hung over the door of their caravan. This horseshoe was considered by her and other gypsies to be the very best deterrent against evil spirits. It would protect him from any evil that might want to invade his afterlife.

Surrounding the coffin were candles which she lit. These candles had to burn continuously in the presence of the corpse. Under no circumstances were they to be allowed to burn out. Gypsies feared the likelihood of repercussions the dead might take in the darkness. The candle also provided light for the deceased to travel into another world.

She walked to the tent's partition and summoned the clan members. They filed in and sat down, each grieving Miset's death.

*

The three days of mourning swiftly passed .

On the day of the funeral, Chovinne was attired in symbolic red. Red, the color of blood, would give the dead eternal vitality. When worn by the living, the gypsies believed the color red was able to ward off any evil spirits and protect them in an extremely dangerous environment.

The jobmaster and the funeral director had followed her instructions. She saw that the six horses used to pull the hearse had red plumes in their trappings. The hearse also included red trappings and red plumes. The sight was truly magnificent. Her father would be pleased.

The jobmaster, she had hired, sent out his best horses and carriages for the gypsy entourage as she had requested. The mourners were escorted to their carriages.

Chovinne looked around her at all the carriages, giving them a last minute inspection. Everything had to be perfect for her father. Reassured and satisfied that it was, she climbed into her own carriage and the funeral procession began. The hearse was followed by the mourning coaches. The funeral cortege slowly made its way through the countryside.

Upon their arrival at the Abbey, the gypsies were graciously escorted into the nave by the attentive monks.

The pallbearers, the strongest men in the clan, shouldered the coffin.

Chovinne's attention was so intent on watching the coffin that she did not notice Abbot Paul as he approached her. He put his arm around her shoulders. She looked at him, tears brimming in her eyes.

"I would like to escort you inside. May I?"

Chovinne couldn't speak. The emotions she was feeling precluded any utterances on her part. She nodded her head yes.

Inside they both placed their fingers inside the Ballaun, a shallow stone dish used to hold holy water, and blessed themselves.

When everyone was seated, Abbot Paul addressed the multitude of gypsies who had congregated to pay their last respects to a beloved, former voivode.

My dearest friends,

Crime, wickedness, jealousy and brutality have brought us together prematurely. Heinous behavior of this kind is always with us. Our existence is infested with this malignancy which insidiously intertwines and affixes itself solidly within our lives.

Whether known or unknown to us, we can without notice become victims of unscrupulous individuals. The deliberate callousness of murder is always difficult to absorb.

Miset met his fate in such a manner. He was murdered, the ultimate transgression against another person.

The gypsy community will never again mention his name. Those are your beliefs and I respect them. I, on the other hand, will process and sort my memories. There are many that bring me joy; I will cling to them.

My dear friend asked to have his requiem mass said here, so that is what I shall now do.

"I am the resurrection and the life, saeth the Lord,..."

The celebration of the mass began, a ritualistic somber rite; the essence of collective beliefs and hope in the existence of another better dimension. The monks began chanting the funeral dirges. The caressing tonality of their combined voices had a peaceful quieting effect upon Chovinne.

She temporarily lost her focus when her eyes wavered to the stained glass windows. She recalled the story associated with them. The Abbott had recounted to her how he had found the three intact stained glass pictorial windows in a dark recess of the cellarium, perhaps hastily placed there by a frightened abbot during the time of the confiscations and dissolutions of the abbeys.

One was of an angel holding a scroll, another was St. Ann teaching the Virgin Mary, and the last was the Christ child. The windows were truly beautiful. The bare flesh was depicted on each window; the faces, necks, hands and feet were cut in pink glass, while the remainder of the glass was a harmony of blues, pale greens, whites, browns and yellows.

The sun streamed through the windows and cascaded long colorful hues within the nave.

The sound of Abbot Paul's voice brought her back to reality. The Requiem Mass had ended. The bells in the bell tower began to ring out their mournful sounds. Everyone rose as the pallbearers reclaimed the body to be escorted to the cemetery. Abbot Paul walked out with her and the gypsy entourage followed.

At the cemetery, the coffin was opened once more for the gypsies, to allow them a final farewell. Family and friends filed by saying their parting words and placing objects in the coffin. Coins and clothing were the most common. They felt Miset would need these most in his afterlife.

The gypsies then joined hands and created circles around the coffin, a symbolic gesture of unity to once more reinforce family solidarity. Their heads bowed they waited for Abbot

Paul to begin reciting the final committal prayers at the graveside.

"For as much as it hath pleased Almighty God of his great mercy to take unto himself the soul of our dear brother here departed, we therefore commit his body to the ground..."

Chovinne knelt down beside the coffin and touched her father's face. This was the last time she would touch him or see him. She felt a hand on her shoulder. Looking up she saw that it was Abbot Paul. She felt the love, warmth, and reassurance that he was offering her. He helped her to her feet, put his arm around her and together they watched as the lid was closed and the coffin lowered into the ground. The monks began shoveling the dirt to fill in the grave.

Chovinne sprinkled beer over his grave. This was symbolically necessary to offer her father liquid nourishment in his afterlife.

Abbot Paul blessed the grave...

"The grace of our Lord Jesus Christ, and the love of God and the fellowship of the Holy Ghost, be with us all evermore. Amen."

The service finished, the gypsies began to disperse, saying their goodbyes to everyone. Soon Chovinne, Abbot Paul, Dudras, and Subina were the only ones remaining at the graveside.

"Chovinne, I have something for you," said Abbot Paul.

"With everything that has happened, I don't think anyone had time to think about a grave marker."

He handed her a bronze cross.

"Here," he said, taking her hands and placing the cross securely in them, "Everyone should be properly marked."

She had never expected anything like this. Looking at it, she noticed the inscription "Papa" engraved on it.

"How like you to always do something kind and generous for someone. Thank you, it's beautiful!"

She walked over to the grave and placed the cross within the soft, fresh, brown dirt.

During this time, the others felt it was appropriate to discreetly leave. They felt she needed this time to spend alone with her father.

Although she was focused on what she was doing, she was aware the others had gone. She was free to speak aloud if she wanted to.

"Everyone has gone, Papa. It's just the two of us again. Isn't the cross beautiful? Abbot Paul made it himself, for you. As always he still thinks of helping others.

The service was as dignified as you had hoped it would be. You must be very pleased.

I promised you that I wouldn't cry. I'm afraid I'll have to break my promise this one time. I should never have made it."

Her eyes misted, and tears fell. She wept quietly for a long time.

Subina and Dudras were very worried about Chovinne, voicing their fears to Abbot Paul. They told him she was still at the cemetery by herself. She hadn't said anything to them about wanting anyone to be with her. They didn't want to intrude, but they felt she should have someone with her.

"Don't concern yourselves about her," he said. "I'll care for her. I was planning to return to be with her. I know someone has to temporarily replace her with the gypsies. Go and do what you must without any worries."

Their concerns alleviated, Subina and Dudras left for the encampment.

Abbot Paul knew Chovinne well enough to know that she would remain beside the gravesite until the following day. He swiftly gathered some pillows and blankets and left the confines of the Abbey to be with her.

Upon his arrival at the cemetery, he found her asleep. He hadn't arrived too soon. He touched her face and hands. They were cold. The night air had already begun to chill her body. He placed a blanket on the ground. Next, he proceeded to pick her up and lay her down on it. She was so exhausted that moving her didn't wake her. He knelt down beside her and carefully raised her head to place a pillow beneath it. The blanket was large so he folded it over her and tucked it in on the sides. While tucking the blanket closer to her, he noticed something on the ground. He picked it up. It was a charm on a chain which contained a small strand of hair inside. While she slept her grasp on it had relaxed, and it had fallen out of her hand onto the ground. He knew Chovinne would be devastated if she lost this charm. He placed it in his pocket for safekeeping.

The night air was cold, but not so cold as to chill him to the bone like this, he thought. He pulled the blanket closer for extra warmth, but it didn't seem to help very much. There wouldn't be any sleep for him this night. He would keep a vigil for them both.

He worried about Chovinne and her extended family. How would they survive? What would she do to see them through this crisis. Whatever she did would take much thought and careful planning to keep the gypsy clan unified. Only time would tell.

He was distressed to see her sleep so fitfully, moving her head from side to side and muttering incoherently. He could do nothing except watch over her.

Finally the long dismal night was almost over. A chorus of erratic chirping birds was the unmistakable forerunner of imminent daylight. The bleakness of the night was erased as daylight stretched across the countryside.

Chovinne felt the warm rays of the sun upon her face. Confused, she hurriedly sat up and looked into the reassuring face of Abbot Paul.

"I didn't know that you would be here, that you would come to be with me. I'm so glad that you did. I hope that I wasn't any trouble for you."

"How could you possibly be any trouble for me?"

She felt a need to explain.

"I didn't ask you to stay with me because I didn't want to impose on your generous kindnesses to me."

"Listen to me carefully. This is important. I want you to know that I'm here for you. You can count on me. I'll always be your friend, always!"

She understood his sincerity.

"I'm sorry, it won't happen again."

"Now that we have an understanding, let's go down to the Abbey and have something to eat. I'm famished. You must be as well."

"I'm very hungry. I would love some tea and plum cakes, lots of plum cakes."

"Then you'll have them. Let's be on our way."

"Would you mind starting without me? I'll be along shortly."

He understood her need to be alone with her father.

"I'll walk slowly," he said.

She noticed that the fresh dirt on the grave was already drying out. Blades of grass would soon begin to grow over it sealing the earth for eternity.

"Papa," she said aloud, "I'll do as you have asked me. I'll be happy, as much as living on this earth will allow me.'

She knelt down touching the inscription on the marker.

"I love you, Papa."

"I must leave you for now. The task of providing for my family awaits me. You have taught me well. Now it's for me to remember and use my mind in order for us to have a good life."

Taking one last long look, she turned and ran to catch up with Abbot Paul.

They were both quiet for a little while. He broke the silence.

"Share your thoughts with me?" he asked.

"I was thinking about my promise to Papa. He wanted me to be happy. I'll try to do that. It'll be difficult, though."

"It's a good idea to leave the bad memories behind, just think about the good ones. You had many of those. Concentrate on them and I'm sure your life will be a happy one."

Nothing more was said. They continued walking together toward the Abbey. She held his hand tightly.

When they arrived everything was in readiness for them. The smell of the plum cakes permeated the air exactly as she remembered. She was ravenous. They went directly to the refectory table and sat down. Abbot Paul said the blessing and then they began to eat. She savored every morsel of the plum cakes.

"I just love eating here. You must put something special in the plum cakes to make them so irresistible."

"I'm glad to see you enjoy yourself again."

She kept talking to him with her mouth full and even in between bites.

He smiled at her. He loved this woman very much. He had missed his chatterbox.

"I have always been very spoiled here, and I love it. I wish I could stay longer, but I cannot. My family needs me. I just wish I could take you with me, but you are needed here.

"Have you given some thought to what you are going to do once you return to your family?"

"At times, but I could never really formulate any tangible ideas. My concentration was always broken by thoughts of Papa."

"Now reality is right here with me. I must find a way to provide for my family."

She drank her tea while they spoke of many things. She

drank all of the tea except for a small amount of liquid on the bottom.

The tea was from China. This tea left a minimum of tea dust, so it subsequently produced extraordinarily well-defined leaves to study and interpret.

Holding her tea-cup in her left hand, she moved it three times in a circular, counter-clockwise direction. She had questions in mind and would seek answers from inside the teacup. Slowly she inverted it on the saucer, resting it on the edge and the middle, leaving it there for a few minutes to enable the liquid to drain away.

Switching from her left to her right hand, she placed the tea-cup right-side up. Sections of the cup represented different periods of time. The handle of the cup represented the inquirer "the house." The rim included the present and near future. The patterns on the inside walls were not as immediate and those on the bottom were remote but their representation no less meaningful.

Carefully she surveyed the cup from all angles. The tea leaves were definitely symbolic, and not lacking clarity.

Close to the rim, near the house, she saw in detail an aviary. A large cage containing birds meant the advent of new ideas. The crossed lines next to the aviary meant important decisions were to be made, new ventures to be embarked upon.

On the other side of the handle, again close to the house, was a horseshoe, a clover and a galloping horse, his mane blowing in the wind. She was thrilled with the horseshoe. This symbol was a sign of good luck. Fortune was preparing a pleasant surprise for her. The clover next to the horseshoe meant her good fortune would be immediate. The galloping horse signified an immediate journey.

As she progressed from the rim, there were more symbols on one side. The unmistakable forms of an ant and a hammer were easily seen in close proximity to one another. The ant signified that she must persevere in her arduous labors if she was to be successful. The representation of the hammer was another unmistakable sign foretelling her to fashion her fate relentlessly, once it revealed itself.

On the bottom was a small ship and it pointed away from the "house." A journey was indicated in the not too distant future. This symbol left her really wondering. She couldn't imagine why she would be taking a voyage.

These symbols gave her hope, which she hadn't had in a very long time. The tea leaves were never wrong and they never lied. Revelations were forthcoming. She was enthusiastic and very excited. In a short time everything would be revealed to her in a chain of events that she would recognize.

"Did you see something important in the tea leaves?" he asked.

"Yes," and she proceeded to tell him about them.

"The ones telling me I will have to work hard I understand, but one has left me guessing. In time, though, I will understand its prophecy. Tea leaves have a way of clearing the chaos from my mind. My senses will be more acute now. I'll become more observant and receptive to messages."

She reached across the table and took his hand in hers.

"My family has waited long enough for my return. So much has happened. They feel lost and vulnerable. I must now assume the legacy Papa left to me."

"I'll walk with you to your horse. Dudras brought him here knowing you would need him to get back to your family. He's ready for you. He was fed and watered in readiness for your departure."

Together they walked in silence to the stables where her horse was sheltered. Reliant showed his pleasure at seeing her. He was holding his head high in anticipation as she approached him. She spoke aloud, her soothing voice held his attention. He seemed to understand what she was saying.

She mounted her horse in preparation to leave.

"Chovinne, please take these cakes that I wrapped for you. I thought that you might get hungry along the way."

She looked at him with a twinkle in her eyes.

"You know me too well. I won't be very far from here, and I'll already be eating some. Thank you."

She put her hand to her throat to touch her locket.

"Abbot Paul," she said. He noticed there was panic in her voice. "My locket, with a strand of Papa's hair inside. It's missing! I must go to the cemetery to find it. I can't be without it. It means too much to me."

She was about to dismount her horse.

"Chovinne, stay there. Don't be alarmed. I have it. I meant to give it to you, but somehow it slipped my mind. I found it on the ground last night. It had fallen out of your hand while you slept."

He took it out of his pocket and gave it to her. She hurriedly put it around her neck and fastened the clasp.

"I'm so relieved! I was careless. This must never happen again! This locket is my last connection with Papa. I want it with me forever."

"Now that I have everything, I must go. I love you more than you will ever know."

"I love you too. You will always be in my thoughts."

She left him standing there, his eyes focused on her until he could no longer see her. He hoped that only good fortune would be at her side. This, however, was the real world and nothing came easily. The good and the bad would be hers, as it was with others. Whatever came her way, he knew she would handle it.

He didn't see Chovinne, hidden, in a copse, by some trees, looking down at the cemetery. She blew her father a kiss and continued home to the encampment, toward a new life for herself and the ones she loved.

CHAPTER 13

The configuration of the tea leaves that she had seen in her teacup continued to baffle her. Deep in thought she paced the floor inside the caravan, occasionally stopping to glance outside the windows. No longer able to stand the confinement of the caravan she left. Perhaps if she went riding she could clear her mind.

As she looked around her, she could see that most of the gypsy clan were tending to their various tasks.

To get their attention, she spoke loudly. "Everyone, listen, I have something to say to all of you."

They all stopped what they were doing to hear what she had to say.

"I'm going to the city for the day. I don't know exactly when I will return. I want all of you to know that anytime I must be away from you, I want all of you to continue doing your normal everyday activities. In my absence you will report to Dudras and Subina. Whatever concerns you have they will report to me and, together, we'll work on them when I come home.

I'll be away from you a good portion of the time in the near future seeing to our welfare. When I have something to report to you, I'll do so as soon as possible."

It was still early, the very best time of day Everything was still undisturbed, quiet, serene and peaceful. Chovinne thought that perhaps it would be a good day after all. She felt optimistic for the first time in a long while.

Arriving in the city, she found herself being drawn to the maritime district. She hadn't been there for a time. She knew a lot of the underworld people. Street people knew each other and what they did and word got around swiftly. They knew she was a gypsy from whom they could steal nothing except her horse. They had tried once to take him by force and were nearly killed themselves. He could be violent if and when the occasion ever arose. Her horse offered her the only protection that she needed. It was an extremely dangerous environment where murder and robberies were not uncommon. Fencers, burglars, pickpockets and shoplifters all lived in the cheap boarding houses that lined the streets adjacent to the docks.

Shops here catered to the needs of the sailors and dock laborers. Shipowners were the primary patrons of those shops that displayed in their windows bright brass sextants, chronometers, and huge mariners' compasses. In the sailmaker shops, huge ropes were displayed in the windows. The unmistakable odor of the tar they used on their lines permeated into the street.

Marine shops displayed their items on trays and tables outside as well as inside. Chovinne stopped to look at the display because she found it very interesting. There were models of ships in bottles which she had never before seen. In addition, there were prints of naval battles, silver watches in thick leather cases, tobacco boxes with anchors on the lids, and cases full of guns. There was quite a collection of buttons, keys, compasses, tins, bottles, boxes, sealing wax and candlesticks. If people could not find what they wanted here, she seriously doubted they would find it anywhere.

The next shop she saw was a clothing shop. The merchants here strategically organized their clothing for optimum viewing. Easily seen items meant more sales.

Oilskin hats, rough blue jackets with mother-of-pearl buttons, red and blue flannel shirts, canvas trousers and boots, pilot-coats and thick, shiny, woolen black dreadnoughts were available in quantity for the sailors and dock laborers who could afford them.

Chandler shops specialized in candles for ships. Ships required many candles to light their interiors.

Swag-shops scattered around the docks sold mostly to sailors. The merchandise they carried included pen-knives, pocket-knives, nail-files, scissors and shears, sailors' knives, oyster and fish-knives, bread, ham, beef, and cheese knives.

Sailors could find cheap shoes at the shoe-mart shop. Leather patches could also be sewn over holes to give renewed life to their shoes.

Grocers in this district sold meat in cases and biscuits. The sailors were guaranteed that these provisions would keep in any climate they ventured.

Laundresses who lived here made their living by taking in the sailors' washing.

The lodging houses were also brothels.

Being a professional rat-catcher provided a lucrative living. The catchers visited the ships to rid them of their swarming vermin.

Carpenters and smiths were numerous along the waterfront. The congestion of the Thames river frequently caused collisions of vessels and other accidents. Consequently, their services were often needed.

On an average day, three thousand men looked for work at the various docks. The news that ships were due at any particular dock spread and the gates of that dock were besieged in the morning. Burly men with determined faces were hurrying to the dock, a diverse group of experienced and inexperienced laborers.

Jobs at the dock consisted of dock and wharf workers, dockyard laborers, corn, wheat and fruit porters, tea workers, wool workers, leather dressers, millstone and brick makers, cement workers, coal heavers, backers, porters, whippers, tippers, ballast-getters, lightermen, mechanical laborers, coopers, oil millers, timber runners, warehouse men and granary workers.

These men scurried swiftly past Chovinne. They were late. It was almost half-past seven. The "calling foremen" would soon be making their appearance. The ships were waiting to be "made-up", and these men did not want to miss the opportunity to be called.

A great number of men stood at the "cage." They were herded together like cattle behind iron bars placed end to end to form a restraining gate to protect the "calling foremen" from them. Many called out their names hoping to be recognized and given work for that day. They began fighting. Their coats, hats, and ears were being torn off. If men fell to the ground, they were crushed to death in the struggle. The strong literally threw themselves over the heads of the others. They kicked, punched, and cursed. They rushed to spots that gave them the advantage of being more easily seen.

It was a savage spectacle of the human struggle for existence. Chovinne was aghast at the melee she observed from a distance.

The gates opened and those who were given work were allowed through. The constables standing nearby saw to it that decorum was restored once they were allowed in.

This had been quite an education for her. Although she had spent much time in the city, this was something she had never seen, and, something she would never forget.

She brushed it from her mind for the time being. There were other things on which to concentrate.

The ships captured her attention. There were many of them. Their masts and flags were only temporarily obscured when black smoke gushed out of the ships' chimneys.

Cargoes were waiting to be loaded or unloaded by the dock laborers. Corn, wheat and flour was to be shipped to the continent. Raw cotton from America, once unloaded, would be sent to English textile mills to be spun. Sugar, tea, coffee, beer, spirits, wine, tobacco, wool, glass and timber would also be unloaded to be distributed to the various factories, markets, or to be stored in the warehouses all around the dock.

Dismounting from her horse, she wisely hugged the side of the street, staying close to the shops. She didn't want to be trampled by the onslaught of workers.

"I wouldn't do that if I were you!"

Startled, she turned around just in time to see a small boy, about ten years of age, his arm and hand outstretched, poised to pick the pocket of a man standing in front of a storefront. This man was very tall and heavyset. He wore a loose cotton neckerchief, a strong shirt, canvas trousers and boots, and a loose great coat.

He turned around and his large hands reached out and effortlessly scooped up the child. She noticed that his hands and fingers were so large and long they easily wrapped themselves around the small body. Frightened to death, the boy began to sob. He could barely speak. When he found his voice, he begged the man not to hurt him.

"I only did it because I'm so hungry. It has been two days since I've eaten."

The man held him high looking into the boy's face.

"I won't hurt you, but you shouldn't steal. If you keep stealing, others much bigger than you will beat you and really hurt or kill you. Or even worse, you could be sent to a workhouse. Do you understand what I'm saying?" he asked.

The boy nodded his head, indicating that he did.

He slowly eased him back on his feet. Looking at him he knew that his admonition had fallen on deaf ears. He would continue to steal. It was his only sure way of surviving. The city of London was overflowing with many children just like him. Their parents were either dead, too sick to work, too tired, or too drunk or drugged to care.

"Here is some money," he pressed some coppers into his hand, "Go now and eat something." He turned him around and tapped him on the rump.

"That was a very nice gesture," Chovinne said.

Embarrassed that someone had heard and seen him, he replied, "I don't want to see anyone starve."

He took a few steps and stood in front of her, hands on his hips. She was dwarfed by his stature.

"What are you doing here, Miss?"

He didn't wait for her to answer, continuing to speak.

"This isn't a place for a lady like you. No good will come to you here. It would be best if you turned around and were on your way out of danger."

"I came to see for myself what happens here. I'm curious and I'll stay as long as I must. Tell me," she asked, "why aren't you working?"

"I hurt my leg badly about a week past, and I'm waiting for it to mend. The "calling foremen" don't take kindly to a man who is temporarily down. I still have two good arms even if my leg is temporarily slowed. I can still do more work than two or three good men, but they won't listen to me, so I must wait."

"Is the dock always this busy?" Chovinne asked.

"The season determines how busy we are, sometimes we have a slack season. Let's go closer. The constable won't let us pass through the wicket, but we'll be close enough to get a much better look. What you'll see happens every work day, all the day long."

She watched the people going about their business through a light grey veil of unfiltered air. She could hear the seagulls, but couldn't see them.

This world was very different from the one she had just

left. She was amazed at how vibrantly alive it was.

The sailors were raucously singing their chanties in unison while they worked. Their rhythm and motion fascinated her. Some of the songs they sang were in English, others were in their native languages which she could not understand.

Emigrant passengers, handkerchiefs in hand, wiped their tear-filled eyes and were clinging to family members they were soon to leave behind. Homeless girls who had been trained to be houseservants were emigrating with their new families.

The intermingled fragrances of coffee, spices and molasses gently floating on the wind smelled sweet and aromatic. However, this was short lived for soon the air reeked from the pungent stench of hides. These hides would then be loaded into wagons and taken to the tanneries. Sulphur, which was used for making paper, matches and gunpowder, was quite acute and made her eyes burn.

Animal noises pierced the air. After months of languid confinement on the ships, these animals were unmanageable, loudly conveying their distress for everyone to hear.

A ship's captain could be heard, in the background, cursing. Apparently, something had gone wrong.

Casks being rolled on the stones made a rumbling sound similar to carriages when their heavy wheels passed over and pressed on stones in the roads.

The traffic on the Thames never ceased. There were Chinese tea clippers with tea from China and wool from Australia. Oyster boats whose cargo was being swiftly emptied by laborers also were present. There were tiers and tiers of anchored vessels, scores of masts, and labyrinths of idle tackle. Most ships were moored by massive rusty anchors and chains.

She watched the half-penny steamboats incessantly chugging along up and down the river, navigating carefully.

The kickback from their steamboat paddles unearthed from the riverbed slimy, muddied old wooden hulks that had been broken and splintered into many pieces, sending them to the shoreline along with floating coal slime. Other debris such as rusted anchors, rusted pistols and knives, copper nails, iron, chains, broken baskets, bones, oars, tackle, coal pieces, and seashells were also dislodged.

This litter was enthusiastically retrieved by mud-larks, both young and old people in dire need who frequented the shores of the river waiting to find anything salvageable from the waste to sell on the streets.

Inside rowboats, with splashing oars, were grim-faced men whose faces showed fear when large vessels came too close to them. Capsizing was not uncommon and they always prepared for the worst. Lumbering barges slowly wound to their destinations. They would bump up against other vessels, and the noise sounded much like breaking walnuts with hammers.

She could see bridges, arches, warehouses, church steeples and house roofs.

The shipbuilding yards were busy with clamorous anchor-smiths, the incessant saws cutting timber planks for building ships as fast as they could. Engines were pumping ships, and men were working the capstans, an apparatus mainly on ships consisting of a spool-shaped cylinder around which cables are wound for hoisting anchors and weights by hand.

She was so intent on what she was seeing and thinking that she didn't hear the man next to her speak. It wasn't until he waved his hand in front of her face to get her attention that she noticed him.

"I'm sorry. Did you say something?"

"I'm Benjamin, Miss, Big Ben, they call me." He extended his hand to her. Smiling at him, she took it in hers.

"I'm very happy to formally meet you Ben. I am

Chovinne."

He turned his attention to the tall ships.

"Look," he said enthusiastically, "here we are with the world of commerce before our very eyes. It's amazing, isn't it, Chovinne, the excitement, the thrill of having connections with the rest of the world. Our country is growing and expanding its markets. Look at the clippers, Chovinne, they are bold, reckless and gloriously dazzling. Their sleek hulls, with their deeply arched bows and their myriad of canvas swelling above their decks give them elegance. They are the epitome of perfection."

"I agree."

"There's so much money to be made. The sailors speak of their many adventures. They tell me glorious stories of the places they have seen, but mostly about America. They tell me it is a wild, green, clean and unspoiled place with fresh air, clean water, plenty to eat, and full of promise for people willing to go and settle there. I can empathize with them. My father was a seaman on clippers and I went with him on many voyages. I learned everything I know about the sea from him. My father became ill and died. Shortly after, my mother did also. Luckily, I was old enough to seek and find work when I found myself alone in this world. I am a self taught man, but, since I have no formal education, all I can hope for is manual work."

"My dream is to own many ships. I know though that it is only a dream and will never come true. The reality is that my life will continue as it is, existing from day to day, with no way out."

"Don't be so negative, perhaps your luck will change, you can always hope."

"I don't think so. Many times my back has felt like it was broken. It's hard work that I do, hard, hard work. Unless someone bequeaths me a lot of money, this is where I will be spending the rest of my life."

"I don't know what to say to you Ben."

"There isn't anything to say, really. We live, we work and we die. Pretty grim, isn't it. I won't dwell on it though. It serves no useful purpose."

"I have told you about my hopes and dreams, it's your turn. Tell me Chovinne, what do you want for yourself more than anything else. What would make you happy?"

"In order for you to understand what I'm going to tell you, I'll start from the beginning and give you some background about my life."

"I grew up having two families. My gypsy family and my abbey family."

"Abbey family! Do you mean that you lived in an abbey with monks?"

"I did, six months out of every year, since the age of ten."

"All the abbeys were dissolved and destroyed by Henry VIII."

"Yes, that is true. It wasn't a real abbey in the sense of previous generations."

"The Abbot's parents had bought a parcel of land at auction that the Abbey stood on. Upon their deaths, it was stipulated in their will that it be bequeathed to their son, the Abbot."

"He wasn't happy being in the fray of the everyday duties of a priest. He wanted to live a more cloistered life."

"He decided that he would renovate the Abbey. It wasn't too ostentatious, it was small in comparison to others, and it still retained a great deal of its originality. The pillaging had been minor in comparison with the others, and the Abbot knew it could be refurbished on a small scale to make it habitable again."

"That is where my father and the rest of the gypsy clan came in."

"I first came to know these wonderful monks when they gave my father and the rest of my family work when none could be found, and they were on the verge of starving. They helped the Abbot with the restoration work in exchange for food."

"The monks already there had been passers-by who had also stopped, asking for employment. They were given soup, bread and tea, and a good night's sleep. They grew to like the retreatist way of life, the simplicity and camaraderie. A sense of belonging and accomplishment soon pervaded their everyday lives and they wanted to stay and work together as a community. They donned robes and became monks. It didn't matter that it wasn't real. It was real for them and that's all that mattered."

"The Abbey belonged to the Abbot and he could do what he wanted. He was still a priest, choosing to call himself a monk. He would administer to anyone in need. Helping whenever he could was for him the charitable thing to do."

"It was a world very different from the one I knew. It was the stability of living in one place for a length of time that was different from always moving from place to place."

"At the Abbey, the routine was predictable but not boring. I was allowed access to the cornmill, brewhouse, workshops, smithy, piggery, stables, gardens, bakeshop and refectory. The infirmary had its own apothecary and small isolation room. That is where I learned about herbs and their uses. The herbarium housed the herbs. The cellarium was used for storing wine, making cider and storing root vegetables. I spent a lot of my time in their scriptorium. I have read a lot and acquired considerable knowledge about many things from their many books."

"I had my own room in the hostellary. The only places I was not allowed to go to were their personal rooms. If I became sick during the night, I could summon the Abbot to my bedside by ringing a bell on a nightstand next to my bed."

"Food from their bountiful gardens was plentiful for the

first time in my life. My stomach was always full."

"I felt safe there. You never feel safe on the road in a caravan. Thieves and constables were and are a constant problem. I felt secure knowing these gentle and kind men would never harm me. The Abbey provided a base where I could stay without interference and without worry."

"Why did you stay at the Abbey when your family moved on?"

"My father asked the Abbot if he would consider keeping me to give me an education. From them I learned how to read and write. Their books provided answers to whatever I wanted to know. I also gained much practical knowledge tagging along after them, asking many questions, making a nuisance of myself. They were so patient with me, explaining everything in detail."

"I began to see life differently and that is when I began to daydream of living in a house, having a real home, on land that I would own, my own piece of earth that would belong to me and my family."

"I hope our dreams come true. Tell me. Have you seen enough?"

"Quite, and I am very grateful that you accompanied me. Now I must go. I have many things to think about."

"I'll see you safely out of this district."

"You don't have to do that. I know many of these people by sight and they know me. I'm careful."

Ben insisted.

"I told you earlier. It isn't safe here and I would feel much better if I accompanied you a safe distance away. Now that I have made a friend I wouldn't want anything to happen to you."

"Well then, friend, let us go."

Together they walked to her horse, Reliant.

"What a magnificent animal you have. How did you get him?"

My father and I found him abandoned on the road. He was a young colt and extremely sick. Whomever had owned him must have given up all hope of his survival to not even have brought him to a veterinarian. I suppose they expected him to die. The veterinarian, my father and I nursed him back to health."

"Aren't you afraid someone will steal him from you?"

"No, he can be very unpleasant if someone was to approach him to try to touch him. See for yourself."

Ben put his hand out to touch him. Immediately, Reliant's ears began to lay back showing anger. His head became more erect. His tension was visibly rising, a sign of hostility to a stranger.

"Ben take your hand away before it's too late"

"He was really upset, Chovinne. Why did you do this?"

"I wanted you to learn something. Here give me your hand and you'll know why."

He obligingly gave her his hand.

"Now, I'll introduce you to my horse"

"I've taken your hand to show Reliant that you aren't to be feared."

She took the reins and together they stood in front of him.

"Touching you shows him that he has nothing to fear from you because I have accepted you."

"Now you and I will touch him together."

This time Reliant's reaction was quite different. For a brief moment he hesitated, then he became his old calm self. Slowly Chovinne took her hand away while Ben continued to stroke him.

"You'll never have to fear him again. He has accepted you now and he'll remember you."

"He is a beautiful animal."

"Well, new friend, this is where we part company. You're safe now. Take care of yourself, and don't come back down here."

"I won't, at least not alone. I promise."

"Good. Don't tempt fate, it's easy to lose out."

"I'm often in the city. I hope our paths will cross again," she said.

She watched as Ben, on his way back to the docks, stopped to buy some fresh pastries from a baker's cart.

She placed her fingers on her forehead and closed her eyes. Her mind was racing with endless thoughts whirling round and round in her head.

Two men who were standing not too far from her were boasting about all the money they had made betting on the races.

"It was bloody easy. I just bet and won," said one.

She stood as if mesmerized. This was it, the galloping horse in the teacup. She had her answer. She was ecstatic.

She had to go somewhere to think. She mounted her horse and went to Hyde Park. The nobs were riding in or driving their carriages. There was also the usual ostentatious display of status seekers. There was an unwritten social register that someone was always trying to break through. Any acknowledgement whatsoever by a person of exceptional wealth, breeding or prestige bestowed upon another of lesser quality was a very high compliment. These were the many "nouveau-riche" middle class people whose fortunes had only recently been accumulated parading up and down the park in their new ornately decorated carriages for all to see their success.

She left the noisy, bustling main thoroughfare inside the park and directed her horse to her favorite patch of green grass, far from the crowd to a shady spot on a hillside. Here the traffic was less dense.

Chovinne read the newspapers daily. They recounted England's economic growth. She was in a period of transition. They told how the cessation of wars and resulting political stability allowed England's material progress to prosper. Industriousness and private enterprise became the focus of more people. Private ownership increased accommodating the middle class with money to invest. The Victorian virtues of industry and honesty were rewarded by material prosperity.

She knew that the importation of cotton alone which entered the British ports for the textile mills and factories was in the millions of pounds. London was predominantly a finishing center.

Engineering firms were making machines and machine tools for industries.

The age of railways that had begun in the 1830's provided a network by which coal, iron and other commodities could be more easily transported from one place to another. Rail networks provided the transportation needed to bring the coal from the mines to the cities.

Canals were nearly completed as another avenue of transportation.

Main roads were being remade for smoother travel with less wear and tear on all coaches, wagons, omnibuses and all other smaller transportation that used them.

England led the way for swift ocean travel. There was really no competition. The markets of the world were open for manufactured goods. Her supremacy of the sea was a well known fact.

The euphoria that Londoners felt came from the fact that they had not engaged in wars for some time, and could now devote their energies to securing a better life for themselves.

This acceleration towards an industrial revolution gave her a lot to think about. She felt exhilarated now, more alive than she had been in a long time. She knew what direction she would take, and the steps to take, to achieve her goals.

"Chovinne hello!" said Andrew, "I recognized your horse as I was passing by. Have you been here long?"

"Only a short time. I was at one of the docks very early

this morning and stayed awhile."

"Why did you go there?"

"I went to see my future."

"Your future." He looked at her questioningly. "No one can see the future. Would you explain that to me?"

"I didn't know why I felt compelled to go there. While there I met a man, a dockworker. We began to speak of the vast economic opportunities that the expanding world markets could bring to a person who owned many ships."

"I read tea-leaves to help me understand significant symbols that I saw in my tea-cup. I saw a ship which left me confused until today when I went to the dock."

"Now I understand that the ship in the tea-cup means I will somehow be involved in trade. I will think about that and with time more will be revealed to me. The uncertainty I had about my future is gone. Now the future looks very promising."

"My concerns were intensified because of the untimely death of my father, which was unexpected and left me completely shattered. I lost my father and my very best friend. Since then I have become the voivode of the clan. The responsibility of seeing to their welfare then became mine."

"I'm sorry to hear of your loss. The death of a loved one is very painful for the ones who must remain. Tell me about him."

"I can't. It's still too soon, but I will someday. I'll tell you all about him and our life together."

She quickly changed the subject.

"Andrew, do you have some time," she asked.

Her tone of voice indicated that she had something important to say to him.

"I have a few hours before I must see someone," he said.

"Come, let's go inside my carriage." He opened the door for her.

They were hardly seated when she started talking.

"I need your help. I must find a broker, one whom I can trust. I need your recommendation before I can begin making my future investments."

He looked at her and smiled.

"I can finally repay your kindness since that almost tragic day we met."

She shook her head.

"I don't understand what you are saying."

"Chovinne, I am a stockbroker! That's how I earn my living. I would be delighted to direct and assist you in any way that I can."

What incredible good fortune, she thought. She had worried about finding someone upon whom she could depend to work only in her best interests. With a few words, he had allayed all her fears.

"I can't believe how fortunate I am." She smiled broadly. "I gladly accept your kind offer."

"Where do you want to begin?" he asked.

"First, I need some money. I don't have any yet, but I will."

He looked at her, but said nothing. She was leading up to something. He didn't interrupt her. He knew it was best to hear what she had to say.

"The capital I need is unavailable to me through conventional means. The banks of England rarely loan money to a woman and even less to a gypsy."

"I can get the capital for you."

"I can't let you do that. I'm responsible for my family. I must do it my way."

"How will you get the money?" he asked.

"The Classics."

He raised his eyebrows. He was surprised but he shouldn't have been. He knew she was resourceful.

"I have to go now."

"When will I hear from you again?" he asked.

"I will see you at Epsom. Stay close to the paddock. I'll be sure to find you there."

"Chovinne, it will be wonderful seeing you there. We'll finally be able to spend some time together."

"Yes, that will be very nice for me too."

CHAPTER 14

The leather bags she held in her hands contained all the gold, silver and copper jewelry that her father had made especially for her, plus his own. She would have to pawn them to get enough money to wager at the races, and to also buy herself some clothes and other essentials.

She hated having to pawn the jewelry, but it was her only recourse.

Pawnshops were poor people's banks and they flourished. These shops provided the poor like herself who were in need, piecemeal money to subsist a while longer.

Pawnshops were more than just isolated shops. There were many and their accessibility within the city and their convenience strengthened the bond between the pawnshop and the borrower. Habit, convenience, crisis, temporary difficulties, poverty and unemployment nurtured the growth of pawning.

She stood outside the pawnshop, its three unmistakable brass balls symbolically denoting this centuries old tradition of merchant identification.

When she stepped inside she saw that the shop overflowed with clothing, bedding, furniture, and numerous cheap, personal items. The shop reeked from the stench of old fish, cabbage, spoiled curdled milk, manure, mold, urine, vomit, oakum, and much more that had been left unwashed on the clothing by the people who had brought them here.

She saw the owner at the far end of the store standing behind a display case working on his ledgers. What she didn't realize was that he had one eye on his ledgers and the other on her.

As she approached him he extended his hand and cordially greeted her.

"You have something for me," he asked.

"I have come to pledge some jewelry."

She placed the leather bag on the display case before him.

He opened the bag and emptied the contents.

"Lovely, lovely," he exclaimed, "such exquisite gypsy jewelry...a cat's eye ring, a black opal ring set in heavy gold, large golden earrings, a parure set of necklaces, earrings and matching bracelets set in stamped gold, coral cameos on the finest filigreed golden mounts!" He held the earrings, necklaces, cameos and bracelets in his hands caressing each piece.

"There was some jewelry popped today, but yours is remarkably more beautiful. They are exquisite."

"You are aware the interest is high," he asked.

"Yes, I know."

"Your pledged items will be here waiting for you to redeem them."

"The terms are that if you cannot meet your repayment, your jewelry will be forfeited."

He reached down behind the display case, produced a cash box, opened it and counted out the loan.

"I hope that this money will help you out of your difficulties."

"I'm sure it will."

She turned to leave.

As she reached the door, the shopkeeper called out to her.

"I wish you luck."

She thanked him and left the shop. As she walked along

the narrow streets, she dodged soot-softened bricks, stones and mortar which lay on the ground, chipped and decaying from the elements.

She was apprehensive about returning to the shop that had once been the source of such pain and humiliation for her. It was important that she go. Finally, she decided to enter.

Immediately upon seeing her, a broad smile spread over the shopkeeper's face. He walked over to her and took both her hands in his.

"I'm so glad that you have come back to my shop. Tell me, what can I do for you?"

She noticed there was real warmth in his voice.

"I need clothes for my uncle. The most fashionable you have. He wants to make a favorable impression upon some important people and needs to look his very best. He and I are approximately the same height and weight."

His experienced eyes skimmed over her body taking in the dimensions at a glance.

"Consider it done. I have exactly the latest fashions. I'll put them together and package them for you. Please, be seated while you wait."

He escorted her to a sofa.

"You'll be comfortable here. I'll return as quickly as I can."

She sat back against the plush cushions enjoying their luxury. She closed her eyes and relaxed. She didn't have long to wait.

His voice startled her a bit, as he sat down on the sofa next to her.

She opened her eyes and saw his flushed face indicating he had worked at a rapid rate to be finished so soon.

"In this large box are the most fashionable men's clothes to be had in the whole of London town. Your uncle will be pleased with the selection I have chosen for him. They're my very best."

"The hat I have chosen, which you'll find in the smaller band box is also the latest in men's wear."

The pride he felt showed on his face.

"I appreciate so much all the help you have given me. I'm sure my uncle will be very happy." He didn't need to know that the clothes were for her.

"Now tell me, how much do I owe you?"

He told her and she paid it. She took the boxes from him.

Before she could get up from the sofa, he put a hand on her shoulder and looked directly into her eyes.

"I hope that we can establish a friendship. I would like the difficulty of the past to remain there."

"It's done and forgotten," she said.

She extended her hand.

"I'm Chovinne to my friends."

He took her hand with a firm grip.

"My name is Edward. This is a fresh beginning for us. Despite a very turbulent beginning, we have come this far. I hope our friendship will last a lifetime."

"I hope so too. I wish I could stay longer, but there is someone else I must see today."

She rose from the sofa.

"I'll be back soon."

"Until later, then."

She left him standing there.

He smiled to himself. He was pleased that this lovely woman had decided to be his friend. He was happy to have sold her the clothes and accessories at half their actual worth. It was the least he could do after such an unfortunate beginning.

CHAPTER 15

A small group of people had stopped to listen to a street reciter perform a scene from Hamlet.

This young man, who was eighteen years old, was a remarkable actor. He delivered the scene with such powerful eloquence that the onlookers stood spellbound. She knew he did this reciting on the streets to earn extra money. He hoped that by performing in the theatrical neighborhoods an actor or someone with influence would hear him and offer him work in a legitimate theater.

On his person were the most colorful clothes he could find, having been purchased second-hand from a street seller of old clothes.

When he wasn't reciting he worked as a pot-boy in a public house, carrying drinks to the frequenters who spent their days drinking beer and spirits.

When his recitation was over he passed his hat among the crowd. People had been pleased with his performance and were very generous. One coin after another was dropped into his hat.

He waited until the people had left. He then discretely counted the money and let the coins fall loosely into the large pockets of his coat.

"William, that was a wonderful recitation!"

Chovinne was clapping her hands in approval.

He looked at her coming towards him and made elaborate sweeping bows for her benefit.

She laughed at his antics.

"It's so nice to see you," he said as he hugged her. "It has been a long time."

"Too long," she answered.

"Have you been away," he asked. "Have you had troubles with the authorities moving you about?"

"No, none of that, we have been here all along."

She proceeded to tell him about the tragic circumstances that had led to her father's death.

"I'm so sorry. I don't know what else to say. Words are my life and they fail me."

"Thank you, William, I know you are, but let's talk of other things. What have you been doing besides street-recitations and potting?"

"I have been working day and night."

"Doing what, where," she asked.

There is an old shop which is not far from here that was fixed up and turned into a Penny-Gaff. Workers tore it apart inside. Walls were taken out to make a large stage. The band is on one side of it. The fiddler, harpist and cornopean play the tunes to which the gaff goers dance. The new balconies upstairs accommodate even more people."

"What do you do there?" Chovinne asked.

"I'm asked to stay and perform at least three times out of the six performances given during the evening. I occasionally fill in for the singer of comic songs, and I recite although it's not supposed to be allowed."

"The crowds are numerous. When I have finished speaking, I receive a thunderous ovation. I'm very good but the applause is something they feel they must do. They really don't understand what I recite. I don't take it personally, that is just the way it is."

He kept on talking.

"I don't want to be in those places, but my circumstances are such that I can't refuse. The money I earn allows me to eat and to rent a filthy room at a cheap lodging house."

"I hope this isn't the way I'll live forever. I long for the time that I'll be fortunate enough to perform in the theaters.

"You will someday, it takes time."

"I love to perform. It consumes my life. I don't think of anything else. When I'm not acting or working, I write. I know that whatever I write will never equal the great Shakespeare. I feel privileged every time I recite his words.

"Your talent is precious. You mustn't lose it. I have a suggestion, do you want to hear it?"

"Yes, please tell me. I want a good life, to do what I love most. I don't want to end up sleeping in the street, or worse in a work house."

"Make an application to the Theaters for an audition. Offer your help. They always need people to help them with costumes, scenery, props, etc. This would give you the opportunity to know and be close to the actors. It would be an apprenticeship. Listening, learning and cultivating your skills by just being there among them. They would get to know you, and if you asked them to listen to you recite they would be receptive to your requests. If something unforeseen was to happen to one of the actors, a death, an illness, or someone going abroad, you could possible be called upon to replace him."

"I'll do it," he said enthusiastically. "I'll go today. I feel much better now!"

"William, before you go, I need a favor from you."

"Anything for you, if I can."

"I need some moustaches, wigs and Piccadilly Weepers."

He looked at her with a grin on his face.

"Are you asking for yourself?" he asked.

"Yes, but I can't answer any questions you may have. It's important to me, but I can't tell you why I need them."

"Then I won't ask you."

He reached for a leather bag next to his feet. "I always bring extras of everything with me."

"The moustaches, wigs and weepers have never been worn by anyone. They are new."

"Here, take what you need," he said, as he handed her the bag.

"Choose whatever you like. They are yours to keep."

She chose everything in black to match her hair.

"Take some netting. You'll need it. Also some spirit gum and alcohol."

He proceeded to tell her what to do with everything. When he finished explaining, he asked her if she understood. She told him that she did.

"How much do I owe you for all this, William?"

"I buy whatever I need at the theatrical supply shops. They aren't that expensive."

"Are you sure, I really don't like not paying for these."

"The only payment I want is to hear about all this someday from you, every detail because I know it'll be very interesting."

"I accept then. Thank you. You are very generous."

"William, I have something for you. Give me your hand."

Obligingly, he extended his hand.

"Here is a charm for good luck. Keep it with you at all times."

"What is in it?" he asked.

"A small piece of paper that I took from a weathered and tattered theater bill."

"I wanted to see the play very much, but I didn't have the money."

"What was the play?" he asked.

"Shakespeare's Hamlet."

"His best, I'm sorry."

"That isn't important now. You are. I want all the luck this charm possesses to come to you now."

He stepped back from her and in a deep theatrical voice he said.

"Madam, I must go, the theatrical world awaits me!"

"Au revoir and thank you," he said with a smile.

She noticed there was a bounce in his step now. He was more optimistic than he had been in a long time. She knew he would succeed. He had a natural talent and charm. His tendency toward flamboyance was a definite asset. He loved to be seen and heard.

Chovinne knew that for a time he was every person he played on the stage or in the street. His scenes were real for him and, as a result of his deliverances, became for a time real for his audiences.

CHAPTER 16

The grayish-red embers from the evening's cook fires were the only sign of life that greeted Chovinne as she returned home to the encampment. It was late; the others were sleeping. She tended to her horse, giving him water and feed. He, too, had had a long day. When she was finished, she picked up her packages, climbed the steps of the caravan and entered.

Whenever she left the caravan, Chovinne had established a routine of always placing the lamps on the kitchen table for easy access if she came home late and night had fallen. She lit a match and walked to the table. Carefully, she lifted the colorful shades from the squatty glass candle cups. There were fittings at the base to hold the small candles. She thought about how much these Fairy Lamps had changed her life. She felt safer knowing that the constant threat of fire from drafts was eliminated, as well as the smoke and smell because no paraffin was used in making them. The constant annoying flickering experienced from other types was now an unpleasant memory. Having lit them all, she replaced the pink shades on the cups. The caravan was filled with a soft rosy glow. She placed these night lights at strategic places in the caravan. She went directly to the windows and drew the curtains together. The light might awaken the others and she didn't want to be disturbed. She gathered her packages from the floor and placed them on her bed.

She could not deny her curiosity any longer. She had waited long enough to see what Edward had packaged for her. She opened the larger package with great eagerness. Neatly folded and placed right on the top were two black frock-coats. She saw they were made of the very finest cashmerette broadcloth with silk facings on the lapels. She laid them down and was totally captured by the beauty of the four waistcoats; a lovely blue cashmere, a striped satin with a floral pattern, a brocade and a dotted velvet. Beneath these were four cravats, five stand up collars and three separate velvet bags.

She wondered what could possibly be in them. She didn't know which to open first. She decided on the center one. Hastily, she eagerly reached inside anticipating its contents. She was amazed to see a gold Albert watch on a large gold chain. What a lovely splendid watch! It must cost a small fortune she thought. She knew only the very well-to-do wore them. They were the only ones to whom money was no object.

In the next bag was a round-framed gold monocle which hung on a fine gold chain to be worn around the neck.

The final bag held tie pins and ornamental buttons for the waistcoats. Gold cuff links and jeweled shirt studs were included. Edward had also added three rings among the array of beautiful jewelry.

It all took her breath away, and there was still more! As she reached in she withdrew fine kid gloves, shirts, trousers, socks, and square toed pumps. At the very bottom was a gold handled walking cane with a rich black ebony finish, inlaid with bits of ivory. She unscrewed the handle and revealed a hidden compartment for hiding money or papers, small daggers and other things.

Lastly, she opened the bandbox and lifted out the black silk plush topper.

Edward had really seen to it that nothing had been left to chance. No man would be dressed more fashionably than this!

It was time to begin changing her appearance. Taking her long hair she divided it down the back of her head and wound the two sides so they would cross over. She pinned the hair into place.

William had provided her with some very fine netting material, She used it to wind around her hair to further guarantee the proper fitting of the wig. It fit tightly on her head. There were no gaps to reveal that it was not her own hair. It fell evenly to just below her ears.

All the additional necessary items were placed on the table before her, the Piccadilly weepers, moustache, brush, antique oil to help set the curls, curling tongs, spirit gum and alcohol.

She took the wig off so that the hair wouldn't impede her while she fixed her face. She took the weepers and the moustache and fit them on her face for size adjustments. Moving her head from side to side, she saw by the reflection in the mirror that they were too bulky and needed to be trimmed.

William had stressed the importance of angle cutting the hair vertically. It was the way facial hair grew. He explained that only in this way would the hair lie on the face in a real and natural manner. She did the same thing with the moustache to give it a genuine appearance.

Cautiously, she clipped the hair until it looked right. She looked at herself again and again. Finally it looked perfect and natural. She was sure she wouldn't be detected.

Now the really difficult step, the application of the spirit gum. There was no room for error here. She applied the spirit gum with a brush to the sides of her face. When the gum became tacky, she pressed the weepers firmly into position, right up to the natural hairline in front of her ear.

She did the same with the moustache holding it above her upper lip.

Blue shading on her jaw, chin and around her bottom lip suggested the growth of stubble.

She combed the antique oil into the wig hair. The curling tongs would insure the curls would stay set.

Finished, she again put the wig on her head. Looking at herself she smiled broadly. The disguise was so perfect that even she couldn't see any similarity to her old self.

Now came the clothing. The gold cuff links when placed on the shirt were dazzling. Next came the stand up collar and cravat. The tie pin pricked her finger as she inserted it in the cravat to hold it in place. She waited until her finger stopped bleeding before continuing. Assuring herself that it had, she proceeded to step into the trousers. This accomplished, she put on the socks and square-toed pumps. She was a little indecisive as to which waistcoat to choose; the brocade prevailed. Acquiring an adeptness for fastening the ornamental buttons with a button hook wasn't an easy task. With practice it got easier. The round framed monocle looked distinguished hanging from her neck. The gold watch with its Albert watch chain was indeed stunning. It gave her the look of prosperity that she desired to achieve.

The kid gloves she put on her hands felt as soft as her own skin. The black frock coat and the black silk topper were next. From the chair beside her she took the walking cane into her hands.

The picture was complete. She had acquired the refined finishing touch that she wanted.

The transformation was total. She stood up and scrutinized herself. The picture was excellent. She looked every inch like a very prosperous, dignified man.

There would be much to accomplish in a few days. She would have to look, think and act like a man. It would take intense concentration to transform herself for a time. It was good that she had been around men all her life. She had heard their thoughts and opinions on religion, family-life, politics, occupations and leisure time.

In addition, newspapers did much to educate the public. They printed the pros and cons on any subject as accurately as possible. Because she was literate, she was prepared to discuss whatever subject that would arise during conversations from the male point of view, assuring that her arguments would be convincing and educated.

While in a gentlemanly state, she would have to maintain at all times an acute awareness of even the most subtle nuances of the mannerisms of the male gender. Actions always speak louder than words. Even the most trivial shouldn't be taken for granted. Walking, sitting, standing and common courtesies, if not done in a proper manner, would cause immediate suspicion if said or done out of the ordinary.

Dudras tapped lightly on Chovinne's door. He waited a few minutes. When there was no answer, he tapped again. Still no answer from inside the caravan. It was late. She must have fallen asleep, he thought. The lights meant the candles were still lit and burning.

He slowly inched the door open and looked inside. He saw a figure at the far end of the caravan. What he saw was not Chovinne, but a man's silhouette, his back to him.

This was very strange. He didn't know what to think. He was nervous. This was not what he expected to encounter.

He looked around him, trying to locate Chovinne. Not seeing her, he became alarmed. Perspiration was forming on his brow. He wiped the sweat away with his fingers. His heart was racing. He felt each heartbeat thumping loudly inside his chest.

Strangers had intruded in the encampments before. They waited until everyone was asleep. Then they stole whatever they could find that was valuable.

A look of pain and horror spread over his face. This person was in Chovinne's caravan and he couldn't see her anywhere. He immediately assumed something terrible had happened. He was worried sick.

He quickly stepped inside, closing the door soundlessly behind him. He walked toward the table. On it lay some sharp-edged knives that could easily wound or kill someone. He reached for the largest one. His strong hand securely gripped the handle, his fingers seemingly glued to it.

Focusing his attention on the intruder, he slowly and deliberately walked towards him. When he was close enough, he lunged at him. In that one swift motion, he wrapped his muscular arm around his neck. The other hand held the knife against his throat defying him to move.

"Where is my cousin? Tell me what you have done with her. I will kill you if any harm has come to her. Talk now!"

"Dudras, let go of me. You are choking me!"

He heard a very faint, raspy but unmistakable voice. He was stunned. He released her.

"What is happening here?" he shouted immediately.

She began to cough and take deep breaths.

He walked around the chair and stood in front of her.

Looking at her incredulously, he said, "Chovinne, have you lost your mind? Why are you dressed this way? I could really have hurt you or worse."

"I have a plan and dressing this way is part of it," she said between breaths.

"You must dress like a man? For what purpose?

"Let me catch my breath and I will tell you."

He listened closely to everything she said.

"You will be taking a big risk. You could lose everything you have pledged at the pawnshop and the money you had left after the funeral."

"I won't lose. Tea leaves always have meaning. I believe that, but it is up to me to select the right horses."

"I always read what the newspapers report about the races with great interest. It's exciting reading about the fillies and the colts, their development, their successes and their losses. I have stored all of this information in my mind."

"I repeat myself Chovinne. Betting on horses is a disastrous business."

She wouldn't allow his pessimism to influence her.

"The field for the meetings is very big this year. With so many entries, betting will be high. I will win more money than you have ever imagined."

"Two horses in particular, a filly and a colt, are entered in the Classics. I know these three year olds will be special. They are ready to prove they are the best. Their trainers have not overtrained them as others have. This makes them good candidates because they most likely have not grown sour and quite sick of racing from being subjected to pain and distress. They have been brought close to winning quite a few times."

"The filly has remarkable speed. She will easily win the Oaks."

"The colt will also prove to be an excellent choice. He has speed and endurance for the Derby. You know that those are the two overriding factors that are considered in that grueling horserace. He possesses the stamina that is necessary.

"The owner has changed jockeys. This new man has an extraordinary judgment of pace. He will be the turnabout for him."

"Many people would disagree with all of my ideas, but to me they are and always will be the uppermost considerations. They supersede the others."

"I can see that you have thought about this thoroughly to defend it so vigorously. You have convinced me."

"Now I need your help. Will you help me rehearse, Dudras?"

"Of course, I will."

"We have a week before the Derby. The next two days will be spent rehearsing until I become a perfect gentleman, then, a day on the coach, a day spying on the horses to be raced, and one day coming home. Then we will all leave for the Derby."

*

Dudras began the training.

"Chovinne, these are the basic rules of etiquette that men follow."

"When riding on horseback or walking along the street, the lady always has the wall."

"When meeting a lady in the street or in the park whom you know only slightly, you wait for her acknowledging bow. Then, and only then, may you tip your hat to her, which, by the way, is done using the hand farthest away from her to raise your hat. You do not speak to the lady or to any other lady unless she speaks to you first."

"If you meet a lady who is a good friend and she signifies that she wishes to talk to you, you turn and walk with her if you wish to converse. It is not "done" to make a lady stand talking in the street."

"When climbing up a flight of stairs, you precede the lady. When going down, you follow."

"In a carriage, a gentleman takes the seat facing backward. If he is alone in a carriage with a lady, he does not sit next to her unless he is her husband, brother, father, or son. He alights from the carriage first so that he may help her down. He takes care not to step on her dress."

"At a public exhibition or concert, if accompanied by a lady, a man goes in first, in order to find her a seat. If he enters such an exhibition alone and there are ladies or older gentlemen present, he removes his hat."

"One more thing, a gentleman never smokes in the presence of ladies."

"Chovinne, you must know and remember these rules. One mistake and you'll be humiliated. You could also be labeled a social outcast."

"Tipping your hat and mastering the cane is what we have to work on right now."

"Let us begin then. We have much to accomplish."

"After being acknowledged, show me how you would tip your hat to the ladies."

She put her hand up, grabbed the had, tipped it, but brought it down too quickly.

"No, no," he said with some impatience. "Go slowly, smile."

"This isn't going to be as simple as I believed."

"Just put your mind to it. You told me how important this is."

"When I become this other person, I'll have to leave myself behind. I'll look upon this as yet another challenge for me to master and conquer."

After some time had elapsed, Chovinne told Dudras that she had had enough of hat procedures for the day.

"Show me what you would do with your cane."

"My cane? I just carry it beside, me, I suppose."

"You suppose wrongly!"

"There are various ways to hold the cane."

"Take the cane next to you and, step by step, I will teach you what to do."

"Are you ready to begin?"

"Yes."

"This will take some time. You aren't too tired are you? If you are, we can stop for today."

"No, I want to continue. We don't have much time, only two days."

"Good, then we will begin."

"Place your thumb and forefinger at the top of the cane. Now, curl your other fingers inside the palm of your hand, but not too high. Just so your nails do not show."

"How does it feel to you?"

"It feels like I had better hold on tightly or this cane will fall out of my hand."

He sat back in the chair next to her. "Practice, release your grip and repeat the procedure until I tell you to stop."

It was a full half hour before he stopped her.

Her fingers were sore, but she didn't say anything.

"Now a simplified way. Take the cane and set it squarely in the palm of your hand, wrapping all your fingers around it. Good," he said as she held it perfectly. "This is the preferred way to hold your cane if your other hand is occupied holding a glass or anything else. What is important is how you stand. Your left leg remains straight while the other one is set apart and pointing away from your body."

"Hold your cane in the palm of your hand just like before, only this time take your other hand and rest it on your hip. Place your feet slightly apart and point them in different directions. This stance is an extreme example of self-importance carried to the limit by the Gorgios."

"Slant your body forward, now move your right leg outward and bend your knee slightly. Keep your left leg straight. Tilt the cane backward and hold it with your thumb and forefinger."

Surprisingly, she didn't have many problems mastering the cane.

Under Dudras' watchful tutelage, she practiced and refined the fine art of the finesse needed to portray a man of substance.

CHAPTER 17

"I have called upon you to come together with me because I have something very important to talk to you about. What I have to say will drastically change our lives. I'll do this only if you are with me. The family must be united in this venture for us to succeed."

She proceeded to tell them her plans.

"I'll bet on the Classics if you agree. With the money that I'll win, I'll buy a large home for all of us. We'll have land to till and enough food to fill our stomachs. We'll have cows, sheep, pigs, chickens, and horses–many horses that we will need for our carriage service.

"This may sound impossible to you all, but I can do it. Tea leaves have foretold our destinies. They showed me a path to follow where there was none before."

"How will we be able to live in the Gorgio world? They spit on us; they hate us. It would mean adjusting to their world."

"Yes, we will need to adjust to their world when we must. But our home, that will be the exception. There, we'll be free. It'll be ours. For the first time in our lives we'll have something that will belong to us and only us. No constables to come around to send us on our way. Think how wonderful that would be."

"We cannot wipe out centuries of contempt, suspicion

and anger against us. It can never be wiped out!"

"We won't have to. We'll go about our business as we always have. Those who want to accept us will, those who won't we can live without. We are a family. No one and nothing will ever change that."

"We will have to work very hard, at first, but we do that now. We struggle and scrape every day, just to stay alive. That is very hard, and we have nothing to look forward to. When we have our land, we'll never want for anything so desperately again. I promise you."

"I'll leave you now. Take this day to think and talk among yourselves. I must have your decisions this evening. If you agree that this is the right course for us, I'll leave for Newmarket and the secret trials tomorrow morning."

She left them to digest everything she had said. They had a whole life change to think about."

The waiting seemed to go on forever. The sun was beginning to set when she heard a knock on the door. Opening it, she saw them all there.

"Don't keep me waiting any longer. What have you decided?"

"We have all agreed that we can gain nothing if we don't take the risks."

"We'll work hard and reap benefits we have never known before. We'll become prosperous gypsies. More importantly, we'll still be together, and that is what is paramount."

"While I'm gone to Newmarket, I want everything repaired that needs it. When I return, we'll be leaving immediately for Epsom. Ladies practice your fortune telling skills. The Gorgios are waiting for us."

CHAPTER 18

"Dudras, isn't it exciting! At last I'm on my way to find out what we need to know about the horses so we can continue with our plans."

"Seeing you smile like that is contagious."

"The sun is shining. That is a good sign."

"Especially here, it rains so often. Look I can see it from here," her finger pointed to the inn. "Let us hurry."

At their urging, the horses began to trot at a faster pace. The pounding of their hooves on the ground echoed loudly.

Inns outside of London were the places that had the booking offices for coach operators. Posters were printed and displayed on the walls. Patrons only had to look at them to learn where and when the coaches would run. Journey times indicated which day of the week coaches would depart and the approximate arrival times at their destinations. All the towns served and the distances between each town and the fares, as well as the amount of luggage passengers might carry for a modest sum of money per pound was also indicated.

Guidebooks with notes inside were gratuitously given to the passengers outlining places of interest they would be seeing on their routes.

This was all made possible because of a nationwide network of inns, offices, coachmakers, post-boys, blacksmiths, saddlers, harness makers, stables and repair yards. Farmers supplied the hay for the horses. Waiters and maids at the inns looked after the travelers.

Chovinne bought her ticket and was told the coach was ready for boarding. Dudras walked with her to the coach.

"Chovinne, I'm not going to tell you how to take care of yourself. You're more than capable. You've handled emergencies that would have left other women helpless and afraid. I can't let you go, though, without this admonition. You are a woman alone, don't be friendly and especially don't smile. Smiling is often taken as some kind of permission and weakness. A smile allows an intrusion into your life. More often than not, it isn't to your advantage. Maintain your distance, this allows you to go about your affairs without interruptions."

"I knew that already, but rest assured I won't forget. I hear you."

"Good, much luck. It will seem like an eternity until I see you again."

She was the first inside the coach and sat next to the window.

CHAPTER 19

The journey to Newmarket by coach was a torturous body-jolting experience. The deep ruts in the road caused the coach to bump which in turn made it sway precariously. Many times along the way, the passengers hung on to the sides of the coach or to their seats to avoid being catapulted to the other side. The linen side-curtains were closed in a futile effort to keep out the road dust, leaving the interior of the coach in almost complete darkness. Within Chovinne's reach was an upright coach lamp with a candle inside and matches beneath it. She knew it would be an impossibility to light the interior of the coach, because it swayed so violently. When it finally arrived at the Countryside Inn, she was relieved that her ordeal was over for the time being.

As the coach slowed, she opened the curtain to get a good look at the inn. Two old wooden entrance gates had been opened and the coach entered into a cobbled courtyard.

The inn was two storied. It had a thatched roof, shuttered windows and an unbroken parapet which carried its lettered sign.

Opening the door of the inn, she stepped into a dining room with heavy fine carved beamed ceilings and timber uprights. The most obvious piece of furniture was the large dining table in the center of the room. Chairs were pushed in and neatly arranged around the table. A decorative linen tablecloth covered it. A massive sideboard was placed in close proximity. The sideboard was utilitarian as well as a showpiece. On the upper half were general shelves which held crystal glassware and decorative pieces. The center drawer contained the linens and silverware that were just below a large marble open shelf. This shelf was used to hold items before they were served to the guests or to place items removed from the table when the meal was finished. Large enclosed cabinets beneath held a multitude of items that were to be placed on the table, among them–silver serving dishes, cruet sets, sugar bowls, cream pitchers, and goblets.

To the left was a large stone fireplace that heated the inn, with two deep inglenooks on each side. A worker was busily taking logs from the wood tender and placing them over others on the andiron. Using tongs, he adjusted the logs on the fire and, with a poker, moved some burning logs. When he had finished that, he used a copper bellows with leather folds to blow air onto the fire. Next, he proceeded to take a short handled broom to remove ash and clean around the fireplace. He neatly replaced everything when he was done.

At the far end of the dining room was a beautifully carved mahogany bar. The staff were positioned before foot-and-a-half-long hand cranks, filling tankards and pewter mugs with real ale from casks. It was thick, rich and dark. Inns had special cellars where the ale was allowed to ferment longer, thereby softening the edges.

At her immediate right was a hall stand, a tall piece of furniture placed against the wall. It had hooks for clothing and a mirror so that each guest could check his or her appearance. It also had a storage box and a drawer for gloves. There also was a hat rack hung on the wall next to the hall stand. Close by stood a tall case clock.

The innkeeper's desk was next to the clock. It was in a strategic location, not too far from the front door, allowing him a perfect spot to see to the smooth everyday operation of his business.

Chovinne signed the register and was given her room number and key. The innkeeper wished her a pleasant stay. He apologized that he was temporarily understaffed and would she mind taking the stairs not far from them by herself? He assured her that she would have no difficulty finding her room. The landing was wide and looked like a full stair, but it was only an illusion. When she turned to climb the stairs, she found it curious that it was such a narrow curved staircase. The stairway lamps lit her way. When she reached the second floor, she stepped into a pink corridor. The walls had soft pink tinted flower prints on them. She walked to her room which was the last one on the right side of the corridor.

Inserting her key into the keyhole, she noticed that it was a very solid door. It made no sound as she pushed it open. There would be no question that the smallest squeak would not be heard. This was unsettling; she didn't like it. It was too quiet. She filed this in her mind to remember.

She stood on the threshold cautiously looking to see what was beyond. The same print on the corridor walls continued into the room. It wasn't a large room, just large enough to be comfortable. The brass bed caught her eyes; it was so shiny, it glittered. A delicate lace bedspread covered the bed. Lace cushions had been placed next to the pillow shams. The pink walls, the lovely lace and the gleaming bed were startling. The beauty of it all created a dreamy color scheme.

The window was gracefully framed by two elegant see-through lace panels which linked the inside with the outside. The laced window dressing suffused the room with a tranquil light. The panels were swagged around a thick wooden rod held by brackets. The bottom of the panels lay extravagantly puddled on the floor. If someone wanted to open the windows for fresh air, these panels could be drawn back by passementerie, corded tasseled tiebacks, and held there.

She continued taking in her surroundings. The one large armchair in a corner of the room had antimacassar lace protectors on the arms and back to prevent soiling. Next to that was a simple armoire, a free-standing closet.

A framed art wall hanging was suspended by a golden braided cord with a tassel at the top and at each end.

The mirrored vanity had a hand mirror, brush, comb, perfume bottles, face powder, scented oil, lavender soap, and a red velvet jewelry box. A dried flower bouquet in a crystal vase stood on one end.

The commode was a one-piece unit. A mirror at the top and at the center was a flat surface with a standing splash backboard made of waterproof marble. This space was for the bowl and pitcher. Below this were drawers to hold the towels, and, then, a larger compartment to store the bowl and pitcher when not in use.

She walked over to the bed and placed her leather bag on it. It was wide on the bottom concealing a secret compartment. It graduated to a narrow top, much like a doctor's bag. Taking off her outer clothing, she placed them on the bed. Taking a hairbrush from inside the bag, she brushed her long black hair to rid it of the accumulated road dust.

She poured some water from the pitcher into the bowl. Cupping her hand, she scooped up some water and let it fall slowly down her face, back into the bowl. She did this a few times before taking the towel to blot off the excess water remaining on her face.

Next, she cleaned her clothes and shoes with brushes that she had brought for that purpose.

Finished, she put her clothes back on, hung her change of clothes in the armoire, and placed her leather bag there also. She left the room and locked the door. Then, Chovinne walked to the stables behind the inn. Inside were three horses and carriages, and three horses and post-chaises for hire. These were always ready and waiting to be at the disposal of the travelers who stayed at the inn, who might need them for getting about.

She inspected each horse and post-chaise carefully and settled on the one with the Cleveland Bay. She paid the hiring fee, received her receipt and left for a specific area where she knew the secret horse trials were held.

She stayed a reasonable distance away, high on a hill overlooking the course. Chovinne tied the horse to one of the many trees around her. She felt secure in the knowledge that they provided her the camouflage she needed to get a concentrated view of the activities that were due to begin momentarily.

She focused her field glasses on the course. There they were. She could see the colts being brought out by their trainers. The five runners were restless. They wanted to run; they loved to run. They were difficult to hold down when they knew what was expected of them. With her knowledge of horses, she knew that the first requirement of a potentially excellent offspring was being the progeny of a fast runner. The second was that the dam of this lineage thoroughbred have a kind and gentle nature.

She moved the field glasses slowly over each one until she came to Britilen, the one upon whom she placed her hopes. Her eyes liked what she saw. A large, handsome colt, his physical muscularity and wide, but not fat, girth was impressive. He was heavy, but not clumsy. He was eager and impatient and conspicuously restless, but not nervous. He was there to run and win. He was mentally adjusted.

Her attention now was diverted to the other colts. They, too, were ready, but were not nearly as sharp as Britilen.

The signal to begin was given. The colts set off with reckless impetuosity, the bursts of speed had the pack running firm. Britilen lengthened his stride. This aggressive competitor continued to press, opening up, increasing the distance between himself and the others. Full of running, he sailed on to beat the others by seven lengths.

"He is incredible!" she said aloud. Barring any unforeseen circumstances, he will win the Derby outright. She was ecstatic. In her wildest dreams, she had never dared to suppose that such a magnificent animal existed.

The sporting intelligence carried by the newspapers had definitely missed calculating this horse's capabilities.

But, despite all that she had seen, she knew that she had to maintain a detached assessment at all times. The only true indicators of outcomes were how the horse performed in four or five recent races and his looks and overall condition on racing day.

When she returned to the inn, Chovinne noticed that a bed warmer was on the floor outside her door. It was a copper pan filled with hot coals to put beneath the covers to keep warm. She unlocked her door, picked up the warmer, went inside, locked her door and placed the warmer on the floor next to the bed.

Chovinne wasn't thrilled about an overnight stay at the inn. She was apprehensive and didn't believe in fairy tales. She knew that evil people existed and that bad things could and did happen to anyone, anytime, anywhere. Standing next to the bed, she took the square pillows out of their backless shams. Then, she turned down the bedspread and exposed the linen sheets. She passed her hand on the fine linen and let it linger there. All this luxuriousness was totally indulgent. She was accustomed to sleeping on coarse, unbleached sheets which were rough to the touch.

Sitting on the edge of the bed, she removed her boots, then got into bed fully clothed. If anything happened, she would be prepared. She sank into a soft, deep mattress. Her feet were cold so she sat up and reached for the warmer on the floor and placed it under her feet. She pulled the sheet and blanket up close to her chin. It was midday. She closed her eyes. The trials she had just witnessed played themselves over and over in her mind. The young colt had displayed a fierce competitive instinct. He was bold and enthusiastic. This made Chovinne hopeful and she drifted off to sleep.

A horrendous noise resonated throughout the room, waking her from a sound sleep. What an awful way to summon the guests to dinner, she thought. There had to be a better way than striking a brass gong. Her body hurt and she wasn't in the best of moods. She gave commands to her body to move, but it didn't respond. The coach and carriage rides had taken their toll. She just lay there. Her entire body was utterly stiff and achy.

She felt like she was a hundred years old. Very slowly she sat up, and then eased her feet to the floor.

Looking at her clothes, she could see they weren't wrinkled even though she had slept in them. She put her boots on and stood up.

I'll feel better, she said to herself. Just a little more time, I'll get through this.

Once downstairs, she sat in the inglenook next to the blazing log fire in the hearth. A waiter rolled out a Sweet Trolley with an assortment of pastries, scones and strawberry jam, china, spoons and a silver teapot. He poured Chovinne a cup of tea. Chovinne had brought some white willow bark with her for the pain that she knew would ensue, and put some in her tea along with a lot of sugar because the bark was very bitter. Soon the pain and soreness would only be a memory. She sat back, gazing into the fire. She noticed a metal fireback inside the open fireplace. This was to protect the brickwork at the back from the fierce heat of the flames, and to throw the heat into the room. She tried to see pictures in the flames, and was disappointed when she couldn't. The willow bark was beginning to relieve her pain. She was feeling a little better and was enjoying herself. The sweets on the Sweet Trolley were delectable.

A man, whom she recognized as traveling in the coach at the same time as she had, approached her.

"Do you mind if I sit here next to you?" he asked.

A very perceptible, disagreeable odor of alcohol wafted to her nose.

"Yes, I do mind. I prefer to sit alone."

She moved away from him.

He gave her an icy stare and took a swig from the pewter mug of mulled ale he held in his hand.

"Did I hear you correctly? You, a gypsy, are too good for me. I wipe my feet on the likes of you. You are such low-class people. You should be flattered that I even acknowledge you."

He was very loud. Everyone was looking in her direction. All the old hurts and humiliations she had always choked down were intensified once again. She should be accustomed to this by now, but she wasn't. All the old spiteful wounds plus this new one hurt her once more. She hurt physically, and, now, she was suffering emotionally as well. What more could go wrong?

Looking at him, she made a decision that she would no longer allow others to cripple her emotionally. She wouldn't give anyone that satisfaction again. It had to stop, and there was no better time than the present to deal with the scurrilous language and other vulgarities directed at her from the multitude of Gorgios like him, that she would always encounter. She would never be able to insulate herself from all abuse, but she was strong and would handle whatever she had to.

"Your words fail to shock me. You haven't said anything that I haven't heard before. It's obvious that you're drunk. I'm sure if you were sober you would be aware and realize how your foul mouth is offensive and self-deprecating. You are totally without good manners, sir."

She stood up and returned his icy stare. She would no longer let words or intimidation or strength empower these people.

He raised his arm to strike her.

She was prepared and wasn't going to let him hit her. She lifted her arms and with the palms of her hands she pushed hard against his chest. He was already unsteady on his feet and completely lost his balance. He fell backward onto the floor. The force of the backward motion caused the ale from the mug in his hand to become a projectile that splashed his entire face as the liquid came back down.

He was so incensed that he tried to grab the mug to throw at her. She kicked it away from his reach, and then with her booted foot swiftly clamped down hard on his fingers, hand and wrist. He writhed in pain. In her hand, she held the silver teapot that she had hastily grabbed from the Sweet Trolley and was prepared to pour the hot tea in his face, if he persisted.

She felt a hand on her shoulder.

"I'll handle this now."

She turned and looked up to see a friend, a constable who had befriended her in the city of London. One of the few who had always been kind to her and her family.

He helped the man get to his feet.

"The lady wants you to go."

"Lady, what lady, she is nothing but a ..."

He didn't get a chance to finish his verbal assault. The constable grabbed him and literally threw him out the door of the inn.

The constable came back to speak with her.

"He's gone. He won't bother you again."

"Thank you for helping me."

"It's especially gratifying to help a friend. I had the authority to assist you, and I did it by tossing that rogue into the street."

"It's close to the dinner hour. We both must eat. Let's have dinner together. I would like your company, if you approve."

"I would love to dine with you."

The waiters had begun setting the table. White earthenware dinner plates were placed on the table, along with the cut-crystal goblets, cutlery, silver butter dishes, bone holder, spoon holders and linen napkins. Four deep-dish serving dishes were also placed on the table.

A calling bell was rung and Chovinne, along with the constable, left the inglenook and walked over to the table to join the other diners. When they were all seated, the waiters filled their plates.

Chovinne looked at the constable.

"I never expected this! We're having Fidget Pie."

She remembered having this at the Abbey. It was filled with pheasant and partridge, potatoes, onions, apples and spices. It had a thick light golden brown, buttery crust and was absolutely wonderful. Bread and butter accompanied the meal. There would be Cherry Tarts for dessert.

Since everything couldn't possibly be placed on the table, one only had to ask the waiter, and he would get it for them from the sideboard.

She didn't drink any champagne or port. She didn't approve of alcoholic beverages. What had happened to her earlier in the evening proved her point of the deleterious effects of alcohol to impair and alter a person's personality.

The dinner was very pleasant, and they both chatted quite a bit. The time passed swiftly, much to their dismay.

"This evening has ended too soon. The company and the food was delightful. I enjoyed myself very much," he said.

"I did also."

"I'm glad I got this opportunity to know you."

"I, as well."

Most of the diners had already left. It was an informal

dinner, and the guests left when they wanted to.

"It looks like we are the last to leave. If you wish, I'll escort you to your room."

"I would like that."

When they arrived, she unlocked her door.

"Do you mind if I go in with you to see if everything is in order?" he asked.

"No, I don't mind.

She went in and lit the candle while he waited at the door.

"You can come in now."

He thoroughly inspected the room, looking in the armoire and under the bed.

"Everything is in order. My room is down the hall and he gave her his room number. Don't hesitate to call me if you need me."

She sat down at the mirrored vanity. She began brushing her hair. She was thinking about everything that had transpired earlier. She had questions that needed answers. The constable insisted on thoroughly investigating her room. She supposed that although it was unusual in her mind it wasn't to him. Being a constable, he always expected the worst. What had occurred earlier in the evening would have been enough to prompt him to be watchful.

The quietness of the door had left an indelible imprint in her mind. All of these questions nagged at her, plus she heard her father's admonition, be careful, be watchful. That was enough, in itself, for her to take precautionary measures. He was reaching out to her from the grave.

She went to the armoire and took out her leather bag and carried it to the bed. She opened it and with her hand reached down into the secret compartment for the pistol case that was there.

Dudras had given it to her for protection. He told her she might need it to defend herself. She had practiced shooting with it and wouldn't hesitate to use it, if confronted. She was proud that she was a very good shot. Dudras had gotten it from an American whom he had helped. The man didn't have the money to pay him, so, instead, had given him a Colt Navy. An American, Samuel Colt, had invented it in the early 1850s. It had been displayed along with others at the Crystal Palace exhibition. It was gold inlaid and engraved. Six revolving chambers provided the convenience of six shots before reloading. It was highly prized, widely reproduced and sought after. She opened the lid and removed it from the case.

She held the pistol in her hands and loaded it. Such a seemingly innocuous weapon could quickly snuff out a life. Such was life that made these weapons necessary.

There was one thing of which she was sure. She knew she would have to be vigilant. Taking two pillows, she put them beneath the sheet and blanket, to make it look like there was someone asleep in the bed.

A good place to hide was very important. She was fortunate. There was the large armchair to hide behind. It was the only place in the entire room that really offered a plausible place for concealment. The inn was close to the street, and the gas lamp imparted a faint light inside the room, just enough to discern large objects.

She put a shawl around her shoulders. It would have to suffice for warmth. She needed to feel the cold night air to keep her awake. Wrapping herself in a blanket would be warm and cozy and make her sleepy.

Sitting on the floor, behind the chair, the pistol next to her, she prepared herself for any eventuality.

Time passed slowly. She thought about the past, and she thought about the future. She needed to do this to stay awake.

Suddenly, her body seized up. She heard a faint, almost imperceptible, click. Someone was unlocking her door. Now, the person was pushing it open ever so slowly, more and more, until she saw a man step inside the room. She was in an acute state of awareness, the type of nomadic life she had led had prepared her to become self-sufficient. He stood there for a minute looking at the bed, then noiselessly closed the door. As he walked toward the bed, he lifted his arm. In his hand was a long bladed knife. As he got closer to the bed, she got a glimpse of his face. It was the man with whom she had had a confrontation.

Ever so slowly, she picked up the pistol with a steady hand, then stood up to watch his next movements. He wouldn't notice her. He was too intent on what he was about to do.

His face contorted with rage, he plunged the knife into what he presumed was her body. He soon realized he had been foiled. He became even more of a madman, obscenities spewed from his mouth. He was crazed with hatred. He looked frantically around the room, now knowing that his arrival had been anticipated.

"I've been waiting for you," Chovinne said.

He turned his head in the direction of her voice, then the rest of his body to face her.

"You came here to kill me."

He lunged at her. Her finger squeezed the trigger. The first shot hit him squarely in the chest. He kept coming toward her. She shot again and again. Only after three shots did his knees buckle. Clutching his chest, he dropped the knife from his hand and sank to the floor. When he fell his body hit the armchair, causing it to pin her against the wall.

Soon her room was filled with people. Someone lit the candle illuminating the faces of the wide-eyed guests, who were horrified to see the enormity of the situation.

The constable moved the body just enough to allow Chovinne to step out from behind the chair.

"He came after you. I gave that some thought, but I didn't think he would go as far as this. How did you know?"

"When you asked to inspect my room, I knew you were worried he might have come in here to wait for me. I also heard my father's voice telling me that I should be careful, and I had my own suspicions. I could not dismiss all these forewarnings."

"This is all my fault. I made a grave error in judgment. I should have stayed here with you. I just never thought he was capable of going this far."

"Please don't torture yourself over this. I'm glad that this is over."

She looked at the body, as he lay on his back. The front of his shirt was covered with blood, as were his hands, the result of clutching his chest. His blood had splattered on the armchair, and as she looked farther into the room, there was blood on the linens as well as on the floor.

Strangely, through all of this, she was rather calm. She had killed a man who had tried to kill her. Another terrible waste of life. She didn't like it, but she faced it and had done what she had to. He had come to kill her, but, instead, had lost his own life.

"Do you know this man?" she asked.

"Yes, he is a locksmith in the city. He has a shop."

"It was not just a coincidence that you were here, was it?"

"No, guests have come to us for a year now complaining of being robbed of their money and jewelry. I have been here quite a few times as a guest to solve the robberies, but each time nothing happened. It took what happened between the two of you to precipitate this attack."

After hearing this, Chovinne remembered seeing him have a tete-a-tete with the innkeeper earlier that evening. She made the connection. They were working together. She told the constable of her suspicions.

No sooner had she said the words, the innkeeper was there beside them.

He was speaking rapidly to the constable.

"I want to keep this quiet. This will give my establishment a bad name. I will be ruined. I don't want this to be known. People won't come here."

The constable told the guests to return to their rooms to get their money and jewelry and to return there. Everyone returned without any possessions; all their money and jewelry had been stolen. They were beside themselves.

"Everyone, listen, we'll all go with the innkeeper downstairs to his desk. We'll ask him to open his document box for us."

"I lost my key," he said.

"There are other ways of opening it. Be assured, if you don't open it, I will."

The innkeeper realized he didn't have a choice. When they were all around his desk, he produced the box. It was covered in fine leather. When it was opened, a discernible gasp arose from the guests. All began identifying their missing jewelry, and the amount of money he had taken from them.

The constable took some papers from the desk. He dipped the pen in the inkwell.

"I want your names and addresses. All of you will have to appear in court in the future to testify against this man."

"Chovinne, extenuating circumstances beyond your control caused you to kill a man. I will tell the magistrates the whole story. You, too, will have to appear and tell your side. I foresee no problems for you. It was, after all, self-defense.

CHAPTER 20

The distinct sound of the clamoring coach could be heard as it came closer and closer to the coaching inn.

Dudras was thinking that it had been forever since he had last seen Chovinne. He had missed her and was eager to hear about her sojourn.

The coach stopped and the passengers stepped out. The last one off was a grim faced Chovinne. The traditional greeting and small talk was forgotten as he went to meet her. He took the leather bag from her hand.

"What on earth is wrong?" he asked.

"A disastrous incident happened. I killed a man, I shot him. He came into my room to kill me. I didn't have a choice."

She related all the details of the progression of events that had led to the explosive conclusion inside her room.

"I was very fortunate. The constable had been there to witness the hostility of the dead man toward me earlier in the evening. He told me to go home, while he stayed behind to inform the local authorities of the events as they had happened, and, to vouch for my character. It was a relief to get out of that inn and come home."

"Because of your insistence that I should bring a gun with me for self-defense, I was able to defend myself and save my life."

"I shudder to think that you could be dead. Chovinne, I don't want you to go anywhere without one of us again. It is too dangerous!"

"I don't like it either, but I can't live in a cocoon. I can't succumb to fear. Freedom to move about is imperative if I'm to conduct our family matters. I was very cautious. I'll have to become even more so. Being aware and observant is what saved my life. I hope that it will continue to work for me."

"I'm really having a lot of trouble reconciling this. Living is hard and people escape through alcohol and drugs. This, in turn, makes the world an unfit place to live."

"Try not to dwell on this, Dudras. I believe it was inevitable, just because I was there. I was singled out because I was a woman alone and perceived as a passing distraction. I'll find a place for us; a haven where we'll be able to retreat from the world and be alone, away from all this insanity."

CHAPTER 21

The caravan left for Epsom several days before the official start of Derby Week. Their intention was to find a perfect location on the Downs. It was essential that they be highly visible when the throng of merrymakers descended upon the course grounds. The gullible Giorgios, eager to have their fortunes told, would cross their palms with silver many times. They believed that the gypsies possessed powers to reveal their futures.

The following day wagons filled with men and lumber came rolling in to build the makeshift booths, stalls and marquees. In no time, they were all standing next to one another, each ready to accommodate the various diversified entertainment within.

There would be puppet and peep show booths, as well as boxing, wrestling and roulette booths. Comedic and melodramatic sketches would be acted out in other booths. Gingerbread, fried sausage and boiled beef stalls were always favorites. The Gin and Beer Sellers would ensure that everyone enjoyed themselves.

Carts with steaming pies of every description would abound. Hokey-Pokey, a refreshing ice cream treat, delighted the young and old. Fruits and vegetables, coffee and tea carts could be found everywhere on the green. Ballad singers and fiddlers entertained on the downs.

Race day finally arrived. She got out of bed and watched as the sun rose in the early morning sky. Today was going to be one of the most splendid and thrilling days of her life.

The sun was barely visible in the horizon when she heard the loud procession of carriages, coaches, buses, wagonettes, traps, and donkey carts all winding their way towards the Downs.

She ate breakfast, then dressed. Finally, the time arrived. Her disguise in place, Chovinne left the caravan. She walked behind the marquees and booths out of sight. This way if someone should see her they would assume she had been taking in the sights. When she finally came out into the open, she walked down the green to the paddock, observing the colts as they were being saddled. She saw that none measured up to Britilen, four were too spirited, three were fretful. This meant trouble. They would be too hard to handle. The others were good, but not on a par with Britilen.

She looked up and saw the touts not far from her. Everyone knew who they were. They had already arrived many days before the commencement of the races. Their job was to report to all the parties by whom they were employed only, and there were many that would be there today, their observations and the potential capabilities of these colts. On their word alone they would place their bets. To do this, months before, they had traveled to wherever they knew secret trials would be held. They had hidden themselves in the bottom of hedges or ditches, or as she had, in a copse of trees at the break of day to assess all the racing competitors. They noted almost instantaneously how they would measure up, barring any unforeseen circumstances on racing day.

Before coming to Epsom, they knew the precise odds by hanging about the betting rooms. This combined with their knowledge of horses usually, but not always, made them remarkably accurate as to predicting the results of the forthcoming great events.

Already a fashionable crowd was standing around the paddock. Chovinne noticed Andrew close by watching the colts. She eased her way through the crowd and stood next to him. She had to get his attention so she intentionally stuck her foot out to loosen his grip on his cane as she pretended to lean forward to get a closer look at the colts. This made him lose his balance.

She had to muster all the contriteness she could.

"I'm sorry," she said.

"No harm done."

She decided to put an end to the charade.

"Andrew, it's me."

He looked at her.

"I'm sorry, you have me at a disadvantage. I'm afraid I don't know you."

She put a finger to her lips instructing him not to speak. She crooked her finger indicating she wanted him to follow her.

They walked to where the crowd was sparser and far enough from other people so there wouldn't be a chance of being overheard.

"I said that I would meet you here."

He looked at her from head to toe. Finally, he found his voice.

"Why the disguise?"

"I had to do this. I won't be conspicuous dressed this way. I'll be as free as you are to make decisions with no interference."

"I'll admit that you have done a masterful job of concealing your true identity."

"Introduce me as a friend who has been living in India. You met me again when you went big game hunting there last year. I came to England this year on business. I'm now one of your clients wanting to invest in England's growing industries which, after today, will be true."

They walked back to the paddock. She listened to him as he talked about the colts.

"Well, don't keep me in suspense any longer. Who did you choose?" she asked.

"I chose Lonslee."

"He will come in last."

"How do you know"

"He is an anxious horse, among many. Look how he is sweating and lacking in concentration to be reliable. He doesn't like his new jockey. See how he is always trying to get him off his back. He won't run for him."

"Who else have you chosen?" she asked.

She listened to him accentuate the good qualities of yet another horse.

"I'm afraid that choice isn't good either. That one has been raced too often and too hard and has lost too many times. He has been ruined by this. His heart isn't in it. His self-esteem, which is fragile, is gone because of his repeated failures."

"I can see that I seriously lack your expertise and knowledge about these colts. I don't belong here. How do you know so much?"

"Experience, observation, and reading the papers. I, like the touts, had to see for myself, so I went to the secret trials at Newmarket. I was amazed by one particular colt, Britilen. She pointed him out to Andrew. Just look at him, very strong and confident. He has never been raced with horses older and stronger than he is. That is why his spirit has never been broken. Also, his trainers have always treated him with kindness, and he is being ridden by a jockey he loves. His jockey is a beginner, a stayer, and a finisher. There is no better jockey in England. He is an artist at the finesse of handling horses. He never thrashes them mercilessly with his whip. He only uses it when it is important, and then only as a last means of communication between them. He would never push a horse to a punishing finish. He is both a horseman and a jockey. As a horseman, he understands horses and has the ability to control and master them because of his great love for them. Without the love, you can't expect greatness. As a jockey, he has balance and coolness of thought. He is more than capable of making lightning decisions. His judgment of pace is excellent and he is always relaxed. This is how he and his colt will win. You are looking at the Derby winner."

"My touter told me who to choose. You mean to tell me that he's wrong."

"I believe he has misjudged the winner this time."

He stood there looking at the colts, then looking at her, indecision evident on his face.

"The touter told me the colt has been brought close quite a few times in his last races. He was right for the win."

"He won't win the race. I know this. He doesn't have the necessary stamina and speed. He won't meet the challenge. He will falter before he even gets to the winning post. One more thing about Britilen's jockey. He's a kidder. He is a genius. No one knows for sure what he'll do in any race. He has many tricks at his disposal."

"Andrew, it's the first race of the day and the one to lay. The field is large with many entrants, and because of it, so is the handicap."

"It's your money and your decision. You could bet on them both if that would make you feel better."

"I respect your opinion and I've made up my mind. What you've said changes everything. I'll go with your horse."

He motioned with his arm to his bookmaker who wasn't too far from them. He was one of the respectable ones that operated in London, who made it a point to be at Epsom. He was next to them in an instant.

Andrew tore his old racing card and began filling in his numbered bets in the new one. When he was done, he gave it to the bookmaker.

The bookmaker's eyes widened when he saw the changes he had made.

"You have certainly not picked the favorites. There's still time for you to change your mind."

"I won't be changing my mind," Andrew said.

"Give me your racing card."

He took it from her hand.

"My friend also wishes to stand by him."

"You will vouch for his character?"

"I will."

"Then, it's done."

"Well, we surely committed ourselves. We can't go back now," he said.

"We'll both be rich when the race is over. He's a superb horse. You'll see."

They watched while the horses took a final canter in the parade ring. Britilen's face showed eagerness and anticipation.

The throng on the course was dense. Suddenly, the constables formed a line and herded the multitude of people back to the Downs.

The starter ordered the field to line up at the post.

The flag fell and with a burst of speed the field was away. The horses were locked in battle on the great wide course. The challenge of the long uphill rise lay before them. The crush was on. They struggled mercilessly, their flying hooves pounding the turf. Tons of horseflesh were now caught up in the swift descent to the mile post pressing for good positions. The left handed cross would become crucial and their placement critical at Tattenham Corner. The field was dangerously bunched up, but Britilen remained in front. Jostling was at its height and danger at its peak.

Chovinne watched as Britilen gained precious ground. The others soon were in close pursuit. Two horses soon flanked him. Their jockeys were hand-whipping their mounts, trying to shut off Britilen. The Britilen jockey was dauntless and unafraid. He wouldn't allow himself to become unbalanced. Not even the thought of a fall or being kicked to death beneath flying feet swayed his determination to win the Derby. Chovinne could see Britilen stand his ground. He was a big horse and wouldn't be moved. His back legs thrust his muscular body forward, and he easily gained the momentum needed to take the rising ground which was the final test of this grueling race. Chovinne noticed that he showed not the slightest signs of weakening. He maintained hard gallops down the straight and likewise down the stretch. His strength combined with quality and speed made him more than capable of staying the distance. He won comfortably by four lengths.

CHAPTER 22

The deafening roar of the crowd abruptly ceased. The favorite had been defeated. Many who had bet heavily on a horse that they had been assured couldn't lose had done just that; he had lost the race. Faces all around showed shock and disbelief. The realization of the financial difficulties they were now in was very real. Debts would now have to be paid. Settling day had to be met. They would have to ask their moneylenders, bookmakers and friends for time to pay. Andrew turned to look at Chovinne. She was jubilant.

"I told you we would win. The tea leaves never lie."

"Yes, you certainly did say that! We have made quite a tidy sum from this race."

"Come to my caravan with me. We need to talk."

He had never been inside a gypsy caravan before. He found it small, but pleasant and comfortable.

"Please sit down at the table. I'll make some tea for us."

It wasn't long before two steaming cups of tea were ready to serve. She placed them on the table, along with some blueberry tarts.

"Help yourself," she said, as she handed him the plate of tarts.

"These are delicious. Did you make them?"

"No, I bought them on the Downs. I really don't have time to cook."

"Well, then, you do make a perfect cup of tea."

"How difficult is that?" They both laughed at her comment.

"While you finish eating, I'll go behind the dressing screen to remove my make-up and clothes. This disguise is beginning to wear on me."

She continued talking from behind the screen.

"Andrew, I need to ask you yet another favor. Would you come with me and help me with my transactions. I've never been inside a bank."

"Of course, I will. Today, I'm a much, much richer man and I owe it all to you. I personally know a banker, a childhood friend. He'll see to it that every detail of yours and my wishes will be carried out."

She walked back to the table and sat down to finish her tea.

"It's been quite a day, " she said.

"I've had such fun," said Andrew.

"For me, too, it has been a very long time since I enjoyed myself as much as I did today."

"Chovinne, what are you going to do with your money?"

"My immediate plan is to buy a home for myself and my family, make some investments, and fulfill a dream for a friend. What will you do with your money?"

"Investments. There are many lucrative ones. They'll make even more money for me. I'll tell you which ones are sound later, when you are ready to invest."

"So let us set a date for this momentous occasion."

"I would prefer to call on you where you are staying. We could go together in my chaise."

"All right, then, I agree."

She told him where the caravans were.

"Is five days from today good for your calendar?" she asked.

"Yes it is, and I'll arrive early. We'll go to the bank, and, then, we can make a day of it. I'll bring you back home so you can change, and, then, we'll return to the city and spend some time together, if you want to."

"I want to, that will be really nice. I'll see you, then."

Andrew left.

*

Later, while she was contemplating her change of fortune, Dudras came to see her.

"How did we do at the races?" he asked.

"I won a lot of money for us all."

"Chovinne, that is wonderful!"

"Dudras, let's go to the pawnshop to reclaim the jewelry."

The sentimental memories associated with them was their value to her. Her father had made most of them for her.

Together, they went to the pawnshop.

CHAPTER 23

On the appointed day, Andrew was there, bright and early.

Chovinne introduced him to the gypsies. Then, they both climbed into the chaise and left for the city. The sun was shining. Andrew had pulled back the collapsible roof top, so they could enjoy the warmth of the sun. The drive to the city was extremely pleasant as was the conversation. Crisscrossing traffic, they arrived at their destination.

"Andrew, you said a bank. You did not say The Bank."

"I wanted to surprise you."

"Surprise is an understatement. I'm overwhelmed. I never dreamed I would come here."

Standing with Andrew before it, Chovinne remembered reading how The Bank of England's facade had been built to resemble The Temple of Venus at Tivoli. It was an imposing structure.

"Let's not hesitate any longer. Let's go inside," he said.

Once inside the bank, Chovinne had to conceal the wonderment she felt in this auspicious building. She had been transformed into another world. One she had never known, but was now going to become an integral part of her life.

In a voice barely above a whisper, she said to Andrew,

"I'm really impressed. This bank is huge."

He looked at her and smiled. He felt very smug at his fait accompli. This had turned out just the way he planned. The bank's interior absolutely took her breath away, as he knew it would.

The bank was filled with officers and clerks.

As they began walking through, they were questioned by men, dressed in blue and scarlet, as to their business inside the bank. Satisfied that they were there as clients, other employees dressed in buff coats, red vests, and dark pants with a bank medal attached to one of the buttons conducted them through the bank. Chovinne asked him how many people were employed by the bank. She was told an estimated one thousand men were employed as clerks, porters, and watchmen. Every measure was taken to prevent robberies. Forty soldiers guarded the bank at night to prevent that from happening. Chovinne counted sixty departments. She saw bills counted out in vast amounts as she walked by, as well as the stamping of paper, and the distribution of it to the customers. Below the bank were vaults that housed bars of gold.

They were ushered into a large office. Andrew's friend was sitting behind a huge desk piled high with papers. Seeing his old friend, a warm smile spread across his face. He stood up as Andrew and Chovinne, in disguise, walked over to him. They shook hands. He and Andrew talked about old times. Minutes passed before Andrew told him why they were there. Andrew introduced Chovinne as a friend and client, who was there to open accounts for future business transactions. When all of the paperwork was finished, they left the bank. Andrew drove her back to the encampment. She removed her disguise, changed her clothes, and, once again, they were off for London.

"Where are we going?" she asked.

"I can't say except that I have a marvelous surprise for

you."

In the city, Andrew left his carriage in a mew next to a friend's townhouse.

He and Chovinne walked to the stairs at Westminster and took a boat to the Vauxhall Pleasure Gardens. There were other gardens, but this one maintained its high reputation.

"This is it," Andrew said, "my surprise for you. I hope that you like it."

He paid the admittance fee for both of them.

The principal entrance was already crowded with people from all walks of life.

"Let's take a walk, so I can show you this beautiful place."

All of the attractions the spacious gardens had to offer were laid out on tracts of lawns with trees throughout. Walkways were everywhere, leading to all the different features the gardens had to offer. As they walked along, they came upon a gaily decorated alcove where people were being entertained by marionettes while having supper. Farther down was an ornately decorated temple featuring a deity.

The pavilions she saw were strategically placed in the gardens, because they were places for entertainment.

These partly enclosed structures with their peaked tops and wooden floors were used for entertainment. Concerts were held there in the summer months. The bands were respectable. The performers, both instrumental and vocal, had the highest professional reputation. These pavilions reminded Chovinne of the summerhouses of the rich in the country. They were structurally designed with large open windows that allowed cooling summer breezes inside.

Lastly were artificially created cascading waterfalls.

Andrew pointed out to Chovinne that the most stupendous feature of the gardens was the thousands of lamps in various colors. Some were designed to look like the sun, others, the stars, and still others, the constellations.

"Let us sit here in this alcove," Andrew said, "the lights will come on soon and I want you to experience the enchantment of the gardens when this happens. I'll get some punch for us while we wait."

She didn't have long to wait. Suddenly, the various colored lamps lit up the gardens. It was totally transformed into a magical wonderland.

The waterfall, next to them, became even more beautiful when the lights cast different hues on the cascading water.

The concerts began at eight o'clock. They sat and talked to one another, not really paying attention to the music. They finally had time to really learn about one another. She told him about her life; he told her about his. His parents were deceased. He was an only child, educated at Eton and Oxford. He had sold the country estate. Now his home was a townhouse in the city.

The finale of the evening was a grand display of both fireworks and balloon ascents on one of the grand walks.

"The evening has ended much too soon. When may I see you again, Chovinne?"

"I have to attend to some business this week that is of tremendous importance to me and my family, and someone else. If everything goes according to plan, how would you feel if I went to your townhouse Sunday, and, together, we would go to the country, and I could show you my surprise?"

"Yes, that sounds perfect. I'll see you then."

CHAPTER 24

Important matters needed her attention. She, again, assumed her disguise and went to London. Chovinne immediately went to Lloyd's. A few days earlier, while perusing the newspaper, she had read that Lloyd's had some ships for sale. There she would find all the information she needed. She was aware that Lloyd's classified their ships according to age, build, and seaworthiness. The ones she inquired about were classified number one by them. Lloyd's were underwriters of marine insurance. The integrity of their reputation as honest dealers, who promptly repaid the value of vessels or cargoes lost, was well established. Last, but not least, was the fact that the post always provided Lloyd's, the guardians of shipping, a never ending stream of information. The shipping news in the daily papers provided readers with special interests about the departures of vessels and any casualties or delays, such as a ship being wrecked or in distress or any other incidents. This service alone provided comfort to people worried about the welfare of husbands, fathers, sons, brothers, or friends in distant seas.

Now that she had undisputed factual information, she could proceed with her other plans. At the bank she told Andrew's friend of her intentions. She informed him that she wanted to purchase clippers. Again, the knowledge she had amassed at the Abbey proved invaluable. She had read that

British clippers were of composite construction, wooden planks on an iron frame. An iron-framed clipper, although a comparatively small vessel with a weight of 1500 tons, could be driven harder than one made entirely of wood. Their copper-sheathed wooden hull fouled less quickly than iron plates. This was an extremely important factor when cutting through water and when smoothness of movement determined that these fast sailing ships would be the first to dock. Ben needed ships of quality and speed, if he was to succeed. She filled out the paperwork necessary for him to remove from her account the assets necessary to purchase the ships. Andrew's friend also promised to send one of his top men to attend the ship auction for her. The man was a wizard in acquiring for a client whatever they needed, and, at a good price. She was to return later in the afternoon. By then, all the transactions would be completed.

When she did, everything was done. She held the Bill of Sale in her hands. What a wondrous surprise it would be for Ben. She couldn't wait to give the paper to him.

It was still dark outside the next morning, when she again left for London. She had to get there early if she expected to find Ben before the men were called to work.

She didn't venture too far down into the maritime district. She had given Ben her word that she wouldn't go there alone again. She waited where she had met him before, knowing he would show up there again. It wasn't long before she saw him, with some of his friends, coming toward her.

She was still sitting astride her horse when he saw her. His arm flew up and he waved his hand furiously at her. She waved back.

"Hello, Chovinne. What are you doing here so early?"

"I came especially to see you. I have thought about you often."

"I have also. I'm thrilled to see you."

"Ben, have you been working every day since we last

met?"

"No, many days I'm not called."

"That is why I have come to see you. I have something for you."

She reached into her leather bag and handed him the Bill of Sale.

"Hurry, open it and see what it is! It is a gift from me to you."

He opened the paper, read it, took a deep breath, looked at her and read it again.

"It says here that I'm now the owner of three ships. You did this for me. Why?"

"I remember the conversation we had when I first met you, how you longed to have adventures in you life, and how seeing the world was your dream. I never forgot how depressed you were, knowing that coal-whipping and other heavy dock work would always be what you were destined to do, and that you would be there forever. I didn't want that for you. Since last we spoke, my life has also changed. I have some money and decided to do this for you."

"Chovinne, you hardly know me. No one, except my parents, has ever done anything for me. I am speechless. It's so unexpected and so wonderful!"

"We parted as friends and you were in my thoughts and I was in a position to help you, so I have."

"I woke up this morning thinking that today would be a day like any other. Now, there is this! He held the Bill of Sale in his hand. This paper gives me a new life. I'm now the possessor of three ships!! Do you have any idea how incredulous this news is to me? I'm now a man who will be in charge of my life. I'll be able to do everything that I've always wanted. I'm now a person of means. A minute ago, I had nothing, absolutely nothing. Now, I have everything, because of you."

"I have so many friends who have worked with me,

whom I can trust. All of them at some time have worked on clippers. I'll employ them on my ships. This is so good, because I know them so well. We have talked about the work they did. I know what they can do best. They are a fearless group of men, and I know they will do their best work for me. Their lives, also, will be changed forever."

"I will pay them more than a decent wage."

"I repeat. I'm so excited and so thrilled!"

Chovinne smiled as she listened to him talk. He was so animated and filled with such happiness at the prospects of what the future held for him. He was now liberated and so full of hope. He was freed from his shackled life. He couldn't wait to undertake this new venture. His life would never be mundane again. It would always be filled with new adventures.

"I'm so grateful, Chovinne. What do you say to someone who has just given you a new life? Thank you is so woefully inadequate."

"It's enough. Seeing you so happy makes me happy too. I know the China trade will be profitable for you. If you are the first to return to London from Canton or Foochow with Chinese tea, opium and silk, you will be paid premium prices for your cargo. The world is yours now, Ben, to live it as you want, to enjoy it to the fullest, and to prosper."

In his heart, Ben knew he would find a way of repaying her someday. He would make sure of it.

"One last thing, you have to know is that you are insured with Lloyd's. You don't have to worry on that count."

"Go see you clippers now, Ben. I know how anxious you must be to see them."

"Stay in touch, and let me know how things are with you. I'll most probably be buying a cottage while you're gone."

She told him where she would be living, if she did, and to look her up whenever he was back in the city.

"There is an estate advertised for sale. I plan to look into it. When you come back to the city, I'll be there or I won't. I can't give you more information than that. If I'm there, you know you'll be more than welcome at my home."

"Well, Ben, this is goodbye for now. The best of luck to you!"

With that they both went their separate ways.

CHAPTER 25

Auctions were routinely advertised in the papers. One, in particular, caught her eye. She read the Introductory Particulars. The main cottage estate included worker cottages and the gamekeeper's cottage; all of these to be taken in its entirety. It was a grand residence and could make a sound investment for someone of taste. Delightful grounds were described in a secluded area with pasture and meadow ground, grazing land and fine tillage. Also included were stabling and coach houses of fine quality.

This couldn't be more perfect for what she needed. It was exactly what she had in mind. She was very, very interested. The custom was for potential buyers to investigate the residence and acreage to be sold.

Disguised yet again, she rented a Cabriolet to investigate the cottage estate that was for sale.

The winding hedge-lined country lane sloped gently upward. On each side were verdant meadows. The patchwork of fields, meadows, dells, and hedges was the very essence of the English countryside. She stopped the Cabriolet to admire the beauty of the foaming white blossoms on the hawthorn hedges. Chovinne thought about all its inhabitants. The hedges provided an ideal home for many small creatures. Living there were the hedgehogs, also known as fuzzypigs, hedgepigs or urchins. They were a tiny, short-legged animal weighing about a pound and a half. The spines on their bodies, three quarters of an inch long, normally lay flat, but when imminent danger threatened them, their out-thrust quills protected them from many of their predators. Chovinne caught many of them to sell by listening closely for the sound of their rhythmic snoring while asleep on some moss or leaves in the hedgerows. These animals were highly valued and commanded a good price when she sold them because they were remarkable destroyers of pests. People purchased them to keep their gardens pest-free. Also sharing the hedges were the the field voles, the hedge sparrows, skylarks, crested wrens, the song thrushes, and many others.

The mice in the hedgerows provtded hunting prey for barn owls, kestrels and gray partridge.

She saw her first swallow skim the fields.

In the summer, caterpillars became butterflies in the hedge, and wildflower seeds, from the fields, took root next to the hedge and lived once more. Summer also brought the honeysuckle among the twigs, and pink dog roses would brighten the lanes even more. Foxgloves burst forth each spring from the tall hedgerows creating a spectacular flower border. Hedges marked boundaries, restricted livestock, gave shelter and shade, and protected the crops from the wind.

Next to the hedges, at a distance from her, a beautiful red fox, with his white underbody and bushy tail tipped with white, had his black booted feet firmly planted on the ground. His front paws were trying to reach inside the hedgerows for a tidbit to eat.

Foxes, being omnivorous, will eat rabbits, squirrels, woodchucks, grasshoppers, mice, rats, moles, birds, fish, fruit and berries. His most favorite food was poultry.

She found foxes fascinating. She marveled at their cunning, unending ingenuity. They always learned from experience, and their ability to escape from captivity was phenomenal.

A shy cuckoo called to her from the woods. The cuckoo had a long slender body and was grayish-brown on top and white below with a slightly curved bill. On her many excursions into the woods, bird-catchin,g and at the Abbey, she had only seen the evasive cuckoo a few times. While to many people, the cuckoo's call was irritating because it couldn't sing, to Chovinne, it was another wonderful reminder of life and joy. He was calling to her, telling her he was there and to remember him, even though his call was guttural, repetitious, monotonous and melancholy.

In an adjoining meadow, young lambs were wide awake. They were leaping, dancing, butting and crying in their young diminutive voices. There was a gentleness, a sweetness and an innocence in their enjoyment of life. Close by, their mothers kept an ever watchful eye over them.

She hated having to leave such an idyllic locale, but leave she must. Reluctantly, she held the horses's reins in her hand, and with her free hand, she took a moment to stroke his nose.

She again climbed aboard the Cabriolet on her way to meet with the owner of the cottages. The elms next to the lane had branches that swept down like garlands, almost touching the ground. They crowded the lane preventing her eyes from penetrating any distance. The slight breeze caused a flickering mix of shadow and sunshine in her eyes.

Finally, at the end of this bucolic scene were the cottages she had come to see, a main cottage and twelve detached cottages.

Her eyes beheld a scene of extraordinary beauty, a wonderful rural retreat concealed from the rest of the world. It was so beautiful that it took her breath away. She knew in her heart that she was home.

She passed through an ancient gateway made of iron and

stone that was very ornamented. Rugosas had been planted close to the gate and around the property to serve as an aesthetic, dense, luxuriantly foliaged living fence in the spring, summer and fall. They averaged six to eight feet tall. Their thorns were more lethal than other roses, so they were very effective against unwelcome deer, dogs or other intruders. These roses thrived on neglect. They required no pruning, feeding, or fussing of any kind. These pink, deeply crinkled, five-petaled fragrant roses gave a long display of flowers.

The main thatched cottage was more like a smaller version of a country home. It was a commodious dwelling.

It was owned by a nabob, an Englishman who had made his fortune in India during the East India Company's monopoly on trade. He had returned from the East a very rich man.

Primogeniture wouldn't be a concern in this matter. This man had no heirs.

Because nature's beauty is random, English gardens were planned accordingly. Simplicity in design was left to the originality of the gardener and this gardener was indeed a master. A stone walk meandered, instead of marched, to the front door. Low-growing perennials like creeping phlox, candyluft, alyssum, rock cress, forget-me-nots, lady's mantle and creeping thyme had been planted to achieve a garden symphony in front of this cottage. When taller varieties of perennials would shoot from the earth these would still make beautiful ground cover beneath the taller plants.

At the sides of the walk peonies, irises and bleeding hearts would bloom. As the spring crescendoed into summer, delphiniums, daisies, coreopsis, and astribe would take on the starring roles. Growing some plants for their leaves alone, like the silver-gray foliage of lamb's ears and artemisia and the fern hart's tongue, would facilitate the transition from one phase to the next. The walls were beginning to be softened with honeysuckle and ivy.

She tapped the door-knocker against the large wooden door. The man who answered identified himself as the owner and greeted her. She gave him the name of her assumed identity. He invited her inside. They went from the entry hall directly to the front parlor.

He asked her to be seated, then proceeded to tell her that the peasants who had worked for him had left to find employment in the coal and iron mines and cotton mills. This, in turn, created too much work for his Indian houseservants. Overburdened with work, they all returned to India.

To complicate matters, his wife had recently died, so now he found himself rambling alone in a cottage that was far too large. He decided it would be in his best interest to sell and live in a townhouse in London. He told her he was leaving the cottage furnished, except for a few of his treasured mementos, and that the furnishings would be added to the price.

He asked her to follow him, as they went through every room in the cottage. The first floor had a front parlor or sitting room containing the main fireplace. It had a great central chimney and all of the flues placed together, crowned by the shafts. Behind this room was a spacious kitchen supplemented by a large pantry, china closets and plentiful storage space. The utilitarian fireplace was for cooking meals and for warmth. The scullery, a room adjoining the kitchen was where the hard work was done. It was large enough to also serve as a wash-house. Buckets, necessary to get water from the well, were stored here, as well as wooden tubs and coppers for washing clothes. The warmth from the kitchen permeated the scullery when an adjoining door was left open. Linen cupboards in the scullery kept a good supply of linen, sheets, pillowcases and towels. Undergarments were kept there also.

She looked through a window in the scullery and could see a well not too far from the door. This was very fortuitous, usually wells were situated far from most cottages and workers had to walk long distances carrying water buckets to and from them.

About one hundred and fifty feet from the well, discreetly camouflaged by vines clinging to the wooden structure, was the earth closet, a very necessary place. She knew it would be tasteless to broach the subject with him. She could see that the sewage followed a structured path to the nearest irrigation ditch.

The second floor had a study or library, a sewing room, one bedchamber for the master and the madam, and two additional chambers which served as servant's quarters or guest rooms. The downstairs rooms were interconnected via large doorways. There was a main stairway to the second floor. The upstairs rooms were linked by a central hallway. The cottage had all the amenities she could possibly desire.

She followed him through a back door of the house to the backyard garden. Immediately, there was an intimate connection between her, the cottage, and the landscape. A stunning arch top wooden arbor beckoned her to pass through. When she did, an herb garden was on her immediate left. The owner began telling her about the herbs planted there just beginning to show themselves. He bent down and gently touched the herbs, looking up at her while explaining each one's benefits, chamomile and lavender to alleviate anxiety, peppermint and rosemary to clear the mind and sage for a happy feeling, and on and on. Chovinne had learned all this at the Abbey. She knew how his heart must be heavy, knowing he had to leave everything he loved behind, so she did him the courtesy of listening attentively to what she already knew.

Sweetbriars had been planted in the eastern exposure. In time their green apple scent would permeate the garden.

Their bright red, fragrant hips would make excellent jam and syrup later on.

A short stacked stone wall was a perfect height for sitting. It was close to the flower beds filled with bright flowering perennials which tumbled over each other.

A bench had been placed in a corner of the garden. This would give her a place of her own where she would be able to go to sit back in comfort and be by herself, where she could occasionally distance herself to enjoy the visual images, and where she could have the tranquility to pursue her thoughts.

In close proximity, just beginning to sprout, were the infamous legendary flowers, the souls of the garden, each with a story to tell. First, were canterbury bells, said to ring every June 23rd midsummer night's eve to ward off evil spirits. Sweet Williams, known for their fragrance, received their blood-red hearts when Orlando, a fabled knight, was mortally wounded. Who could forget the tale surrounding foxgloves? Legend said they were a gift from mischievous fairies to foxes. Slipping the flower over their paws made it easy for them to steal into hen houses at night.

Nestled in different locations were four contemplative gargoyle sculptures. She wondered what they were thinking, and if they would like their new tenant, if she was fortunate enough to buy this wonderful estate. These stone creatures evolved from the fertile imagination of medieval times. They purportedly had powers to ward off evil spirits. Chovinne found that it would be nice to have these sentries around.

There was so much to see. The apple trees were in bloom, the Rosemary Russet, Orleans Reinette and Quarrenden.

The owner was very enthusiastic about the lily pond. He called it his oasis of calm and the perfect setting for quiet reverie. A depression in the ground had convinced him that it would make a very attractive pond. It was an informal pond and a work of art. Differently shaped flat stones had been placed around its perimeter. Perennial flower beds protectively wrapped the pond and its inhabitants. The reflective qualities of flowers, trees and clouds resting upon the water lent it a mesmerizing aura. Inside the pond, the aquatic perennials, the water lilies, were anchored by thick stems to the rich mud at the bottom of the pond. In due time, the splendid flowered water lilies would emerge, floating on the water's surface, spreading their pointed petals wide for all to appreciate. Frogs, who had tired of splashing in the water, lept onto newly formed lily pads at the pond's edge and began snapping at flying insects near the surface of the water. Soon the flowering perennials would attract pollinating insects, dragonflies, butterflies and hummingbirds. Their foliage would also provide shelter and security for them from the harsh weather and many predators. Small mammals would find their way to the pond.

From there she inspected the coach houses, stables, barns, cow-sheds, sheep-fold, gooserie, and piggery. She found them very adequate. While in one of the cow-sheds, she noticed that the carts and wagons had been sheltered while not in use. The country wheelwrights took great care in the choice of woods they used for the different parts. The framework had been made of oak, the sides, floors and wheel-maves of elm, and the shafts, wheel-spokes and fellies of ash.

The design of the carts and wagons in the cow-shed varied considerably in their design. Some had two or four wheels double shafts or single poles. The wheelwrights built some with straight, upright sides, and others that sloped slightly outward. She was really happy to see the five ship-like harvest-wains. They were built high on all sides to hold the harvests securely in place.

All wagons were built for strength and durability. Wagons to be used on the roads were built for extra strength and durability. A ton of wheat or hay was the usual load they were expected to carry. Four or five horses were needed to pull the wagons and three or four men were required to accompany the wagon on its long journey on formidable, treacherous roads. Again, she had attained all this invaluable knowledge while at the Abbey.

Plows and other implements had been placed here also for shelter.

The only matter that concerned her was the fact that it was more than time to rid these buildings of the rats. Since they had been vacant for some time, the rats were reproducing at an alarming rate.

Walking back to the main house, she saw a dovecote adjacent to one of the barns. She asked the owner about it. She asked to see it more closely. He recounted to her that, when he bought the estate, it was already there. Tall, thick ivy had concealed it, a solitary pigeon-house, seventy five feet in circumference and made entirely of stone. Small openings had been left all around for ventilation. The wattled roof had been repaired as well as the door. He theorized that it had been built during the middle ages, and, then, forgotten when estates were redistributed. Back then only monks, rectors, or lords of the manor were allowed to have dovecotes. These were indispensable, because they provided the only fresh meat consumed during the winter months. Everything else was highly salted for preservation. They were highly prized, carefully stocked and zealously guarded, because it played an important part in the economy of former days. She went closer and peered inside. It had been finished in daub. It housed one hundred and fifty nesting places. A ladder inside enabled a person to reach any particular nest. It had also provided him with fresh meat, just as it had his predecessors.

Niches, twenty inches deep in the southeast front of the gamekeeper's cottage, held ten skeps from the wind and the rain. These skeps looked like baskets placed upside down. Hinged iron bars fit across the bole and secured the skeps from theft. In cold weather, the bars were useful by keeping straw, bracken or heather in place to insulate the bees.

His employees had made mead for him and themselves from fermented honey. Water, spices, and fruit or malt were added to the mix for this alcoholic liquor.

The other cottages had housed unmarried men who were in charge of the animals and who did other work associated with the estate, the herdsmen, shepherds, head teamsmen, waggoners, regular laborers, keepers of the woods, hedgers, thatchers, mole catchers and farriers.

The upper level of all the cottages was constructed in dormitory style, a long, single room to accommodate the many workers.

This man had obviously cared about his workers. The twelve cottages were well-built and maintained.

This estate was a showcase of beauty, but the lily pond was, by far, what she found to be most aesthetically pleasing. The water lilies when they bloomed, would be magnificent creations, endless in their structure and beauty. She would have to wait until summer for the gorgeous blooms. Their radiance left anyone who looked upon these cupshaped flowers spellbound, awestruck by these floating beauties of nature that would cover the pond.

Walking slowly back to the main cottage, the owner was quiet. She interpreted his silence as her cue that it was time for her to voice her observations concerning the estate. She told him how enchanted she was with the utter beauty of her surroundings achieved by his diligence for perfection. It would be a joy to live in a place such as this. The owner abruptly stopped walking and looking directly at her asked if he would be permitted to visit. Without hesitation, she told him he would be more than welcome anytime. With that answer, he told her that she was the new owner of the estate and that it wouldn't be necessary to go on with an auction. He informed her that other prospective buyers had been hesitant and evasive when they were asked that question. He could tell that she loved the estate as much as he did. It pleased him so much to know this. In addition, the added pleasure of knowing he could visit this beloved estate, whenever he wanted, greatly eased his mind about leaving his home.

"I'll inform the gamekeeper today about the change of ownership. During all the years in my employ, I have found him to be very conscientious and loyal. He is beyond reproach."

"Would you tell him to expect me at his cottage within the next two weeks?"

"I'll tell him."

He gave her directions for the least complicated and most expedient route to get there.

CHAPTER 26

All of the formalities were over. She held the deed to the estate in her hands. The deed represented permanence, something that had always eluded gypsies. She had come a long way in fulfilling what the tea leaves had prophesied.

The money she had won at the races was enabling her to pursue her, and her family's dreams.

Chovinne had carefully calculated the amount of money she could spend on each endeavor.

The estate now belonged to them all. Ben had his dream, his ships. The carriage service would be attended to after they moved to their new home. Money had already been put aside for future investments.

The news that she had purchased the estate was enthusiastically received by the gypsies. They were anxious to see it.

We aren't going to move there until the rats have been destroyed. I don't want anyone to be bitten. When they're eliminated and the areas cleaned, then we'll move.

CHAPTER 27

A rat catcher lived on a street in London that was, in reality, an alley. It was narrow and dirty. Debris lay everywhere.

The sweet smell of opium lay heavy in the air. Small children lay asleep on the ground. She cautiously walked over them, being careful not to step on them. She knew they had been given Godfrey's Cordial, a soothing syrup given to undernourished infants and small children to stop them from crying and to make them sleep, often permanently. The ingredients for this preparation consisted of sassafras, opium, brandy, caraway seed and treacle. The dosage was gradually increased until it reached a teaspoonful. Medicinal use of opium was so common and widespread that it involved neither legal penalties nor public stigma, nor was it used only for children. Britain imported thousands of pounds of raw opium. Opium was available in hundreds of small shops. It was useful as an analgesic and tranquilizer, in the absence of other drugs. Adults used laudanum, an alcoholic tincture of opium, to relieve pain, such as rheumatism. It was rubbed on the gums for toothaches. Opium pills were dropped in any alcoholic drink for a sense of well-being and freedom from suffering.

The ratcatcher, a fearless handler of rats, was coming home from his day's work. He was a flamboyant man. It was essential for his trade that he be noticed, and he did this with a flair. He was easily recognizable. He wore a velveteen jacket, corduroy trousers and laced boots. A large colorful oilskin belt colorfully painted with the figures of huge rats on it with fierce looking eyes and formidable whiskers was diagonally slung on one shoulder with the front and back fastened together at the waist. Several tamed rats were scurrying about inside and outside the arms of his surcoat while others were sitting on his shoulders. The hat he wore was glazed and colorfully painted similar to his oilskin belt. He smelled of oil of thyme and oil of anise. These oils were mixed together and then rubbed into his clothes. The composition of the scents was attractive to the rats. Following on his heels were several terriers, all of whom had been trained by a professional ratter, since he did not have the time to train his own dogs.

Public houses in London had regular rat killing matches. The competition was among dog owners to ascertain whose dog was the very best. Men of every grade of society came to see and bet on the canine exhibition. It was not uncommon for a terrier to kill five hundred rats in little time. The winners were awarded prizes. The ratcatcher attended these matches and purchased his dogs from owners who had tired of the sport.

Chovinne could see that the dogs jumping around her had bodies that were scarred from rat bites. She then turned her attention to the red-eyed ferrets in an iron cage that the ratcatcher held in his hand. The ferrets' work was to chase rats out of holes and burrows and any type of hidden recess and force them out from within. In turn, when the terriers smelled the rats, they became impatient and attacked the rats in earnest. These aggressive dogs with mouths that opened back to their ears had unrelenting grips that quickly broke the rats' necks, killing them instantly, leaving them bleeding on the floor.

"Excuse me, Mr. Jack, do you have some time. I would like to speak with you."

"I always have time, tell me, what it is you have to say."

"There are rats at the estate where I now live. Perhaps you would have some time in the near future to come and eradicate them."

"I can be there in two days."

"That would be perfect."

She told him where the estate was. They settled on a price, and, then she left.

As scheduled, two days later, Chovinne, the male gypsies and the ratcatcher went to the stables. When they opened the door, the rats were running around toppling over each other in their haste of trying to hide. Others were standing straight placing their front paws on their faces as if they were preening themselves. The ferrets were let out of the cage and began chasing the rats with a vengeance. The dogs moved quickly, and, in no time, the rats were eliminated. This scenario was repeated in the other buildings as well. All the rats were buried in a deep pit. When it was over, the ratcatcher held each dog, and, one by one, each dog's mouth was rinsed with peppermint and water so it wouldn't get canker.

"Needless to say, I'm glad that is over! I'm rid of them for now," Chovinne said to the ratcatcher, "but I know more will come because of the oats and other feed. It attracts them and they can eat an enormous amount of food. I'll be seeing you often from now on. I would like to set up future dates with you now, so that something of this magnitude won't happen again."

"I can always do more work." Dates were set up.

"Without a doubt, you'll find enough to keep you busy here. I won't keep you. I know your time is valuable. I'll see you again soon."

She paid him and he left.

The gypsy men cleaned the affected areas. The next day the families moved in. Dudras and Subina elected to live in the main cottage with Chovinne. Others occupied a few of the cottages, but most of them preferred to remain in their caravans. If they decided to move on, they were ready to leave at a moment's notice.

CHAPTER 28

A charming, picturesque village was only a few miles from her home. Chovinne knew that in a few days the village would be hosting its annual hiring fair.

Villages were isolated. It was important for them to have a network of individuals who had a unique craft to allow them to be self-sufficient. Even though many had left for work elsewhere, many also stayed and the continuity was preserved.

Every village had its artisans. The village cobbler made the shoes. The tailor made the clothes for those who could afford them. The carpenters furnished the doors, window frames and other wooden parts. They made the chairs and tables for use in the cottages. They also made the necessary coffins. The saddler made the collars and harnesses for the local horses as well as other leather goods. The wheelwrights made all the carts and wagons the villagers needed.

The village also had general shops and an innkeeper.

The blacksmith was considered the most important craftsman in the village. His forge was the favorite meeting place for young and old. It was the place for the latest news and gossip. The smith was a true genius. He made agricultural implements and plows for the farmers, buisting irons for shepherds to use for ear marking their flocks of sheep. He would also use his creative talent toward ornamental work. He made weathervanes and wrought-iron gates for estate owners, and the finest innkeeper signs.

Of utmost importance was his sound veterinary knowledge. Farmers relied upon him because he was the only man with real veterinary skills. He knew how to treat diseased or damaged feet. His expertise about horn growth and foot expansion allowed for a natural fit whenever he shod a horse.

The thatcher was another very important cog in the network. Whatever material was used for thatching a roof, whether it was wheat, straw or reeds, it was secured to the rafters or to other material, by twine that had been tarred and then threaded through an enormous thatching needle. The material was firmly woven together to offer the greatest resistance to the elements. Any edges that were ragged were trimmed from the eaves and windows. The thatched roofing kept the rooms underneath very comfortable. It was warm in the winter and cool in the summer. Another added bonus was that the thickness of the thatch deadened noises and made the interior nice and quiet. Its only drawback was the danger of fire. Throughout the village, large iron hooks were hung in prominent places so that any passersby who spotted a fire would use a hook to pull out a chunk of material that was either ablaze or smoldering before it started a major fire.

CHAPTER 29

The gypsies couldn't possibly do all the necessary work that would be required for the smooth operation of their home. She, Dudras, Subina and other gypsies would attend the fair expecting to find the necessary people there looking for employment to help them on their estate. She would also need to purchase the animals they would need to procure a livelihood for themselves.

Everyone always looked forward to a hiring fair. Dealers came from near and far to trade and buy quantities of goods. Drovers brought cattle and horses. Merchandisers brought their wares. Quack doctors sold nostrams to cure any ailment. Vendors sold food on the green.

On the appointed day, she and the other gypsies approached the village. The first artifice she saw was the church with its lofty spire. Chovinne thought to herself that she had never seen a look-alike church. It just didn't happen. No apprentice ever followed exactly the methods of building that he had been taught. Each builder, through his ingenuity, devised his own ideas of construction incorporating his skills and differentiation. Geology was a profound factor in styles of architecture. The natural materials indigenous to the districts, such as stone-quarries, clay-pits or woodland timber, gave the buildings their individual charm and distinction. Another factor was that the churches had been built in different centuries and these edifices displayed the architecture of those times.

As they ventured farther, they saw the village green, the center of festivities for the villagers. Many festivities were held there. An especially cheerful celebration was May-Day. Every year on May1st, a Maypole was set up on the village green. It was decorated from top to bottom with alternating red and white spiral stripes. Flowing red, white, and blue ribbons were secured at the midpoint of the maypole, so they would be accessible during the afternoon festivities. As the clock struck twelve, the retiring May Queen crowned the newly appointed one. After the applause subsided, everyone would sit down on the grass to feast on the food that had been made for the occasion. At two in the afternoon the church organist accompanied by concertina and fiddle would begin to play the music. This was the signal to the waiting girls, with flower garlands in their hair, to run to the maypole and grab a flowing ribbon. Holding onto them, they would begin swirling around the maypole pretending to be enchanted nymphs, young and beautiful nature goddesses, that lived in rivers, mountains or trees.

Chovinne was startled to see a pillory, stock, whipping post, gibbet and ducking-stool on the far side of the village green. The stark reality of these symbolic reminders of antiquity bore testimony of people's inhumanity to each other. When convicted of a crime, offenders were taken to the pillory. This device consisted of a wooden board with holes in it for them to place their head and hands. They were locked in and exposed to public abuse, ridicule, scorn and shame. Villagers threw stones, rotten eggs and apples at the individuals. Chovinne tried to fathom how much it must have hurt to have had these objects thrown at them. The high degree of velocity must have broken noses, jaws and cheekbones, caused blindness and blackened eyes and caused severe injuries to their heads. Their bodies, also, must have sustained many black and blue bruises. The stock was similar to the pillory. It had a frame for confining the ankles. The wrists were sometimes encased. The offenders suffered the same fate as those who had been pilloried. Other offenses required different legal punishments. The whipping post was yet another. Offenders were whipped until they fainted from the pain and terror they had to endure. It must have seemed to them to last forever. Criminals to be executed were drawn through the streets on a hurdle. After they were executed, they were placed in gibbet irons that were shaped like the human body — head, torso, and legs. Birds must have pecked for food from the rotting corpses. The irons, undoubtedly, creaked and groaned whenever strong winds blew. This scene must have left a haunting imprint on the minds of anyone who witnessed such a spectacle. The ducking stool was yet another barbaric method of administering justice. The offender was tied to a chair that swiveled on the end of a long board. This board was fastened to a frame on wheels. Whenever the need arose the ducking-stool was pushed down to the water's edge. The offender was frequently immersed into the cold water. She tried imagining who those people were that had invented those sobering instruments of torture and death in previous centuries. Even as cruel as these inventions were, as deterrents to crime they had failed. She believed people behaved then, as they did now. Abject poverty hurts and fosters feelings of envy, anger, rage and resentment. Although it was no excuse, these people acted on those feelings making them resort to desperate means to be in the same social class as others. They murdered, stole, and did whatever else they felt they had to do to survive. They justified this in their minds by telling themselves they were just as deserving, so, in retaliation, they did and took whatever they wanted.

The din on the green was now ear shattering and brought

her back to the present. The marketplace for the animals was not held on the green. Six acres, adjacent to it, was set aside for that purpose. All of the animals were brought there for sale. Many hundreds of animals—horses, sheep, cows and pigs—would be exhibited and sold. Oxen were also sold. The lowing of the cattle, the thudding of the horses' hooves, the gabbling ducks, the cackling geese, the bleating sheep, the shouts of the sellers, and the music of the hurdy-gurdies transformed the quiet tranquility of the villagers' lives. The fair was both a great source of profitability and fun for them.

Chovinne needed sheep so she set about finding a man she knew. He was a renowned drover. With only his sheepdogs, he conducted flocks of sheep through many difficulties on highroads, lanes, streets and commons. He delivered them on time and in excellent condition. To reach their destination, he and his flock rested at night stations along the way. Here he would feed and water his charges, as well as himself.

Those who sought employment distanced themselves from the multitude of people. They were more easily noticed. In addition, they stood in long rows. To identify the type of work he/she was seeking, each laborer had an identifying mark added onto his/her clothing, or else held his/her identification in his/her hands. Waggoners had a piece of whip-cord twisted around their hats, thatchers had a piece of woven straw on their hats. Shepherds had a tuft of wool on their hats and carried a crook. Carters carried a whip and dairymaids carried a milking-stool or pail. Herdsmen, teamsmen and regular laborers, as well as house servants, held a sign conveying to prospective employers their chosen station in life.

After selecting the farm laborers, Chovinne sought to find domestic help. There would be much work to be done on the estate. The gypsy women would be working alongside the household servants, laying fires in the fireplace and carrying wood and scuttles of coal. Carrying buckets of water was always a major undertaking because a household needed a large amount of water for washing dishes, cooking, scrubbing, washings, and baths. Other chores included sweeping, dusting, and polishing silverware.

By late afternoon, she along with Dudras' input had completed the most important business transactions. The horses for farm work were purchased. Other horses for the carriage service would be purchased elsewhere. A set of oxen, cows, pigs, ducks, geese and chickens completed the nucleus of her livestock.

All agreements made with the laborers were for one year. A handshake and a "fastening-penny", usually a shilling was given each laborer by the employer to show good faith.

It had been a very hectic morning and afternoon, but now all her business transactions were over and she could relax. She felt a tug on her shawl. She turned around and looked down to see a young boy about ten years old next to her.

"Do you remember me?" he asked in a tight little voice.

She could see it had taken a lot of courage for him to come and speak to her.

"Yes I do."

She had an affinity for remembering faces. He was the same boy who had tried to pick Ben's pocket.

"What you have to say must be important. Tell me, I'm listening."

"Would you hire me to work for you?"

He was so young and so frail. Chovinne knew the little pickpocket would never be strong. Inadequate food had stunted his growth. He would never have the stamina for hard work.

"Where are your parents?"

"They died when I was small."

"What type of work do you think you could do for me?"

"I could take care of your horses. I know how to

unharness, wipe down, clean, feed and blanket them."

"I'll have many horses, and I certainly could use your help. Yes, I believe you could do that."

"I don't know your name. What is it?"

"Trevor, madam."

"You don't have to call me madam. It's too formal, call me Chovinne."

"Trevor, you know that we have to talk about your past, don't you? There are conditions that you have to meet if I'm to hire you. You must promise to never steal or lie again. I'll never tolerate theft or lies under any circumstances from anyone."

He didn't look at her, but, instead, looked at the ground.

She put her hand beneath his chin.

"Don't be afraid. Look at me Trevor."

Slowly, he lifted his head.

Because he was so young and didn't have a family, she would have him live in the cottage so she could watch and care for him.

"I'll take care of you, but only if I have your word on this matter. You will be living with temptations that will be everywhere. There will be many things for you to see and steal. This can't happen. You'll have a good life with me, living in my cottage. You'll no longer have to worry about food or shelter. There will be no need for you to steal to survive. You'll be earning money to purchase whatever it is that you'll need. You'll have a real home and a real family. Also, remember, if your intention is to lie or steal, you won't get a second chance. It isn't long, but I'll give you five minutes to think about all that I have told you."

Soon the five minutes of waiting were over.

"Well, Trevor, what will it be?"

He had been biting his lip in deep thought.

"I have always hoped that I would have a home. It's hard to believe that I'll have a home with you. I won't steal. I could never steal from you."

"All right then, you're hired."

"Did you mean it when you said I could live in your cottage?"

"Yes, I did."

"Today, can I live in your cottage?"

"Yes, you can."

"Are you leaving now for our home? Can I travel there with you? I don't know where it is."

"Yes, you can."

"Chovinne, will I have my very own bed?"

"Yes, a nice big soft bed."

"I've never had a bed before. I've always slept on a floor or the ground. It will be strange for me."

"Don't worry. I'll be there."

Chovinne couldn't say anymore. It was all too sad. She put her arm around the little waif and together they walked towards Dudras who had been waiting for her. Dudras looked at her questioningly.

"Dudras, meet Trevor. He'll be living with us."

"I'm happy to meet you. Welcome to the family."

"Dudras, would you hoist Trevor up on your horse. He needs a ride home."

Astride their horses, Chovinne mouthed to Dudras that they would talk later in the evening.

When they arrived at the estate, it was already late in the day. Dudras eased Trevor down from the horse onto the ground. Chovinne got off her horse as well. Dudras would tend to both horses which would allow her time to tend to Trevor.

"Trevor, come with me to the scullery. Your face and hair need to be washed and cleaned. You also need a bath."

The gypsy women had been working and heating water for laundry all day, so she knew there was enough to begin right away.

She alternately poured hot and cold water into the copper. She put her elbow in the water to test it for the right temperature.

"Trevor, take your clothes off and get into the copper for a nice bath."

She went to the linen cupboard and took out a washcloth and large towel and some soap. Children's underclothes were also there. She assumed they must have been forgotten by the workers who had left. Since they wouldn't be back to reclaim them, she took what she needed. She asked Subina, who was in the kitchen, if she would go to the caravans and get some outer clothing and shoes for Trevor. She was to tell the gypsies that they would be reimbursed for everything.

She knelt down on the floor and began washing his hair. It was very stringy and dirty and his scalp was encrusted. This was going to be a long process. She told him to close his eyes so that the soap wouldn't sting them. The falling ripples of water ran down his face and neck, leaving paths of different shades through the thick caked-on dirt. As the water penetrated the dirt more and more and cleansed his face, she winced inside when she saw the deep black and blue bruises that were on his forehead, cheeks and chin. She knew this was the result of beatings from older boys, or perhaps he had gotten them in a workhouse. His back and chest also had multiple bruises. Her one consoling thought was that at least he was with her now and would never have to endure such mistreatment again.

When she finished washing him, he no longer looked like the same boy. Underneath all that dirt, he actually had blond hair. Once the black and blue bruises disappeared from his face, he would be a very handsome boy.

Subina had returned with the clothes Chovinne had asked for. Chovinne asked if she would do her one more favor by warming the large towel before the fireplace before bringing it back to her.

When she returned with it, she thanked her for her help. She then asked Trevor to stand so she could wrap the warm towel around him. When he was dried off, she told him to dress himself while she attended to other matters. She took his dirty and torn clothing and shoes and threw them into the fireplace. To her this was more than just burning the clothing. It symbolized the start of a new life for Trevor. She told the gypsy women working in the kitchen that Trevor was an orphan and would now be living in the cottage. They were to consider him to be one of the family. She told him the circumstances that led her to bring him home with her. She then returned to Trevor.

"You must be tired. Come with me and I'll take you to your room."

She showed him all the rooms.

"Chovinne, this is a very large cottage.

Chovinne opened the door to his room.

"Go in, this is your room now."

His eyes tried to take it all in at once. It was completely furnished with beautiful furniture. He walked about the room, touching and asking questions about everything.

Abruptly, without warning, he asked if he could go to bed because he was so tired.

"Is there anything that I can do for you before I leave," she asked.

"Yes, would you please leave the lamp lit for a little while. I'm a little afraid."

"I can do that for you."

"I'll be downstairs for awhile. Don't be afraid. There is nothing here for you to fear. Think about tomorrow. You'll be meeting everyone and getting to know your new home."

She left the room, closed the door, and went downstairs.

Dudras was reading the newspaper when she entered the parlor. He peered at her from over the newspaper. When she was seated, and he had her undivided attention, he simply asked her why she had done what she did.

She told Dudras all about Trevor.

"You believe him? Really Chovinne. I don't know how you can. I think it's a big mistake."

"He came to me, Dudras. His life has been so hard. Somehow I just couldn't say no to him. I'm hoping he won't resort to his old ways. I don't want to have to put him back on the street. I made it abundantly clear to him. I just hope he realizes that I was very serious."

"Are you as tired as I am? I'm going upstairs to bed to try to get a good night's sleep. I have a lot to do tomorrow. I'll see you in the morning."

She washed her face, brushed her hair, and, then, turned down the covers and slipped into bed. She immediately fell asleep.

She was awakened by fingers tapping her face.

"Chovinne, Chovinne, wake up. Please, I can't sleep."

She opened her eyes and in the dim light saw Trevor standing there. She knew he was crying. She couldn't see them, but she knew tears were falling.

This day had proven too overwhelming for such a young child. She moved over and told him to get into the bed with her.

"You have to relax and stop crying now. I know today was intense for you. Too much change all at once. The worse is over now. You're safe here. You can sleep with me tonight, but tomorrow you'll have to sleep in your own room, in your own bed."

She lifted the covers and he got in beside her. She used the top of the blanket to wipe away his tears. Chovinne put her arm around him and nestled his head in the crook of her arm holding him tightly.

"Close your eyes now and get some sleep. I won't leave you. I promise."

"Since you promised, I think I can sleep now."

A few minutes passed and she could tell that he had fallen asleep. He was breathing quietly. He was a street smart pickpocket, but inside he was still just a small, frightened boy.

Tomorrow would be better. Future adjustments would be more gradual and easier for him to assimilate.

When morning dawned, she awoke to find his big, brown eyes staring at her. His face broke out into a big smile. He leaned over and gave her a big kiss on the cheek.

"Thank you for taking care of me. I was really scared. I'll be alright now."

They both got out of bed. She asked him to follow her to his room. There she proceeded to show him how to use the pitcher and bowl, so he could take a sponge bath. She returned to her room and did likewise. When she was dressed, she went out into the hall and called him. She held his hand and, together, they walked downstairs to eat breakfast. Everyone had been told to gather there, and she introduced him to everyone.

CHAPTER 30

The townhouse was a large building, four stories high, accommodating many residents. Names of the occupants were posted in the lobby on a wall plaque. Andrew lived on the ground floor. Chovinne went directly to his door and tapped the door knocker.

Andrew answered almost immediately.

"Are you ready?' Chovinne asked.

"Yes, I am. Let's go."

"Can you tell me about this surprise. I'm definitely intrigued by all this mystery," he said.

"Telling you would spoil my plans. Be patient, we'll be there soon."

She turned her carriage down a now familiar lane, stopping it at the entrance to her estate.

"Well, what do you think of my new home?"

"This is quite the surprise! What a fortunate person you are! This estate surely isn't understated. It's everything you told me you've always wanted, and I can see it is the purchase of a lifetime for you."

"I knew I couldn't adequately describe it to you. You had to see it for yourself."

"I'm amazed at such a visual presence. It's warm, vibrant and beautiful without being ostentatious. Multi-colored flowers have been carefully positioned to create an expression of the utter enchantment that nature provides."

"Birds must undoubtedly extend their visits here, and you, in turn, are the fortuitous beneficiary as you gaze upon their beauty and listen to their melodious songs. Standing here with you, I can see that life in all its various forms gives it the special qualities and meaning that you wanted so much."

"My predecessor's amazing gifts along with his love and patience created this enduring landscape."

"I wouldn't change anything. That is, after all, why I purchased it. It's everything I had ever hoped for and ever imagined."

"No one can ask more out of life than this. I have my heart's delight in this wonderful sanctuary."

"Andrew, tomorrow, many of us, including Dudras, Subina, and I, are going to the forest to get some ponies for the children. The estate is so large. The ponies will give them the freedom to ride and play and have fun. That's how it should be. I want them to ride their ponies and have sweet memories of their childhood. There haven't been many for them, thus far."

"Would you invite me along? It's time that I took more time for fun too."

"It would be wonderful to have you come with us," she said.

"I'm looking forward to tomorrow. At what time should I be here?"

"We're planning to leave before sunrise. I'll show you a vital world many people don't even know about."

CHAPTER 31

The morning mist that had been clinging to the treetops was just beginning to vaporize when they arrived. The gypsies left them as they set out to explore the forest. Chovinne and Andrew would rejoin them later. Together they followed footpaths created by the many trodding feet of people who hunted there. As they ventured more deeply into the forest, they were surrounded by shades of green and brown. They walked upon mosses layered with fallen leaves on the forest floor. It was a delightful walk enlivened by songs of various species of birds. A little chickadee flitted from twig to twig in search of food. Some wood pigeons flew upward in the maze of treetops. A brownish tree creeper crept its way up and around a tree trunk. She recognized the "whit-whit-whit" of the nuthatches flying above them. She pointed them out to Andrew and told him about all of the birds as they walked.

The moss crept over the twisted roots of the trees in thick clusters. Closeby there were mushrooms and toadstools. Chovinne was amazed that all forms of life could co-exist in such a shared environment.

"Andrew, let's stop here for a moment, next to this crumbling tree trunk. There is life here that will interest you. Look to your right and you'll see.

He looked and saw a herd of deer grazing on new shoots

that had sprouted from the soil.

"There are so many of them," he said.

"They aren't aware that we are here because we are downwind from them. Notice how they have a tentative look on their faces. They are cautious and they have to be. There are hunters looking for them."

"Are you ready to move on?" she asked.

"Yes."

They walked another short distance.

"Let's stop here," she said.

"If you look closely at that mossy log a few feet from us you will see a circular tunnel in the leaves that hides the home of a wood mouse. We won't see it because it only feeds at night."

Leaving that area, they walked further along. She stopped next to a tree and pointed out to him the visible damage on its bark.

"Rabbits stripped this tree at ground-level this past winter, because bark was all they could find to eat during the harsh weather. If you look at the higher branches, you will see the bark has also fed voles and wood mice. The marks are easily identifiable because mice leave smaller teeth marks than rabbits. Squirrels will do this also. Fungi is another food they like. They will eat some and knock the tops off others. They will also eat pine cones to the core."

She stopped, bent over, selected a strong twig from the ground and turned over the soil. She unearthed many crawling insects including beetles, slugs, snails and worms for Andrew to see.

"Other insects have made the bark on the trees their home. The moths that you see are often captured in spider webs. The birds also feed on them. Badgers, foxes and owls are here also, but the odds of seeing them are not good."

Finally, she and Andrew stood beneath the ancient sentinel of the forest. The majestic oak had provided protection in past generations for many people who fled from persecution.

"Listen Chovinne, I hear a baby crying. What is a baby doing in the forest?"

"Andrew, that isn't a baby that you hear. It's a hare that has been shot and is dying. You are hearing the sound it makes as it dies."

He stood there looking at her, gradually absorbing what she had just told him.

"The good and the ugly are everywhere," he said.

"We don't have much farther to go. See, the ground is worn from being pounded hard by the ponies' hooves. All we have to do is to follow this path which will lead us directly to them."

"Listen," she said, "do you hear them?"

"They are very noisy aren't they?" Andrew said.

"They are running around and playing."

Chovinne couldn't have chosen a better day. There was sunshine and warmth. She walked faster, anxious to see them. Andrew had difficulty keeping up with her. In her eagerness to get there, she had forgotten that Andrew wasn't as adept on this terrain as she was. It was a path that wasn't entirely straight or smooth. Since it was serpentine, a person had to be careful of what path to take because of the debris and holes which were not visible until you came upon them.

They were both breathless as they got closer. They had covered a lot of ground and had arrived at their final destination. The forest was gone. Their eyes beheld an idyllic locale for the ponies, an open, large, almost treeless glade with small streams running throughout.

"The black, white and brown mares, stallions and colts had not yet shed their shaggy winter coats.

"There are more than I thought there would be."

"Yes, and later on many of them will be living an equally wonderful life on my estate."

Chovinne's great grandfather had been a "whisperer", a gypsy who possessed the power of talking to horses. He could lure horses to him with whispered words, and without moving a finger, by willpower alone, could tame horses. Chovinne possessed the gift as well.

She knew that horses had a herd mentality and were very social animals. They formed family groups much like humans. The presence of others for protection against predators and other dangerous situations made the family units strong.

She watched them from a distance before venturing further. She observed many stallions with their harem of mares. Chovinne watched them closely. The dominant stallion and his harem must remain intact. Chovinne would seek out the young stallions, the bachelor herd, and the yet unpossessed mares to domesticate.

The ponies were familiar with people, because they often left the confines of the forest. They went into the nearby villages and many of the villagers fed them, so, in turn, they became docile and habituated to strangers They were superb riding ponies. They had good temperaments, nice heads and shoulders and short backs, strong quarters and plenty of bone. Their backs could carry an adult, but were still narrow enough to accommodate children.

Chovinne knew it would take more than feeding to convince them to come with her. She had to go talk to them. She explained to Andrew that she had to go alone. What she had to do required concentration, if she was to be successful. She left him and walked out into the glade. She saw a fallen tree and sat on the trunk. The ponies stopped playing and looked her way. Being very inquisitive, they began to inch closer and closer to see for themselves who this intruder was. She deliberately talked only to the bachelors and mares. They had to come as a group. She knew the ponies would not come with her without the familiarity of other family members. She allowed them to see, smell, nudge and hear her. This reconciled their senses that she wasn't a threat. Her measured gestures and well-modulated voice was sufficient to draw them over. In practically no time the ponies stood quietly in front of her. They no longer wanted to run away. The gypsy caravans had arrived earlier and had waited for her. It was now their turn, the preparatory groundwork having been done. They would proceed slowly and take as much time as was needed to train them.

She waved at Andrew to come down and join them. He could not believe what he had seen.

"How did you accomplish what you did?"

"All I did was ask them which ones of them wanted to come with me. It was their decision."

He was completely baffled. This was something he just couldn't understand. He had a feeling that even if he asked her to explain herself, he still wouldn't understand, so he left the subject alone.

Knowing the ponies were in expert hands, Chovinne and Andrew left for the estate.

CHAPTER 32

It was cold in the cottage when they arrived.

"Andrew, would you put some firewood in the fireplace? I'll get some faggots to place over the wood to help the fire burn more rapidly."

They stood next to the fireplace for warmth. It wasn't long before the whole kitchen was nice and warm.

"Are you hungry?"

"As a matter of fact, I'm very hungry."

"I am too. I'll make some furmenty for us."

"What is it?"

"It's hulled wheat boiled in milk. I'll season it with sugar, cinnamon and raisins. It's delicious and filling."

She placed the steaming bowl before him. She noticed he was waiting for her before eating.

"Start eating while it's hot. I'll ladle some for myself and I'll join you as soon as I can."

In no time, they each had devoured the food.

"Do you have any left?"

"I made more than enough."

"Here, have more," she said.

For awhile, they talked about everyday things. Then Andrew broached the subject of her carriage service, asking her if she had looked into it.

"I've done a lot of thinking on the matter. I want only the

best horses and that's why I'm going to Tattersall's. They have the popular breeds, the Cleveland Bays, Yorkshire Coach Horses, and Hackneys for carriage work. They have a sterling reputation. High society would not even acknowledge me if the carriages were not drawn by a perfectly matched pair of horses."

"Andrew, you know very well that horses are expensive both to buy and to maintain. They have to be fed, sheltered and cared for every day. People don't want to go to that expense. They would rather pay someone for that service and be done with it."

"I will concentrate the greater part of the carriage service in the west end. The men's club members and theatre goers prefer to be driven home after an evening out. I will also have carriages at various railway terminals and inns. These people will appreciate carriages that will take them to their front door, or even to their homes, if they are within reasonable distances to bring them into the city and back again. I bought broughams. They are carriages that have dignity and space."

"You have carefully thought this out. When do you begin?"

"I have already leased a townhouse with stable accommodations and a carriage house behind it. My office will be located there in that house. I will be in their midst. The close proximity will be quite advantageous."

"Rotation of the horses and carriages to and from the estate will insure that the horses will be observed by a veterinarian on a regular basis for any potential health problems. I have hired wheelwrights to work at the estate and in the city to mend the wheels because they take the most abuse. This is especially important because it requires a day to make a wheel. They, of course, will have gypsies helping them. Having already bought the brougham carriages that I need, I have contacted the harness-maker, the upholsterer, the cutter, the painter and the gold plater to be accessible in emergencies. My family could do this work, but I need them to drive the carriages. I will be distributing cards at businesses and private homes in the city, as well as, advertising locations in the newspapers.

"My goodness, I'm impressed. I believe that you haven't left anything out."

"I had this all planned in my mind. When the time came, as it did, I merely methodically acted upon them."

"As much as I hate to go, I have to leave now. This day was very special, spending it with you. I did learn a lot. Your life is very interesting. Mine pales in comparison," he said.

"It's being with you that makes the difference. Chovinne, I want to be with you, spend time with you. I'm sure you know how I feel. I want to see you more often. What do you say?"

"I say yes, but I'm a gypsy and you aren't. I must bring this matter to the attention of the elders before this goes any farther. I don't know what their decision will be, but I do know that I must abide by it. I don't want them to say no, but if they decide that we mustn't see one another again, I won't go against their wishes."

"Will I have to wait long for their decision?"

"I don't know. This is important. They have made exceptions before. I hope that they will again. Let's think positive thoughts."

"Andrew, it's quite late, you don't have to leave. There are extra bedrooms. You could sleep here overnight and leave refreshed in the morning after a good night's sleep."

"I will take you up on your offer. I am tired. I'll stay the night."

"Good, let's retire. I'll see you at breakfast in the morning. Until then, goodnight."

Before he left the next morning, Andrew asked her to get in touch with him the moment she knew with certainty, the elder's decision.

CHAPTER 33

It was unacceptable for a gypsy to marry a non-gypsy. She knew this and was prepared to let Andrew go unequivocally, if the elders unanimously opposed their association.

The elders were collectively waiting for her in the library.

"I know that what I have to say won't come as a surprise to you. I'm quite fond of Andrew. He is a good man, a kind, caring, and generous person. When I needed his help with our financial matters, he was more than willing to do anything he could to help me. By helping me, he helped us all. I'm secure in the knowledge that he only has our best interests in his heart. I hope you will consider this in your assessment of him."

"Chovinne, prior to this meeting, we have talked extensively among ourselves about what we would do if you came to us seeking our permission to continue seeing this man. Our decision is based upon what we have seen for ourselves. He loves and respects you. If this leads to marriage, we approve of your choice. There is one stipulation. Any children that you may have can't become the next voivode. This is one concession we won't make. The next voivode must have two gypsy parents."

"I understand and that won't be a problem. When I die, the family succession will be broken, to be continued by someone else."

Chovinne knew Andrew was on pins and needles wanting to know the elders' decision. Knowing this, she left the cottage for Andrew's townhouse in order to catch him before he left. She knocked on the door. When Andrew opened it, small talk was dispensed with. He immediately went to the heart of the matter.

"Chovinne, I have to know. What did the elders say? Can we continue seeing each other?"

"They said we have their approval."

"I'm so relieved! Needless to say, I thought they would say we couldn't see one another again."

"Not as often as we'd like, however, since you're busy with your life, as I am with mine. My carriage service must take priority until it's well established. This arrangement will allow us to concentrate on personal endeavors. Then, we can take more time to focus on ourselves."

CHAPTER 34

Someone was unrelentingly insistent on the door knocker. Chovinne hurried to the door to see who it was. Whoever was there wouldn't take no for an answer and wanted someone to come to the door. Opening it, she saw that it was Ben. The transformation was nothing short of phenomenal. He was impeccably dressed. The man standing there before her was a totally different person from the one she hadn't seen for some time.

"Ben, what a surprise! You look so handsome, so healthy, rested and prosperous. Come in, tell me everything. I can't wait to hear. I have thought about you so often."

"Come, let's go to the front parlor where we can be comfortable. We have so much to talk about."

They both sat down.

"You begin," she said.

"I never thought anyone could be so wonderfully happy as I am. I chose a different venture from most for myself. Life at sea is a precarious one, risky and dangerous. I wanted adventure and that's exactly what I have. I love to think and plan about the future possibilities, to do anything I want. I love the liberation; freedom is exhilarating. You gave that to me Chovinne. It's still difficult to believe."

"There wasn't a day that you weren't on my mind. I didn't want to come back to see you until I could tell you that I was successful. I'm a very wealthy man, Chovinne, but more importantly, I'm a happy one."

They were briefly interrupted when one of the gypsies brought them tea.

"We could be drinking tea that I brought over on my clippers."

"That could very well be true."

"The tea on my clippers is packed in Chinese porcelain containers, which double for ballast stability. It's important that the tea not spoil in the hold if I'm to command a high price for my cargo. When I was out on the high seas, I pushed my clippers hard. I sailed with a competent crew. I bolstered my lee rails to withstand the blowing winds. I didn't shorten the sails when the winds blew. The crew and I went from one wave crest to another. Under full speed of canvas, with sails groaning and the hulls squealing, my clippers were the first to arrive in port. The tea, silk and opium merchants offered me a very substantial amount of money for my cargoes."

"These many past months have been the most ambitious of my life. I can only hope to have the continuous repetition of the fantastic good fortune that I've enjoyed thus far."

"I've saved my most incredible news for last. I'm planning to sail for America. I'm finally going to realize my ultimate dream! I can hardly believe that I'll be leaving in a matter of days."

"I bought larger clippers from Lloyd's. They were thoroughly checked by them for thin, strained, flimsy canvas, worn rigging, crippled spars, rotted masts, leaking hull and for soundness in timber and planking. I've hired extra men for the necessary maintenance of the ship. Caulkers to seal the seams between the planks with tar. Carpenters to replace worn and broken planks and other necessary repairs. Ropemakers, sailmakers, signalmen and cooks have also been hired. I need coopers who will stand guard at the freshwater barrels and carefully conserve it. The majority of the water will be used mostly for cooking. The remainder will be used to mix a half pint of fiery rum from the West Indies with a quart of water when we need to quench our thirst."

"We bathe and swab the ship with salt water."

"Tell me Ben, what do you eat during your months away?"

"All on board eat hard biscuits, salted beef in barrels, and pork, dried peas, oatmeal, brown sugar and cheese. We take along butter, but it usually turns rancid. We can't eat it so we usually throw it overboard."

"We have weaponry and have armed ourselves against possible piracy."

"The Atlantic will be a sailing challenge. It's an angry ocean. It's greenish-gray waters churn constantly. Storms gather and stir up huge towering waves with foaming tops. These turbulent waters cause the ships to roll and toss on the huge swells with great difficulty."

"I'll be sailing first to the American harbor in New York. After I have explored the Eastern coast, I'll go into the interior of the country. I've heard from reliable sources that they have magnificent inland waterways. When I've seen everything that I need to there, I'll move on to the South, and, later, Canada. Knowing the water routes of a particular region, I'll be more knowledgeable about making decisions, when I have to, about where the best resources are to export. This way I'll be able to concentrate on the most expedient means and least expensive ways of transporting cargo to London and elsewhere."

"I have been told by reputable sea captains and sailors not to venture to the West Coast. Portland and Seattle, as well as San Francisco's Barbary Coast harbor district, are notorious for illegal procurement of sailors. Clever crimps see to it that many of the sailors are sent back to sea sooner than they wanted to return. The stories are that, as soon as the anchor of an arriving vessel comes down, the crimpers will be there, coming over the side, bringing with them their bad liquor, promises of jobs with limitless dollars, fast women, and weeks of leave. In no time, clean living men are transformed into unrecognizable, mindless sailors, who, when in a total alcoholic stupor, are easily abducted and brought to another ship, only to recover miles out to sea with no idea how they got there or where they were going. It doesn't end there, there's more. There are also female crimps who own saloons. These women hire runners to prowl for men along the coast. These runners strike up conversations with these men and quickly entice them to go with them to a saloon for a good time. These women usually receive one hundred dollars for every man ambushed. Inside the saloons, the men are treated like important personages and given liquor. The women specialize in chloroform-spiked beer. Another is a drink made of equal parts of brandy, gin and a generous dash of laudanum or opium. Conveniently located, close to the bar, is a trap door built into the floor. The drinking man is nudged until he's standing on it. A signal is given to a person watching from behind the bar. He immediately operates a lever and dumps the man standing there into the saloon's basement. Others with similar fates have their attention diverted so they won't see what is happening near them. They, also, are delivered to malevolent sea-captains."

"Lately, I've heard the crimps are on the eastern coast too."

"I love my crew. We take care of one another. I won't subject them or myself to such atrocities just to make more money. We won't go there until it's safe to do so."

"Well, I've told you everything that I was dying to tell you."

"Now I want to know how you came to purchase this beautiful estate."

"Ben, why don't we go outside and I'll show you why this estate is so perfect."

"This is what I've always wanted, a quiet retreat away from the world. I love it because it gives me the freedom that I can find nowhere else. Here, I can forget for a time that the other world exists. Just knowing I have this place to come to makes it easier for me to temporarily forget the hostility that always exists just beyond this perimeter. Surrounded by all this beauty makes me so thankful that I was fortunate enough to acquire it. It's such a joy to live here."

She then told him about the man who previously owned it, and all particulars from beginning to end.

"Our lives have changed tremendously, Chovinne. You and I both have what we've always wanted. I always remember when that wasn't true and it makes me all the more appreciative."

"This has been such a pleasant visit. The time has flown by. I must be on my way. I have many things to do before I sail."

"What day and what time are you leaving?"

"In two days, on Thursday at daybreak."

"Never ever leave on a Friday, Ben. You will have bad luck. I'll go to the dock to see you off."

"Only if you bring someone with you. I still don't want you down there alone."

"I'll bring Andrew with me. It's time the two of you met."

"Don't leave yet. I have something inside the cottage I want you to have."

Together, they went inside. There in the entry hall was a sea chest and a ditty box. Ben's eyes widened.

"I saw these for sale and thought they would be just perfect for you. Let's go see them."

He picked up the mahogany ditty box by its rope handles. A quality box like this would be very useful.

"I had planned, when I left today, to purchase a box and

chest. Now I won't have to."

"As captain, I haven't had much time off to make myself one."

"I didn't think you did."

"This box is perfect for storing the tools that I require for certain work when no other tools can be substituted for splicing, whipping and seizing rope and canvas. The variety of smaller things that can scatter about, be misplaced or lost, will go into the box and will be together and ready whenever I need them."

They turned their attention to the chest.

"This mahogany sea chest is magnificent, Chovinne. It will last forever. The artist who hand-painted this sea scene on the lid captured the clipper in all its glory. Its unfurled sails swelling aloft-noble, dazzling, and elegant. I also like the way the lid comes down over the sides. It lifts more easily."

"I bought a large chest so that you would have ample room for all your possessions."

"Last week when I was in the city, a retiring seaman was selling all his navigational aids. I thought of you and couldn't resist buying more essentials for you. It wouldn't hurt to have duplicates to rely upon in case you should lose those you did have. I placed them inside the chest. I hope you don't mind that I took the liberty of doing that."

"I'd be a fool to mind. You can never have too many."

"Hurry then, look inside for your gifts."

"I feel like this is my birthday and Christmas rolled into one. This is so exciting!"

The first of the gifts he removed from the chest was a triangular shaped case. He opened it, knowing it was a pocket sextant. It was in perfect condition. Sailors depended upon such instruments to make their navigational decisions.

The next gift was a square brass box. A compass had been skillfully crafted on the center of the top. Surrounding it were several sundials with Roman numerals for use in different latitudes. The sun, moon and stars were elaborately engraved on each side of the box.

"I believe the chronometer is without a doubt the most beautifully crafted that I've ever seen. Silver on the outside as well as on the inside. I'll feel grand making longitudinal celestial observations with this."

He gingerly took a weather glass from the chest.

"This is really old, Chovinne. I believe this glass dates to the sixteenth century. My father had one similar to this one. I don't know what happened to it. Maybe he sold it when we needed money. Ours also had an elegant stand of wood and brass with the weather glass suspended in the center. I'll show you how it works. When the water level reaches a certain point in this glass spout, it instantly shows air pressure that predicts the kind of weather that can be expected. For you to have even found someone selling these ancient devices is phenomenal. The chronometer, as well as the weather glass, I believe were custom made for the wealthy few. They are so elaborate that they could only have been crafted during the Renaissance. I can't really date the sextant. He picked up the weather glass to further examine it. He held it up to look beneath it. When he saw his father's name engraved on the bottom, he nearly dropped it. Slowly, he put it back inside the chest. He was in shock. Many times he had wished for something tangible to see and touch to remember the good times with his father. He had longed for something they had shared together. Having this memento changed everything. He no longer felt alone; the emptiness in his heart dissipated. He felt really alive again. This connection made all the difference. He would show the glass to his friends and say with pride that it had belonged to his father.

Chovinne spoke to him, but he didn't hear her. He seemed to be so far away. It was as if he had forgotten she was there. Chovinne had to grasp his hands for him to notice her.

"What's wrong?"

He shook his head.

"Nothing is wrong. Everything is right."

"You haven't been yourself since you set your eyes on the weather glass."

"What I'm about to tell you, you'll find hard to believe."

She listened wide-eyed as he told her that his father had previously owned the glass.

"Who could have possibly known that when you bought it for me it would be something I thought had been lost to me forever. It's the memories associated with it that are so special. I feel that this is a sign that he has always been watching over me."

"A lot of good things have happened to me since I met you. Do you think it was fate?"

"I've always believed that everything that happens affects people in ways that are part of a greater plan."

"I have more things for you."

"More, you have given me so much already!"

She came back with her arms full, carrying clothing she had purchased for him from Edward.

"This is foul weather clothing to keep you dry. Here is a fur hat, also this scarf and this beaver coat. Put them on. I want to see how they fit you."

He did.

"They fit you perfectly. Now, I won't have to worry as much, knowing you'll be warm on the cold Atlantic."

"One last thing, I haven't shown you the secret compartment in the chest. She showed him what he had to do to open it."

"This place will hold all your secrets from prying eyes–your papers, manifest, maps, diary, logbook and whatever else you want to place there.

"I'm so happy to have all the beautiful gifts that you've given me. I'm practically speechless. Suffice it to say, I didn't expect my life to turn around the way it has. It's difficult to think there is anyone on this earth happier than I am."

"I hate to leave you, but I'm afraid I must go."

They walked outside to the carriage. He carried the chest and she carried the box. He placed them both inside the carriage.

"I'll see you in two days," he said, hugging her.

"I'll be there. I definitely wouldn't miss seeing you off. Until then."

CHAPTER 35

It was raining heavily the day Ben was to leave on his long voyage to America. Already dressed, Chovinne wore a canvas hat and a great-coat, not unusual attire for the gypsies, because they were always out in all sorts of weather. Hearing the carriage as it approached, she selected a hat and great-coat for Andrew, ran out of the cottage and hurriedly climbed inside the carriage.

"Isn't this weather terrible?" Andrew asked.

"You would think that we would be accustomed to this almost constant rain or drizzle, but I guess you never are."

"I brought these for you to wear. You'll be drenched without them," she said.

"Ben is finally going to America. He has wanted to go there for so long. He's jubilant."

They arrived to see that Ben was waiting for them. Chovinne made the introductions.

Andrew was the first to speak.

"Chovinne has told me about how you both met by chance, how kind you were to her by offering her your protection at the docks, when she was really someone you didn't even know."

"The docks are dangerous places. I was there and wanted her to be safe, and I knew she would be with me."

"The day that I met her turned out to be the luckiest day

of my life. Little did I know that she would remember me and change my life forever. She took me out of the bowels of misery."

"My clippers are ready to set sail, but I won't leave until you both come on board. I'll show you everything from stem to stern."

Chovinne saw the pride he felt etched upon his face as he explained the mechanics of the clipper to them.

Soon it was time to leave. Chovinne was both happy and sad. Happy that Ben would pursue his dream, but sad when she thought of the dangers associated with the sea. The possibility that, during any of his voyages, a ship disaster could occur, and that she would never see him again was always be on her mind. It would be something she would have to live with.

"We both know that your departure time is here. There won't be a day that I won't be thinking about you Ben. I hope America is everything you expect and more. I will be waiting for your letters."

"Chovinne, I have a request. I've shown the weather glass to all my friends. It wouldn't be a good idea to bring it with me. There is a possibility that I could lose it in some manner. Would you bring it home with you? That way, I'll know it will be safe."

"I would consider it a privilege to keep your family heirloom for as long as you need."

Ben placed the weather glass in her hands.

"I really can't wait, you know. It'll seem like forever to get there. I'll miss you."

He gave her a big hug and shook Andrew's hand. He smiled at both of them, then walked away.

It stopped drizzling. Chovinne and Andrew watched the clippers until they no longer saw the ships from shore.

"Are you hungry, Chovinne?"

"I'm famished, even though I ate breakfast."

"I am too. Where do you want to eat?"

"Let's buy some coffee at a stall and muffins from a street-seller and eat in your carriage."

"That sounds perfect," he said.

The coffee was steaming hot. They found a street seller with a basket on his arm selling muffins. They were covered with flannel material to keep them warm and were saturated with butter.

They carried everything to the carriage.

"Aren't these just the best?" Chovinne asked.

"I think you have a sweet tooth."

"Yes, I think I do."

She took another bite.

"Yes, definitely, I have a sweet tooth."

"What do you think of Ben?" she asked.

"I don't think you could have found a nicer friend. He thinks the world of you."

"As I do of him."

"Chovinne, I'm leaving for Paris in two days. Some noblemen and business men that I know want to invest their money in England's industries and commerce."

"Will you be gone long?"

"At least three weeks, maybe more."

"Is Chantilly far from Paris?" she asked.

"Not too far, why?"

"Would you go to the races for me and bet on Britilen again? I've been keeping track of him. He's still winning a high percentage of his races."

"I'll make the time."

"That's wonderful. When we go back to the cottage, I'll give you the money I want you to place on him."

"I'll use my money," he said.

"I can't let you do that. I wouldn't feel right about it. As we discussed previously, my family is my responsibility."

"I just wanted to help you."

"You are helping. You'll be the one in Chantilly placing the bet. Since I can't go there, it will be helping me quite a bit, wouldn't you say?"

"Yes, it would. I'll have to learn to deal with your fierce independence."

"When I return from Paris, we will look into investments that will give you profitable dividends.

*

Chovinne had hoped to have Dudras and Andrew accompany her to Tattersall's, but Andrew's business commitments had required him to be elsewhere. Tattersall's, near Hyde Park Corner, reigned supreme as established stock auctioneers of quality. In disguise, with Dudras by her side, they inspected the horses before the auction. They decided on those they wanted to purchase. The horses passed under the hammer and became theirs.

CHAPTER 36

Chovinne knew that the rich wanted elegance surrounding them and this she would provide.

Sumptuous food, drink, gambling, betting, conversation and idle gossip amid resplendent surroundings were everyday occurrences in London's west end exclusive men's clubs. The west was the boundary the rich had chosen to go to when the city of London began to expand. There they had the space to build their mansions and gardens. This was especially expedient since London's prevailing winds were from the west. The land there was on higher ground and the increasingly filthy smoke from coal-burning fires were dispersed eastwardly. They were far sighted visionaries who had the monetary assets to enjoy the healthy, breathable, fresh air.

There was loud talking and laughing in the hall outside her bedroom. Chovinne was in her room and went to investigate the noise. A feather bed was being moved down the hall.

"Where are you going with that?"

"No one wants it in their beds, so we're taking it to the worker cottages."

"I'll take it. Bring it to my room."

She had had a feather bed at the Abbey. Memories of sinking deeply into the soft, comfortable feather bed remained vivid. She couldn't understand why no one wanted it.

She finished dressing, then went downstairs. Just as she got there, she remembered she had forgotten something and went back to her room. As she stood in the doorway, her breath caught in her throat. Trevor was looking through all her jewelry, holding them one by one in the sunlight coming through the window. She noiselessly walked to a dark corner in her room still observing Trevor's actions. After a time, he took the box the jewelry was in and put it back where it had been. Then, he nonchalantly walked out of the room. This was what she had been dreading. With leaden feet, she slowly walked to the box. She wanted to know, and yet didn't want to know, if he had taken anything. Her hands reached for the box. She slowly opened it and looked inside. Everything was accounted for. She breathed a sigh of relief. He hadn't lied and broken his promise. She could trust him now. She went downstairs and ate breakfast with the others. When they all had finished eating and were leaving the table, she asked Trevor to go to the front parlor with her.

"Trevor, I saw you when you were in my room earlier looking at my jewelry. I checked to see if they were all still there. I'm so proud of you. I trusted you and you proved that I can take your word, that you wouldn't steal from me or anyone else."

"I don't know why I did that. I just wanted to see them because they're so pretty."

"I don't want you to ever again enter another person's room without their permission. You must respect people's privacy."

"It's over now. Just remember not to do that again."

"Trevor, would you like to go to the city with me today, all day? It's the first time that I'll be going to my office. I'd like some company, if you don't mind."

"I'd like to see your office and I don't mind. I'll even go

with you more often if you'd like."

"I would like that."

"Wear your nicest clothes. I want you to look your best."

*

"Here we are," she said as she opened the door.

"This is really nice!" Trevor said as he walked around the room.

"Isn't it though?"

The resplendent surroundings gave her a great sense of accomplishment. It had required an inordinate amount of planning to achieve her goals. Sitting down behind her elegantly carved mahogany desk, she checked through all the papers that were on it assuring herself they were all there. Trade cards had been engraved and would be given to all clients. All pertinent information such as the hours, days, distance, and cost would be there to refer to when needed.

*

The day had been a busy one. The last client had just left.

"Trevor, it's time to leave."

He bolted from his chair.

"Chovinne, can we get something to eat on our way home. I'm hungry."

"We'll stop in the city. I have to buy some stationery."

When they got there, she gave him some money.

"Buy yourself any kind of pastry that you like and something to drink. I'll be waiting here for you."

Trevor left her to buy what he needed.

The street-sellers business was declining because stores selling stationery were beginning to dot the streets.

This street-seller was patiently waiting for a customer.

Chovinne walked to his stand, compared the stationery for quality, then bought what she needed.

Trevor was coming back to find Chovinne. He began to run towards her when he saw that a pickpocket was lifting her locket. He took immediate action. He stealthfully followed him. He had seen him put the locket in his pocket. He would get it back for Chovinne. The pickpocket stopped to buy some apples. While he was preoccupied choosing those he wanted, Trevor ever so slowly and smoothly retrieved the locket without any undue effort. Then, he unobtrusively slipped into the crowd.

He returned to where Chovinne was and waited for her to complete her purchases before speaking.

"I have something for you."

"What is it?"

"Give me your hand."

She did as she was asked. He took her hand and placed the locket within it.

She looked at the locket and, then, at Trevor.

"I saw a pickpocket take it, and I got it back for you."

"You are such a darling to have done that for me. What a fortunate day it was when I brought you home."

Chovinne decided, after that episode, to leave her precious locket at home. There were just too many pickpockets and a repetition was inevitable.

Due to advertising in the newspapers, strategic locations of inns and railways, and the reasonable distances offered to and from the city, the west end clientele made Chovinne's carriage service successful beyond her expectations.

People were anxious to avail themselves of the opportunity open to them, which simplified their lives. Though only in operation for one short week, she was doing a brisk business.

The second week was as brisk as the first. Friday, during the afternoon, the postman in a scarlet coat and shining top hat adorned with a gold band, came into her office and placed a letter on her desk. She wasn't expecting anything in the mail. She glanced down and saw that her name was written on it. It could only be from one person. Andrew had sent it. She hurriedly opened it.

Dear Chovinne,

I remembered that you couldn't find the Bronte books in the city. When I saw them in a bookshop, I bought them as gifts from me to you. We did very, very well in Chantilly. I hope the carriage service is steadily getting well established. I think of you every day. I'm counting the days until I see you again.

> *Love,*
> *Andrew*

CHAPTER 37

She had been busy and hadn't stopped by to see Edward for some time. She would do that today. There weren't any people mingling outside his shop. She tried the door. It wasn't locked. She cautiously walked in and closed the door behind her. It was dim inside. It was very strange, something was definitely wrong.

"Edward, are you here?" she asked in a loud voice.

"I'm over here."

She looked in the direction of his voice. He was standing next to the window looking outside.

"Why are you closed?"

"I have two days to make a payment on my shop, or they'll seize my property, and I'll go to prison."

"What, did I hear you correctly?"

"You heard correctly."

"What happened to cause this catastrophe?"

"I made some bad investments, lost too much money, and can't meet my payment."

"Did you make these investments on your own?"

"Yes."

"That was a mistake. You need to work with a professional stockbroker who has experience and expertise about stocks, and will work with and guide you in the right direction."

"I'm glad I came here today. You have invested too much money and time to lose this shop. I'll help you Edward. I'll take care of everything."

"You can help me," he asked.

"Yes I can, I have money now. It's a long story. Suffice it to say that I do. I'll make the next six payments."

"I'll contact my bank. They will send someone here to gather all the information they need to rectify this matter. In the not too distant future, I'll send someone here to help you with your investments."

"Chovinne, I can breathe again. Going to prison isn't a comforting thought. You are as aware as I am that the repercussions are severe when you can't meet a stipulated deadline. I'll repay you as soon as I can."

"Don't worry about that. I'm not. When you are sure that you have enough assets, you can repay me."

"Remember, if anything like this or just anything unforeseen creates a hardship for you, and you need help, please don't hesitate to let me know."

"I will. Thank you so much!"

CHAPTER 38

Although her calendar was hectic, a visit to the gamekeeper wasn't something that could wait too long.

She awakened early, bathed, dressed and was on her way down to make her breakfast when she heard a knock on her bedroom door. Opening it, she saw Trevor standing there.

"Good morning Chovinne."

"Good morning to you too."

"I heard you tell Dudras that you were going to the gamekeeper's cottage, today. Can I go with you?"

"I'd love to have you accompany me. We'll have a great time together. First, we'll eat and then we'll be on our way."

The gamekeeper's cottage stood in a sheltered hollow of the woodlands. The cottage was thatched and gabled like other cottages were. Riding in on their horses, Chovinne and Trevor were greeted by howling, kenneled hounds.

Their keeper had many hunting dogs to help him in his work.

"What do the dogs do exactly?" Trevor asked.

"They ferret out pheasant and other game. They also retrieve them when they're downed and place them at his feet," she explained.

"Chovinne, look over there, on that shed. There are dead animals and birds nailed to it. This man must be an expert with a gun."

211

"He is, otherwise he couldn't be a gamekeeper. When he aims his gun at something, he rarely misses his target."

"Let's go to the cottage, Trevor. He must be waiting for us."

She knocked on the door, but received no response.

"That's odd. He knew that I would be coming here today. Maybe he's in the shed. Let's go there."

She opened the shed door. It was filled with rabbit nets and traps, spades, billhooks, twine and wire, and impounded poacher's implements.

"Chovinne, what's that horrible looking thing in the back left corner?"

They walked over to it.

"That's a relic from the past. It's a man-trap. In days past, gamekeepers would place the trap in tall grass to catch poachers. It's iron jaws would snap together with vicious energy and a poacher would be caught in the iron teeth.

A voice from behind startled them.

"Good morning, I apologize that I wasn't here to meet you. There was a disturbance not far from here that I went to investigate."

His voice was deep, perhaps the tonality was due to shouting in the open air.

Chovinne extended her hand to meet him. "I'm Chovinne, and this young man is Trevor."

Trevor followed suit and did likewise.

Chovinne observed that the keeper was tall and sinewy. His shoulders showed some curvature, a common distinctive feature of keepers. She had noticed this when she had seen them when she had caught birds and hedgehogs for sale. Their work required them to carry a heavy gun. Also, the game that they caught increased this defect over the years. A dog-whistle hung around his neck. He personally trained his dogs. Pups that he sold commanded very high prices.

"Did you ever catch a man in that trap?" Trevor asked.

"Absolutely not. It's one I found in the woods. I wouldn't do that. I brought it here so no one else could use it."

"Rabbits, partridge, pheasant are all plundered by foxes, hawks, weasels, stoats and more. I rely on my gun, dogs, and traps to eliminate many of them. The hardest work I have to contend with is the human poachers. They trespass over private property, where they have no right to be. It's my job to find these notorious leeches."

"Since the work is so hard, why do you do it?" Trevor asked.

"I have a simple answer for you. It's being outside, connecting with nature. There isn't anything that can compare with it. The scents are all around me, flowers, woods, meadows. It's invigorating. The freedom is unequaled and makes me healthy and vigorous."

Chovinne changed the subject.

"My intention was for both of us to formally meet today. As a result of our talk, I feel confident you'll always be conscious of our welfare. Whatever you bring us for our table is fine with me. I'm sure it won't be anything but the best."

"Before I leave, let me tell you that if you ever have anything to discuss with me, please don't hesitate to do so. I want to know everything that happens on this estate, everything!"

"It was very nice meeting you. Trevor and I must be on our way."

*

"How about some lunch? I know of a nice inn where we can stop and have something to eat. Wouldn't that be nice?"

"I won't know how to act or what to do there."

"There's no need for you to worry. Just follow my example and everything will be fine."

There weren't many people at the inn. Chovinne and Trevor were escorted to a nice table.

It wasn't long before a waiter placed a sweet trolley next to the table.

"Let's have tea and gorge ourselves on these luscious desserts. We'll eat sensibly tomorrow."

Trevor's eyes lit up at the thought of selecting and eating anything he wanted.

During lunch, Trevor became more comfortable with Chovinne and began talking more freely.

They both ate and ate.

Chovinne was the first to speak.

"I think I'm too full to move. How about you?

"My stomach is very happy."

"We'll both waddle out of here."

She paid for their lunch and they left.

On the way home, Trevor had something to say about everything he saw and had a multitude of questions for Chovinne. His curiosity was insatiable. He was a very bright child, his quick mind remembered the minutest details. He hadn't spoken that much before, so she didn't know he was so intelligent.

"Chovinne, can we go back to the inn again?"

"Of course, we can."

"Next time, I would like to pay. I'll save my money and buy lunch for you and me."

"I'll look forward to it."

"Trevor, can you read?"

"No, I can't."

"I'll remedy that for you. I will teach you. Starting tomorrow, you will come with me to the office every day to learn. It won't be long before you'll be able to read everything. The family members all know how to read. I don't want you to borrow any books from them. I'll buy you all the books you'll need. After that, when you go to the bookstore, you can make your own selections."

CHAPTER 39

The next day Chovinne was solemn and very worried. One carriage hadn't yet returned to the cottage. The previous night had been foggier than usual. The fog was still shrouding the countryside. How she hated the fog. Light and humanity were obscured under its grey veils. Vision so restricted created an uneasiness of what lay just beyond what the eyes couldn't see.

The anxiety she felt left her when she heard the sound of a carriage just outside the cottage. Opening the door, she was glad to see Andrew was back from Paris, but openly dismayed that it wasn't the gypsies returning.

Andrew had hardly set foot inside the cottage when she voiced her concerns to him. How worried she was about the missing gypsies and how she had to find them.

"We must go looking for them," he said.

"Dudras and I were just about to leave for the city."

"We'll go in my carriage. I'm concerned, too," said Andrew.

The lingering fog made the journey to the city interminable. Once they got there the rows of oil lamps lit by watchmen cast a dull flickering, greenish-white light on the city streets. The streets were almost empty. This would make it easier to spot the carriage. They looked everywhere to no avail. The next logical places to look for them was in the sewer because they now expected the worst. Protection by the police from street brutality was a dismal failure. Surly, villainous street thugs continued to attack and rob unsuspecting victims everywhere. Depositing bodies in sewers was a quick and efficient method of disposal.

Chovinne suddenly spotted the carriage on the roadside.

"There it is!" she shouted.

Stopping just behind it, they all jumped out and ran to it. Dudras, carrying a bull's eye lantern, used it to illuminate the interior of the carriage and the ground around it.

"Do you see anything?" Chovinne asked.

"No. They aren't here."

"We'll have to look in the sewers, then," she said.

"I had hoped it wouldn't come to that."

"I'll go with you, Dudras," Andrew said.

"I will too," said Chovinne.

"No, you can't. You must stay behind. It's too dangerous. The rats are too numerous. It will be difficult enough for Andrew and I to cope with them."

"Stay here while I go back to the carriage to get a pair of boots that I brought for Andrew to wear."

Andrew put the boots on, and he and Dudras disappeared into the cavernous sewer. Chovinne knew it was very dangerous inside. She had been inside before. Bricks that had originally been put there were now rotted in many places and had fallen down. The slightest contact with the overhead bricks would bring them down and injure them if they didn't proceed very slowly. The vapors emitted inside were noxious.

It was common knowledge that the rats in the sewers were very large and really formidable. They wouldn't hesitate to attack a lone man with fury as well as those accompanied by others.

Chovinne hoped the gypsies weren't inside the subterranean labyrinth, but she didn't deceive herself. There was a very good chance that they were.

Finally, after what seemed like endless waiting, Andrew and Dudras emerged. Pain and horror were etched on their faces.

"The worst has happened, Chovinne. They are dead. Their flesh has been eaten to the bone. Rats are still gnawing on them. We didn't dare to go too close, because they would have come after us. I recognized their clothing. That was all that was left to identify them."

They stood together in disbelief. Family members were dead. Most probably, the motive had been greed. They, undoubtedly, were killed for the money they carried.

"Senseless deaths," Chovinne said, "Two very good people taken from us for money."

"I must now tell the families. I dread it. There isn't any way to prepare them for what I have to say."

"Dudras, take the carriage back to the cottage. We will sell it as well as the horses. It would be bad luck for us to keep them under the circumstances."

Chovinne and Andrew followed the carriage back to the cottage. She agonized for the families. She knew only too well how difficult the future would be for them. Grieving would be a painful and slow journey, to be dealt with in whichever way they could. The gypsy clan would always be available to offer their care and support for as long as it would be needed.

"Chovinne, what happened back there to your family is, without a doubt, a terrible tragedy. I want to help. What can I do?"

"Going into the sewer was dangerous. You risked your life for one of us."

"I would do anything to help you and your family."

"You certainly proved that today. Being with me helps tremendously. If I need your help, I won't hesitate to let you know."

"Good, that puts my mind at ease."

Neither spoke again. Each reflecting on the atrocities inflicted upon the gypsies.

The carriage arrived at the estate. She had mentally prepared herself for the ensuing ordeal.

The impacted families were waiting for her in the front parlor. They had been told Chovinne wanted to talk to them. Everyone had patiently awaited her arrival. She had to tell them the brutal truth as delicately as she could. She wouldn't bring in the ghastly manner in which they died. The children were too young to be told something so horribly graphic. The gruesome details would be shocking enough for the widows to bear.

The children began to cry. Their mothers, tears streaming down their faces, had to put their own feelings aside to care for them. The uppermost consideration was to openly discuss with them anything that they wanted to know, especially what would happen to them now. The gypsies discreetly filed into the parlor offering their condolences, reassurance and support. The family unit again prevailed.

Since everyone had congregated in the parlor, Chovinne took the opportunity to speak with the elders to tell them about her plans. They listened and agreed that her idea was sound. It was really the only alternative for their protection.

She hurried outside to speak to the drivers before they left.

"What happened can't happen again. There will be a change starting today. I want all of you to arm yourselves. We must take aggressive action. If you are attacked where the intent is to kill, defend yourselves and shoot only if you must. Then dispose of their bodies. You well know we can't go to the authorities. They won't help us."

"I don't want this violence to happen again. I believe just brandishing the pistol in their faces will be enough for them to flee. Once word gets around, I'm sure these people will think twice before they think of victimizing us again."

*

Life always goes on, no matter what happens to upset it. Chovinne had to go to work and present a cheerful face to her customers. She left early for the office and busied herself with the paperwork on her desk. A knock on the door surprised her. She glanced at the clock. There was still a half hour before it would be time to open for her customers. Opening a desk drawer, her hand reached inside for the pistol she had placed there when she had arrived only an hour earlier. She got up from her chair, paused for a moment, and put her arm behind her back to conceal the pistol she held in her hand. She walked to the door, unlocked it and then opened it. Unexpectedly, Andrew was standing there.

"I came here early because I need to talk to you. I'll get to the point. Tonight we must talk about your investments. I know that it's soon after everything that has happened and that your mind is preoccupied with other matters as well, but I feel we must begin to secure your future. We can't postpone this any longer."

"You're absolutely right. Plan to stay the night because undoubtedly it will be very late when we finish."

CHAPTER 40

Chovinne returned home early. Subina replaced her at the office. She was about to pour herself a cup of tea when she heard her name being called in unison by the children assembled outside. She went to see what the commotion was all about. They wanted her to come out and see how much their riding skills had improved. The older children had chosen to ride the more frisky stallions; the younger children were on the mares. Each child had the responsibility of caring for his or her animal. All of the children owned their respective ponies. It hadn't taken very long for them, as well as Trevor, to master correct riding habits. Trevor was her responsibility, so she had undertaken the task of teaching him. The others were taught by their families. Under her tutelage, he was quickly becoming a responsible, skilled rider. While working together, she impressed upon him that the primary reason for having a horse of his very own was for both of them to have fun. To follow trails through woods, fields and dells, or to race with abandon alone or with other children, to jump over hedges, or to just pleasure ride to look at all points of interest, but primarily just to enjoy each other because a horse is a partner in fun.

She had wondered if there would be a problem for Trevor being accepted by the other children. Her fears had proved groundless. He got along famously with everyone.

When Trevor was finished showing off his skills, he rode up on his horse next to her.

"I did well, didn't I, Chovinne?"

"You did more than well. You were marvelous! I watched you closely and you remembered everything I taught you. You can only get more marvelous from now on."

"Yes, I know," he said, a big grin on his face.

He had acquired a considerable amount of self-confidence. It was good that she had brought him to live with her. He had become very special and dear to her.

When the children had all finished showing off their skills, she returned to the cottage and her cup of tea.

Sitting at the table awaiting Andrew's arrival, her mind replayed all the inordinate change she witnessed in London. Railway companies in their quest to obtain access to the docks were building mazes of rail lines to bring raw material and goods into the city. Tunnels were blasted out and embankments were raised. Viaducts spanned the once picturesque valleys. All these changes were permanently altering the English landscape. Many once familiar places were no longer recognizable.

Coal bunkers, engine sheds and repair shops also dotted the once virgin terrain. Acres and acres were now covered with large machinery, picks, shovels and wheelbarrows. Ticked offices and refreshment rooms accommodated the railway passengers who traveled to and from long distances. When leases expired they weren't renewed, displacing thousands of London residents. They had to scramble to find new homes.

She heard a knock on the door. Andrew was always punctual, not a minute too early, nor a minute too late. She liked that because her life imitated his. The estate and the business put her time at a premium. Tonight, though, she would speak to him about their time schedule. It was important to set aside time for them to be together more.

She opened the door to let him in.

"I couldn't get here fast enough. I've never been this excited to help someone with their investments as I am to help you."

CHAPTER 41

Andrew removed, from his valise, all of the important papers he had brought with him and spread them on the table.

"I have written a list for us of all the most lucrative stocks available now on the exchange. I'll take them individually and explain to you why I know they will reap tremendous dividends for us both.

I don't have to tell you that life, as we knew it, is now only a memory, forever changed. All around us, as far as the eye can see, railroads, shipbuilding and commerce is progressing at a dizzying rate. Our national wealth now depends on our mines and our factories. We are involved in world-wide trade. All this has given way to an impetus of private enterprise on a scale such as we've never known, employing armies of laborers.

The countries of North America are quickly becoming commercial entities. I believe, in time, they will be formidable rivals for us. Our country is growing and exporting its products. We must seize all the opportunities afforded us. With our eyes wide open, you and I will make our mark.

I learned that land adjacent to the river was being sold for commercial development. The land was cheap so I bought acreage. Mills and factories have been built there as well as warehouses. I've already had some built beside our largest dock. I took it upon myself to buy land space next to mine for you also. Your warehouses are waiting to be stocked with whatever you decide to store there. You can repay me. I know how you feel about your responsibility towards your family.

Let's begin. I have much information for you to absorb.

Although the American continent has mills, they are not yet producing enough to sustain themselves. They are sending their raw cotton here to be spun and woven into cloth. We send these finished products back to them. This won't be a long market, though, because they soon will be quite efficient doing this for themselves. Silk and tapestry are being mass produced for export. The luxury trades are booming. There is a large demand for watches, jewelry, clocks, and glass and metals associated with them.

Coal mine shares are an absolute. Railroads and ships would stand idle without coal. Steamships and clippers depend on this resource to power these vessels to America and elsewhere in the world. Homes, commercial buildings, and enterprise are highly dependent on coal.

The need for dock, canal and water companies, gas and chemical works have multiplied.

Breweries for beer, wine and other spirits are increasing.

I can't stress enough the importance of iron and timber shares. Ships cannot be built without them. Iron is also important for a vast number of everyday essentials including iron wheels, bells, fences and gates, window guards, grills, balconies, ballisters, smithing, and eating utensils and more. Timber is also important for making furniture, the printing of books, newspapers, clerical papers and paper for personal stationery, notes and cards.

I always have in mind the seasons, worldwide, for specified commodities. Each country is unique in the ever changeable seasonal rotation of specified commodities like tea, coffee, cocoa, sugar, fruit, rice, spices, and tobacco.

Tanneries for hides are also increasing. Leather is needed for shoes, saddlery, bags, trade and more.

We import rubber, shellac, jute, ivory, copper, lead, tin, glass and furs."

He pushed his chair back and turned towards Chovinne.

"I know this all seems daunting at first, more difficult than it really is. All that's needed is a sharp, watchful eye and common sense."

Chovinne made her selections. Andrew provided his expertise.

"You've made wise choices. I don't anticipate any problems, but if some should arise, I'll need your permission to act in your best interests in an emerging situation."

"You have it."

"In the wake of everything that happened to your family members on my return from Paris, I never did get the opportunity to give you your gifts. I'll do that now."

He retrieved the Bronte books from his valise and put them in her hands.

"They are beautiful. The gold leaf and the multi-colored images on this red background are striking. I'll always treasure them. Thank you."

"That isn't all. I have another gift for you."

"Another gift. I can't wait. What is it? I love surprises."

He took the gift out of the valise.

She looked in amazement at the Chantilly lace shawl.

"It's breathtakingly beautiful. I have never owned anything as lovely as this."

"Here, let me place it over you shoulders."

Her hands touched the soft delicate fabric.

"This feels so luxurious."

"I wanted a gift for you that really meant something to you. I gave it much consideration, and then it dawned on me. There I was in Chantilly where they make the most beautiful shawls. What could be more appropriate for you?"

"Beautiful gifts from my favorite person."

They talked late into the night.

CHAPTER 42

Dear Chovinne,

This letter to you has taken some time to be written. The Atlantic has lived up to its bad reputation. My men and I have encountered very many dirty storms. Luckily, they announce themselves in plenty of time. There has been almost incessant activity since we set sail.

, During these storms the wind momentarily takes charge of the ship. The deck tilts still further as the fore topgallant is released to harden its belly to the wind. The additional thrust makes the spray fly above the figurehead and jib boom. The ship's canvass spreads high above the deck as my topmen work like demons. The wind screams through the rigging, and the forceful waves slap and crash against us mercilessly. The canvasses have taken many beatings. We sewed, patched, trimmed and changed them often. We were almost continuously going fore to aft for other things that we needed.

My neck was sore from looking aloft, and my braced legs ached as well as my arms from holding her at the wheel. It must sound to you as though I'm complaining, but I'm not. I love the ocean, its vastness, power, mysteries, and challenges.

My closest encounter to a catastrophic situation came when I was on watch. I was maintaining the course and gauging the weather. The waxing moon lit up the night. The ocean was calm with barely a ripple. I was scanning what I thought was an empty ocean when, suddenly, I saw a derelict ahead of my ship. The floating hulk showed only five feet above the surface of the water. It had failed to sink after being abandoned and, therefore, it had become waterlogged, the reason why it sat so low in the water. It had lost all its spars and rigging. These ships are carried on the waves into the paths of many ships. They create a grave marine menace and have fantastic periods of longevity before sinking into oblivion on the bottom of the ocean floor.

What is so terrifying to sailors like myself is that derelicts suddenly appear out of the deep. Large floundering phantom ships moving across the ocean day and night in storms or calm. I can only speculate what happened to these ships, because they can travel great distances. They could have hit an iceberg, collided with another ship, become grounded, or had faulty navigation.. Additional very distinct occurrences are fires, storms, piracy among the crew, or criminal acts among the crew.

My crew and I acted swiftly. The stricken vessel had to be avoided. I steered the ship off its course, and it forged steadily past the derelict. As I mentioned earlier in this letter, the ocean was calm which meant that wave pressure on the rudder was minimal, making it easier to maneuver the ship safely around the derelict. Only because I have skilled seamen on board was it possible. Everyone knew what was expected of him. Remember when I told you, one day at the docks, about how important it is to have capable seamen to stay out of serious trouble. Sailors in name only are worthless. It would have been a death warrant to attempt traversing the ocean with unskilled seamen.

I have a good amount of patience, but I've never had a voyage that seemed so interminable. Then, when I didn't think I could endure another day or night of anticipation, I arrived! The dawn broke and with it a beautiful sunrise. A good omen, I felt welcomed to this new world. I was at the helm when my eyes saw the New York harbor for the first time. My heart raced inside my chest. The excitement I felt was profound. I was minutes away from my dream. I had long studied the maps I had in my possession, and I had no difficulty bringing in my clipper, nor my men theirs.

I don't think I told you that New York has a natural sheltered harbor created by natural irregularities in the coastline. You may be saying to yourself, "Why is that so important?" Harbors like these are important because they provide easy entry, shelter, deep water, and moderate climate to protect the ships berthed there during storms. This harbor is enormous, the largest of any in which I have ever anchored. I saw scores of windjammers berthed at the South Street Seaport Wharves. Their long jib booms stretched across the busy street and almost touched the shops of the ship chandlers, sail makers, and other merchants. I was told it was known as the "Street of Ships."

The custom inspectors came on board to check my cargo manifest. Then, they proceeded to inspect and evaluate it. When they were finished they stamped the cargo itself and dated it. The captains from my two clippers brought me their manifests as well. We took the lists to the customhouse and swore that, to the best of our knowledge, they were complete and true. Returning to the clippers, we oversaw the complete unloading of the cargo. When that was done, I was free to begin exploring New York. I had no qualms about leaving the clippers in the hands of my capable crew. I had asked two of my very best friends to accompany me on this auspicious, once in a lifetime, first adventure. For a time, I would leave my sea legs behind for further exploration.

In close proximity was the Fulton Fish Market, a sprawling parcel of waterfront. The catch of the day is all fresh fish, brought here very early in the morning. I heard the boisterous, thick, ear-piercing cries of the fishmongers from their stalls, shouting loudly while vying for all the customers they could attract. I saw raw-fingered men, fishknives in their hands, scaling and gutting their fish while throwing the glittering fish scales and entrails on the ground. Crawling crustaceans are sold as they are. I was surprised to learn that Fulton was fashioned after our own fish markets.

Having seen everything on the waterfront, it was time to investigate the rest of New York. I hired a hackney for my friends and me for the duration of our stay. A very handsome fee to be paid to him later would ensure his loyalty. The driver knew the city well and was knowledgeable about the people and places.

The economic characteristics changed as we wound our way through varied landscapes. Our guide told us there were still many farms, but they were steadily decreasing in number. The people preferred to work in industry. As we continued, we passed modest homes, here and there, with well-kept gardens. As we ventured deeper within the really inhabited heart of New York, I was transformed by the scene that played out before me. It was surreal. It was as if I had never left London. Noise and congestion everywhere. Trade and industry existing among elaborate mansions, townhouses, and apartments built by the wealthy. I saw shipping, trading, and banking buildings, factories, newspaper and publishing enterprises, cathedrals, churches, cemeteries, universities, theatres, hotels, restaurants, and taverns. Our driver and guide said that the streets here are called blocks. Also, many of the immigrants have found lodging in large buildings, called tenements, that have been subdivided into tiny apartments. The more I saw and heard, I couldn't help but notice that there was one very different phenomenon here. These immigrants from different cultures had formed their own neighborhoods. It's like an extended family. They emigrated from the same towns and settled together in one area in order to be there for one another for love, friendship, comfort, compassion, helpfulness, and solidarity. It is all very much like yours, the Gypsy community.

The street hustle is very alive. I spotted a Pop Corn Wagon and just had to see what that was. I asked many questions. Cultivated by Native Americans, who had taught settlers how to cook it, it was considered to be a snack food, to be eaten out of hand. Ordinary corn kernels are dried, then cooked in a large pan in oil over high heat. The kernels expand as they pop to triple the quantity, therefore, its name, popcorn. They are white, soft, and fluffy. Sweet creamery butter is poured over the popcorn. It is absolutely delicious! I bought some for the three of us. Needless to say, we had our fill. Now that I know how it is made, I'll make *some for myself and you when I return, with a bag of kernels, to London.*

We continued to explore further. Our driver stopped the hackney and told us that we could look from afar, but that he wouldn't enter Five Points, the most notorious slum, perhaps in the world. Gangs made their home in the veritable ruin. There was at least one murder a day. I told the driver to move on. None of us had an overwhelming desire to become a victim.

We were hungry and tired, so we unanimously opted to go to an oyster bar on the waterfront. We ordered oysters and lobsters. The oysters are as large as cheese plates, and the lobsters weigh six pounds each. Incredulous, isn't it? Delicious doesn't even remotely describe how wonderful they tasted. For the first time in our lives, we were unable to eat all of our food. It had been a long day, and it was time to get some rest. There was a hotel not far from where we were, so we chose to go there. The driver left and would return in the morning. We literally fell into our beds from fatigue. We all slept with one eye open though. We had to. Thieves want to take what you have. In the morning, we continued our sightseeing.

The driver told us we had yet to see a very special place, where he and every New Yorker, rich or poor, could go to relax, a park. We went to the hinterlands beyond the northern edge of the city. There were some finished areas in the park, but I could see it was a work in progress. The grounds were being cleared, rocks were being removed, drains laid and soil moved. Walks and roadways were being paved. An inordinate amount of trees were being planted. Many were along the peripheries of the park. I surmised the architect wanted it enclosed to envelop the city dwellers and shield them from distractions. This immense location where its inhabitants could enjoy the fresh air is called Central Park. As a whole, this park will afford the citizens of this great city, rural characteristics that are so necessary and so real, the natural scenery of hills and dales, the serenity of a cluster of trees, the softness of grass in the sun, and the radiance of shimmering lakes and ponds, so essential to renewing the fragile human spirit.

We left the park and continued exploring other areas. Time passed swiftly and soon it was the dinner hour. We asked our guide's advice about where we should go. He recommended a grand hotel that also had the finest restaurant in the city. He joined us for dinner. Our luggage was properly secured under lock and key to be retrieved later.

From the varied menu brought to us, we all decided to have pickled buffalo tongue which was considered a delicacy. Peas and potatoes were chosen as accompaniments. I can't describe the taste of the tongue, except that it was different and surprisingly tender and very good. I definitely would eat it again. We lingered over coffee after dinner and talked, not realizing that most of the diners had left. It was late and our driver was tired and was going home. He told me he would be there early the next day to bring us to the waterfront.

I noticed a man not far from us who was dining alone. Since we were the only ones there, I asked him to join us. During our conversation, he told me he was a frontiersman. I told him my story and asked if he would consider being my guide. He charged a very significant fee for his work. I told him I could afford it. His expertise would solidify our safe travel through an unknown terrain. We agreed to meet at a pre-arranged date at an old church that is a significant longstanding landmark in Boston, one he said I definitely would notice. He gave me a list of "must-have" clothing that my friends and I would need, all of which could be purchased in the city. Everything else, he said, was his responsibility.

I was eager to continue my adventure and move on to Boston. Boston also has a huge natural harbor and is a leading port. The approach is full of island marshes that are soft and spongy. They change with the tides making it more difficult to navigate. We maneuvered our clippers down the middle of the channel to the safety of the Boston harbor. The procedure after docking is the same as in New York. The difference this time was that my men would be loading cargo to bring to New Orleans and I would reconnect with them there to come home.

232

Boston is also a delight. There is no pattern to the crooked, narrow streets. I climbed and descended the cobblestone pathways not knowing where they would take me. The walkways are patchy and uneven, but I can only say it adds so much charm to this lovely, walkable city. There is so much to tell you about everything I've seen here, that I cannot describe it to its full advantage. It would take pages and pages to convey to you the intensity of this bustling city. Someday, I will bring you to America on one of my clippers so that you can witness this for yourself. I'm sure you will be just as impressed as I am now.

I met the guide on the specified date and place. He told me that we had all been invited to a friend's home for a thoroughly unique American institution, a Boston clambake on the beach. I was shown how this was done. A fire was built in a stone-lined pit. When the fire died, the hot pit was filled with layers of seaweed, clams, crabs, and lobsters, and then covered. After an appropriate amount of time cooking, they were removed from the pit and placed on a long table for everyone to help themselves and enjoy. To my astonishment, there was yet another surprise. A huge black pot was taken out of the ground where it had been covered with ash and earth. These pots are left on glowing, hot coals for two days to cook the contents thoroughly. I was served baked beans, prepared with pork, molasses, and wild onions, from these pots. They are delicious and wonderfully flavorful. I love to eat so you can expect an accounting of American epicurean delights as I find them to share with you. We were all invited to spend the evening at our host's home.

The next day our guide brought us back to the church. All of us went inside to ask God for a safe trip.

We're on our way into the heartland. This will be much more difficult. I'm so excited. I know there will be much to see and learn. I think of you always. Take care.

My love always,
Ben

233

What an adventure Ben was having. Chovinne was so glad for him. So far it was all and more than he had hoped for. She looked forward to the next letter.

CHAPTER 43

Browsing in bookstores was one of Chovinne's favorite things to do. Today was no exception. While perusing the bookstore shelves, her eyes caught and lingered on a book title that held her interest. She took it from the shelf. It was titled, **Uncle Tom's Cabin**. She read enough pages to get the gist of the story. It was a vivid portrayal of slavery's evils written by an impassioned reformer. Publication had been in 1852. She wondered how she had missed seeing it before now. It must have always been sold out, she thought. Chovinne purchased the book intending to read it that evening.

Returning home after her day's work, Chovinne quickly ate her meal after which she went upstairs to her room. The book she had bought earlier that day had constantly been on her mind since she had purchased it. Chovinne had some serious reading waiting for her.

First, she lit the fireplace. Her room was chilly and she needed it warmer for her bath. Opening the housemaid's closet where the hip bath was kept, she pulled it closer to the fireplace and poured water into it. For a nice scent, she added lavender and rosewater. A covered towel-horse behind her protected her from drafts. She quickly bathed, then dried herself with towels that had been warming before the fireplace. Wrapping one around her, she swiftly walked to her bed. She grabbed her book from the nightstand, adjusted her pillows, and covered herself with an extra blanket. Finally, there was time for herself. She opened the book and began reading. She didn't notice the room growing colder with each passing hour.

She finished reading the book in the early morning hours. Chovinne was overwhelmed by the magnitude of the oppression directed at Negro slaves in America. The book had taken her away to an unknown world. One she knew nothing about, and one that was obviously divided on the accursed issue of subjugation without recourse. She could empathize. She knew what it was like to suffer through the pain of scorn, hatred, and discrimination. Her forbears had been enslaved and had suffered terribly.

CHAPTER 44

Andrew had been waiting to ask Chovinne to marry him, and decided that this particularly beautiful day would be ideal for proposing to her.

He stopped by her office and put the first phase of his plans into motion.

Chovinne looked up when he entered.

"What a nice surprise. I didn't expect to see you until later today."

"I've made some plans for us for late afternoon, when our work is done. Since it's such a beautiful day, I've planned a carriage ride to the park. I will attend to everything."

Chovinne watched the clock. The time moved slowly. She had waited on her last customer. Looking out the window into the street, she saw Andrew drive up in his carriage. She grabbed her ledgers, locked the door, and ran out to his carriage.

"You are really excited about this, aren't you?" Andrew asked.

"I've been thinking about spending time with my favorite person all day."

"Which park are we going to?"

"Regents."

"Wonderful, I love the casual atmosphere of that park."

"I know the perfect spot for us," he said.

It didn't take long to get there. Andrew stopped the carriage, got out and helped Chovinne out.

Spread out on the ground was a huge blanket.

"What a nice surprise. You planned a picnic. It's lovely."

"I hired caterers that I personally know. I told them what I wanted. I knew I could depend on their expertise to handle all the details."

"Chovinne, give me your hand, and we'll sit down."

Andrew motioned with his hand, and soon the waiters were at his side.

"You may proceed."

The picnic basket was opened and a linen and lace tablecloth was spread over the blanket. The waiters next placed fine china, silver goblets, cutlery and napkins.

There were chicken finger sandwiches sliced into strips no more than an inch wide, a veal loaf and various condiments, tea and her favorite plum cakes. There was a bun warmer and a bottle cozy with a champagne bottle inside. The semi-shaded area was an ideal setting. Chovinne and Andrew helped themselves to the food. The waiters discreetly ventured away from them to give them their privacy.

"This is really so lovely, Andrew."

"I'm really glad this pleases you. I was hoping that it would."

"I had a very special reason for bringing you here, Chovinne. You know how I feel about you. I want to marry you. We discussed this subject earlier. I want the two of us to be together always. Will you marry me Chovinne?"

"I can't think of my life without you in it. Yes, I'll marry you."

"You've made me very happy. Let's not wait too long."

"This day has been perfect, Andrew. It's a pity it has to end"

They both reluctantly got into the carriage. Andrew brought her home, then left for his townhouse.

The next day Chovinne called a meeting and told the family of her marriage plans. They all thought highly of Andrew and were happy he would become part of the family.

CHAPTER 45

"Andrew, I wouldn't proceed with our wedding plans without talking to you. Tell me what traditions you want to incorporate, along with mine, in the ceremony."

"Most important to me is that I would like you to do me the honor of wearing my mother's wedding gown on our wedding day."

"This is such a surprise! I was going to wear traditional wedding garments, but I would be delighted to honor your mother and you by wearing her wedding gown."

"It is important to me to be married by a priest in a church or a chapel."

"Those were also my plans. You've met Abbot Paul. What would you think about having him marry us at the Abbey?"

"That would be a perfect setting for our wedding."

"I'm going to incorporate only a few of our traditions. They are simple rites. It's required that you and I stand facing our assembled family members and proclaim to remain true to one another. An elder will pronounce us husband and wife. It is important for us to step over a besom branch. We believe, as a group, that the wood is a valuable charm to ward off evil spirits that seek to destroy loving relationships. Subina will stand for me. Who will stand for you?"

"You've met him at the bank. My very best friend will

stand with me."

"I've covered everything. How about you?"

He got up abruptly. "Excuse me while I go to my carriage."

Chovinne wondered what that was about.

Andrew quickly returned, carrying a large box.

"Chovinne, in this box is my mother's wedding gown that I am giving to you. I have a favor to ask of you, though. Would you open the box only on our wedding day?"

"I have to ask. Will it need alterations?"

"No, you are the same weight and height that my mother was."

"What a coincidence! Yes, I will wait, but I have to tell you it will be difficult for me to do so."

"I asked you to wait, because I know how much you love surprises and I can guarantee that you will be surprised."

"There is something else that I want to discuss with you. My friend has a large, lovely, country estate. He asked if you and I would consider having our reception there for our friends and family. He will attend to every detail."

"How gracious of him. That's an excellent idea. Please tell him that we accept."

*

There were many things to attend to before the wedding, so that time passed quickly.

*

Today was her wedding day and all the anticipation of seeing what was waiting for her in the box was over. She opened it, took the gown out and laid it upon her bed. She wasn't prepared for what she saw. The fabrics were exquisite. The gown was a lovely pale rose colored satin gown with honiton lace on the fitted bodice and long sleeves. A lace panel ran down the front of her skirt which gave even more definition and contrast to the rose colored satin. Upon closer inspection, another surprise awaited her. She saw that it was sewn with golden threads.

There was a knock at her door.

"Come in."

"Can I help you dress," Subina asked.

"Yes, I can use your help."

The gown fit her perfectly. The strand of aged pearls she found wrapped in tissue accentuated the rounded neckline of the bodice beautifully. The wedding shoes she placed on her feet were ones she had, herself, purchased. Lastly, she swept her hair upward while Subina inserted the ornate, pearlized combs to hold her hair in place. Her favorite piece was the shawl Andrew had given her. She placed it over her shoulders and folded it over her. She turned her body around to see how she looked from different angles in the looking glass. She loved that she looked nice for her special day. Andrew had succeeded and truly surprised her.

"Chovinne, you look lovely. Are you ready to see the family?"

"I am ready, and thank you so much for your help."

She and Subina left the room and descended the stairs. Her family had congregated in the front parlor waiting for her. They smiled in approval when they saw her. They knew she had broken tradition by wearing a gown, but they understood why. They each expressed to her their wishes for a long and happy marriage.

It was time to leave for the chapel. Subina handed Chovinne the bouquet she had selected made of red chrysanthemums for love, and ivy for fidelity.

"Chovinne, the weather has cooperated for your wedding. There isn't a cloud to be seen anywhere."

"I was hoping for a nice day."

"Are you nervous, Chovinne?"

"I thought I would be, but surprisingly I'm not. I have no doubts about my decision to marry Andrew."

"What are your future plans?"

"Everything will remain the same. I will continue as I have and Andrew also. It will always be this way because of my position as head of the family. Our welfare will always be a priority for me, and he understands that. His work requires that he be absent for days or weeks at a time to work with clients. He will keep his townhouse in the city. All his free time will be spent at the cottage."

"Chovinne, we have talked so much that I didn't notice until now that we are almost at the Abbey."

The carriage came to a stop just outside the chapel. She looked out of the window and wasn't surprised to see Abbot Paul waiting there for her arrival.

Opening the door, he extended his hand to help her down.

"Everyone is here. They are all waiting for you inside. May I escort you down the aisle?"

"I'd be delighted if you would."

Together, arm in arm, they walked toward Andrew. Abbot Paul lovingly surrendered Chovinne to him. He then addressed the assemblage of family and friends.

"This is such a happy occasion. My Little One is getting married. It's such an honor and privilege for me to have been asked to perform the wedding ceremony. She, as well as all of you, are so dear to me. It is with great joy that I do this."

"Chovinne, Andrew please join hands."

As previously decided beforehand, both family traditions were carried out and they were married.

With the ceremony over, everyone congregated in the chapel to congratulate the bride and groom. While everyone was mingling, Chovinne took the opportunity to slip away to her father's grave.

"I wouldn't leave without coming to see you. I miss you, Papa. I think about you all the time."

"You know why I'm here. I got married today. Abbot Paul officiated. You would like Andrew."

"You know I've never lied to you and I'm not going to start now. It's not all right with me that you weren't there because of an evil person. Your presence was deeply missed. Your not being with me at this eventful time in my life to share my happiness is very difficult. Everyday there is a reminder for me, things I see, places I go, many, many memories."

"I'm told it will get better. Right now, I can't see that far where you are concerned."

"Everyone who could come, came to the wedding. The chapel was beautifully decorated with lovely flowers. The dress I wore was given to me by Andrew. It had belonged to his mother. I looked very nice in it."

"Abbot Paul and the other monks have made an extraordinary exception from their cloistered monastic life and have agreed to attend a reception given for me and Andrew."

"They mean so much to me. It helps a lot knowing that they'll be there."

"I must go now Papa. You are always in my thoughts."

CHAPTER 46

Soon the two days they had allotted themselves were over. It was time to resume their everyday lives. They left the city for the country estate.

Andrew had prearranged with Dudras to care for the carriages and horses upon their arrival so that he would be free to be with Chovinne when they went inside their home.

"I'm glad to be home, Andrew. It's nice in the city, but this place has my heart."

Andrew didn't say anything. He opened the door, and she stepped inside. They placed their clothes on the hall stand.

"Let's go into the front parlor," said Andrew.

When she crossed the threshold, what she saw rooted her to the spot upon which she stood. It was minutes before she was able to speak. She was absolutely stunned at what was before her. The paintings she had sold to Andrew had been meticulously placed in beautiful ornate frames and displayed on the walls. She walked over to look at each one of them, but lingered longest at her father's portrait. As she looked at it, she felt his presence and smiled.

Andrew walked over to her and took her hand.

"What a wonderful surprise, Andrew! To have these paintings back means the world to me."

"I noticed how distraught you were the day you sold

them to me. I kept them. I'm glad I could give them back to you as a wedding gift."

"Andrew, these paintings complete my life. Their loss no longer hangs heavily upon my heart. I've been reunited with my treasures and all the wonderful memories connected with them. I knew you were a special person and this proves it once again."

"There are more gifts for you."

Andrew called out, "Dudras, you can bring them in now. He and other family members came into the front parlor carrying bird cages.

"These are for you, Chovinne."

"I did hear nightingales when I came home. I thought I was wrong and only imagined it."

Three birdcages were strategically placed on center tables next to the windows.

"Andrew, where did you buy them?"

"I bought them at auction; the birds came with them. They have been examined by a veterinarian and have been certified healthy."

She walked over to each cage to get a closer look.

"Andrew, these are beautiful nightingales and such exquisite porcelain cages. Their bell shapes, blue on white motifs, and rounded bases that stand on small round feet beneath are magnificent creations. The visual beauty inside and outside of this estate is so outstanding. My precious paintings have been returned to me. The nightingales and their melodic songs will once again ring throughout our home."

"Andrew, I just love my gifts. Thank you so much!"

"I have gifts for you too, Andrew."

"You bought me gifts?"

"Yes I did. Close your eyes while I get them."

She was gone but a moment.

"I'm back. You can open your eyes now."

Andrew opened his eyes.

"The sticks, you bought them for me! How did you know?"

"You admired them for a time in the shop window. Your eyes never left those two."

"They will be a very welcome addition to the others already in my collection."

He picked up each one for a closer inspection.

"Chovinne, they're even nicer than I expected. This ebony one, with its ivory knob, will assure me of the distinguished look I need for my work. This mahogany one, with its scrolled silver knob, I will use for more formal occasions."

"There is one more thing, Andrew. They both have secret compartments."

"I didn't think to look for that."

He hurriedly took the knobs off each one and looked inside.

"This is wonderful. I'll be able to keep my most personal, private papers inside and in my possession at all times wherever I am, here or in another country, safely and close at hand."

"I, too, am extremely pleased with my gifts! Thank you, Chovinne."

CHAPTER 47

Subina was sipping tea from a teacup, at the kitchen table, when Chovinne came down for breakfast.

"This is a very nice surprise," Chovinne said.

"Come, sit down with me. I've made a pot of tea, and there's enough to eat for us both."

Chovinne had barely sat down when Subina began to talk.

"I have something very important to tell you. George proposed, and I accepted. We are getting married in a simple ceremony tomorrow. Just the immediate family will be invited, because of the time element. He has to return to run his jewelry store in New York."

She reached over and took her hand.

"Congratulations, I'm very happy for you and, at the same time, sad."

"There is something else we discussed. George told me there is a vacant store next to his. When he told me that, I thought it would be a great opportunity for me to open a clothing store. I have saved some money and I hoped you could go to Edward and have him send me starter essentials."

"Is it too much of an imposition to ask you to do this?" she asked.

"Not at all. I'll see Edward soon and I'm sure that he will

be delighted to help you. In return, do me a favor. Keep your money, and some that I will give you, for unforeseen circumstances. I would feel much better knowing that you have some put away for this purpose."

"When are you leaving, Subina?"

"We are sailing in three days."

"So soon?"

"I'm both excited and frightened. I'll miss you and the family."

"I, too, will miss you tremendously."

"I wish so much happiness and success for you. America is the land of opportunity. You're offered this chance to succeed. It is a very difficult world for us. Maybe America will be a kinder place and won't discriminate against us as much. Only time will tell. My one consolation is that there is family there who will watch over you and help you."

"When do you think we will see each other again?" she asked.

"Crossing the Atlantic will get easier and easier. Ben told me that more ships are being steam driven, and they will be much faster than they are now."

"In the meantime, we can write to each other."

"That makes me feel better. I'll write often."

"As will I," Chovinne said.

CHAPTER 48

Seeing Subina going off to America was extremely painful. It was hard to reconcile in her mind the total separation from her by a vast ocean. Always together since they were very young children, the thought of not seeing her regularly was yet another unpleasant change in her life that she would have to bear.

CHAPTER 49

"Chovinne, I've saved enough money so that we can go to the inn again," Trevor said with a broad smile on his face, as he walked into the front parlor waving money in his hand.

"That's wonderful! When do you want to go?"

"Can we go today to the same inn that you brought me to before?"

"If that's what you want, then, yes, of course."

"First, we'll go to the office. I'll speak to Dudras about coming to replace me early this afternoon. We'll have a long, leisurely outing, just the two of us."

On the way there, Chovinne could see that it was difficult for Trevor to contain his excitement during the carriage ride. This was a really big event in his life, something he never imagined, in his wildest dreams, would ever happen to him considering his previous harsh life.

At the inn, she wasn't at all surprised that he remembered exactly what she had done and he did likewise.

"Aren't these sweets delicious, Chovinne? I'll repeat what you said before, *we'll eat sensibly tomorrow.*"

Chovinne smiled at him. He was so changed from the little desperate ragamuffin wandering the streets of London. He was happy now. He knew he had a home, was loved and was safe with her and his new family.

CHAPTER 50

"Chovinne, do you think I could learn to do that?" Trevor asked.

"Do what, Trevor?" she asked.

He pointed to a magician who was performing on the street.

"This surprises me. I didn't know you were interested in that kind of artistry."

"I've often watched them do their routines, wishing I knew their secrets. How they seemingly do their tricks without effort."

"Well, one thing is for sure, you certainly have the sleight of hand for it, which definitely is an asset for you. I'm sure you could become an excellent magician. You are very quick to learn. In the short time you have been with me, you have learned how to read, improved your vocabulary and your other knowledge has increased tremendously. You have learned many requirements of great horsemanship. I am very proud of you."

"You really think that I am all of those things," he said.

"You certainly are. Again, I couldn't be prouder of all that you have accomplished. You are remarkable!"

*

Between clients at her office, Chovinne picked up the daily newspaper to read. On the front page a short announcement got her undivided attention. It read,

> *Due to an injury sustained from an*
> *unfortunate accident when I was*
> *struck by a runaway horse and*
> *carriage that injured my legs, I will be*
> *unable to perform my magic acts at*
> *theatres in the city for the duration of*
> *my three month long confinement and*
> *recuperation. Later, when I am well, I*
> *will honor all these bookings. This was*
> *a most unfortunate circumstance, but*
> *do come to my future performances, as*
> *I can guarantee that you won't be*
> *disappointed.*

This was a man who was at the top of his profession, acclaimed as the best magician in the world, thought Chovinne, as she read about his misfortune. She immediately thought of Trevor. Perhaps, while recuperating, this magician would consider teaching him illusion fundamentals and maybe even more than that. She would make inquiries from her clients as to where he was currently living and go there to talk to him when her work day was over. She would have to convince him that Trevor posed no threat to him. She surmised that no magician would easily share his knowledge, because there would be too much competition. This would take some persuading on her part. Trevor had told her that he didn't want to compete. He just wanted to know for himself, because he was fascinated by magic tricks.

Chovinne's inquiries were successful. Having been told that he was staying at a hotel in the city, she went there, obtained his room number from the desk clerk, and went directly to his room. She knocked on the door. It was a few minutes before he answered.

"Hello, my name is Chovinne. Please excuse this intrusion on your privacy. I have something to ask you. Would you please allow me to come inside and would you give me some of your time?"

He stepped back from the doorway.

"Please come in," he said.

Once inside the room, he asked her to be seated. She had made it this far. Chovinne took this as a good sign.

Walking slowly with the assistance of a cane, he sat down on a chair directly facing her.

"Tell me, what is your purpose in coming here to speak with me?"

"I know a young boy who has acknowledged to me that magic intrigues him. He would be absolutely thrilled, and it would be the highlight of his life if this dream of learning magic could come true. He is quite intelligent and would quickly grasp the intricacies of whatever he was taught."

The magician was hesitant.

Chovinne continued.

"He will not compete with you. It is just something he wants to learn more about."

"Money is no object. I will pay you whatever you deem is appropriate."

He looked at her, deep in thought. Then he spoke.

"The young lad can take nothing for granted. If he is to remain very good as a magician, it will take constant practice. I will teach him how to misdirect attention, concealment, vanishing, and substitution. The success he achieves will depend entirely upon how much he wants to do this, because those skills I just told you about require much effort. The essence of magic is repetition which hones the skills learned everyday. Magic is very detail oriented."

"Do you think he will persevere in this endeavor?" he asked.

"Yes, he will do it, because this is something he himself initiated."

"I would like to propose something to you. I know that, for the time being, you have lost your capacity for earning money. To live here must be expensive, and, undoubtedly, your medical bills are very costly. I will remedy that. I further propose that you could live in a cottage on my estate, rent-free. Living in the country, the fresh air will help during your convalescence."

"You have stated your case very well. I accept. A great burden has been lifted from my shoulders."

"I own a coaching service. I will send one of my drivers to take you to my estate. He will assist you with all of your baggage and bring you to my home."

She rose from her chair and extended her hand to him.

"Until tomorrow, then."

"Yes, I'm looking forward to it."

He saw her to the door, and she left the hotel for her home.

Arriving home, she was hardly inside her door when she called Trevor to come downstairs.

She heard his footsteps in the corridor as he raced from his room and down the stairs.

"What is it, Chovinne?" he asked.

"I have the most incredible surprise for you."

She reiterated everything that had transpired at the hotel."

He stood there soaking in all she had said.

"I can't believe how lucky I am to have you as my very best friend. I love you very much, Chovinne."

He walked over to her and hugged her.

This was the first time he had ever said that. It was a milestone in their relationship.

CHAPTER 51

Chovinne unlocked her office door with Trevor in tow. He was carrying some ledgers that she had worked on the previous night.

The first thing she did each working day was to advise everyone of that particular day's schedule.

"Trevor, I'm going to the carriage house and stable. You stay here and call me if a client comes early."

She was halfway there when a man came running from the carriage house and threw her to the ground. Not expecting anything amiss, she hadn't had time to react. Stunned, she lay there for a few minutes before everything registered in her mind. Looking in the direction of the carriage house and stable, she saw flames leaping from the large door of the buildings.

She screamed, "Trevor, come out here!"

Trevor came running outside and helped her get up.

"Chovinne, we must try to save the men."

She held him back.

"Look the flames and smoke are everywhere. It has spread so rapidly in such a short time. I'm sure that the man who started it placed the incendiary devices where they would take the least time to ignite the materials inside."

"Trevor, you're right, we must try to get to them. There's one thing that we can do. Perhaps we have the time to crawl to the back of the buildings. She took Trevor's hand and together they crawled beneath the smoke. When they got there, they were relieved to find men sitting on the ground. They were having difficulty breathing, their hair was singed, their faces were blackened from the smoke, but they were alive. She started counting heads to see if they were all there, but to her chagrin, three were missing. She knew, at this point, she couldn't go in and save them.

"We can't stay here," Chovinne said, "we have to leave now or else we won't be able to get out. Everyone join hands so that we don't lose contact with one another."

Crackling sounds were all around them. The buildings were on the verge of collapse. There was only one corridor of escape available to them and Chovinne led them through it.

They were all coughing and gasping for air. They all fell to their knees on the ground when they finally arrived at the front of the townhouse. Keeping her wits about her, Chovinne realized the direction of the wind had changed. She watched as the flames hurled themselves against the townhouse. Large red embers, carried by the wind, fell onto its roof. It wasn't long before it, too, was ablaze. Their struggle still wasn't over. They again ran to seek shelter farther away. As she looked, she saw her dreams melting away and disappearing before her eyes. Her brave heart sunk under this unnecessary calamity. The colossal enormity of this fire had totally enveloped and destroyed everything she had worked so hard to achieve.

Fire saving equipment began arriving on the scene, but they were no match against the burning blaze.

CHAPTER 52

Andrew was told that Chovinne's rented townhouse, carriage house and stable were ablaze. Upon learning this, he was in a total panic about her safety as well as Trevor's, the gypsies, and the hired help. He immediately left the client he was with to be there with them.

The street traffic was congested, as it always was, and his carriage moved at a snail's pace. It took more than an hour to get there. The smoke was still thick as he arrived closer to what had been the townhouse. All he saw were smoldering charred remains. Then, as he got closer still, he saw a group of people huddled together. He stopped his carriage and jumped out to investigate. He could hear them talking and recognized Chovinne's voice. He called out her name and rushed over to her.

"I came as soon as I heard. I'm so thankful you and the others are all right."

"We aren't all here. There are three gypsies unaccounted for. I'm afraid they have died in the fire."

"I'm so sorry to hear that," he said.

"Chovinne, how did this happen?"

She told him about being thrown to the ground and how the events unfolded.

"Hatred for us has surfaced again. There are so many people who hate us for being who we are."

"What will you do now?" he asked.

"I'm fortunate that three carriages and horses were outside and ready to leave early this morning. This saved them from destruction. The family will be brought back to the estate in these carriages. The other men will be brought home as well. I will stay here until the bodies are found."

"I have instructed family members to contact the same undertaker we used when my father died. He now knows the gypsy way of dealing with loss and bereavement and will know exactly what we want. They will ask him to come here and wait, for as long as it takes, until the bodies are found. The undertakers will then place them in their respective coffins and bring them back to the estate."

Chovinne, you must be very tired. Come, let's wait in our carriage. You too, Trevor. It will be much more comfortable waiting there, than out here. We'll be notified when something significant happens."

Inside the carriage, Chovinne became very quiet. Andrew understood that she was experiencing a traumatic nightmare. He would help her get through it. Showing his concern, he took her hand and held it, conveying to her that he would be available to her for the duration.

No one slept that night. It was necessary to keep a vigil for the lost family members.

The next morning the search was renewed for the gypsies.

"Chovinne, I'm going to get us some breakfast. What would you and Trevor like?"

"Just some coffee, milk, and muffins."

"There is a cart not far from us. I'll get our food and beverages there. I won't be gone long."

He was back in no time and they ate their breakfast in silence.

"Chovinne, what can I do to help?"

"Just being with me helps a great deal."

"I'm glad to hear that. All you ever have to do is ask me."

"I know that and I will."

"Andrew, this last attack has snuffed out three lives. It was deliberately done to thwart us from having any more success. How stupid was I to think they wouldn't come after us and try to destroy us? We, as a people, have suffered terribly down through the ages. I don't think it will ever stop."

Hours went by.

"I can't stand the suspense anymore, Andrew. I'm going outside to the front of the burned out buildings to wait for word."

"Trevor and I will go with you."

A half hour went by before a man emerged from the charred ruins. He asked them to go with him to see the bodies that had been found.

There was a small grassy area they could walk on to get to the stables.

Arriving there, Chovinne took a deep breath.

The man proceeded to speak.

"We found them all beneath some beams. They didn't have a chance to get out. The beams were too heavy for them to move. I'm sorry," he said.

Chovinne was stoic. She had to be to endure what she saw. The hair had been totally burned off their heads. Their faces were blackened and disfigured by pain, their lips were swollen and wide apart exposing their teeth. Their bodies were bloated to an astonishing size. They had been roasted alive. It was an unspeakably hideous scene, ghastly and macabre.

CHAPTER 53

The estate still had to be maintained and ordinary activities continued even though these every day activities were difficult.

Chovinne's reaction was very different this time. This last act of cruelty had drained her. She knew she was depressed and had to find a way to bring happiness back into her life.

She couldn't stay inside just thinking about these recent killings. Subina had asked her for help. She would address that today.

Edward's shop was again bustling with activity. She had barely gotten inside the shop when he noticed her and flew to her side.

"Chovinne, what a wonderful surprise! I can't thank you enough for what you did for me. Money that I have put away is waiting for you. Is there something special that I can help you with today?"

"There is. My cousin has emigrated to New York and is opening a clothing shop. I was wondering if you could help her."

"I know just the thing to do for her. Women on the American continent want to look nice and wear the latest fashions. On a regular basis, I import beautiful fabrics from China and the Indies. I will send her broadlooms of these fabrics. I also have less expensive materials. Fashion babies are regularly sent to me from Paris dressed in the latest fashions from their head to their feet. France's designers set the mode for fashion. These also include infant's and children's clothing. There is so much to the clothing business, Chovinne. Before you in the showcases are all accessories that are current. These are the finishing touches that enhance whatever is worn. Your cousin needs these also, if she is to be successful."

"That's wonderful, Edward. I'll write to her today informing her that you'll be sending her all these things. She will be so happy to know this. I will pay you in advance for her supplies."

"No need, Chovinne. The money you gave me earlier for my difficulties will cover all expenses."

"I'll give you her address. Soon, Subina will have everything she has always wanted."

"Chovinne, she will be successful. I will send her only the best merchandise."

CHAPTER 54

"Chovinne, I would like for us to have our first small celebration, your friends and mine together. It would be an informal occasion. How does a week from today sound?"

"I don't have any immediate plans, that will be perfect."

"Chovinne, I'll have caterers here to serve food and drink. You won't have to do any work whatsoever."

"I have to leave for work now, take care. Today, I'll be very busy. I have clients that want to invest more money in certain areas. That will take time. I don't know at what hour I'll be home."

"I'll be waiting up for you, whatever the hour."

When Andrew left, Chovinne decided to visit Charles, the magician, and Trevor who were inside a cottage practicing and honing their magic skills. She knocked on the door. Soon Trevor was there inviting her inside. She wanted information and didn't waste time asking.

"Charles, how is your protégé progressing?"

"Very well. Trevor is a very quick study."

Chovinne looked at Trevor and saw a big grin on his face.

"Perhaps I could persuade both of you to give me a sample of what magic tricks you have been working on?"

"You came at an opportune time. Our props are still set up. We'll be glad to give you a command performance."

Chovinne watched in amazement at their skills of illusion,

concealment, substitution, and vanishing. Trevor was a capable assistant and very confident in his newly acquired skills.

"Thank you for indulging my request to see your artistic demonstrations. I was absolutely enthralled. Both of you kept me spellbound the whole time."

"Chovinne, while you're here, I want to let you know that I'll be leaving soon. I'm well now and I've enjoyed being here with all of you. I have made wonderful friends. All of you are my kindred spirits now, and I shall never forget you. I want all of you to attend my comeback performance, free of charge."

"I can't wait to go. I may not be able to speak to you after your performance, so I'll tell you now. I, and the family, won't forget you either. I know you will be very busy resuming your career, and it will take you to far away places. I hope our paths will again cross."

"As I do. I will be touring many countries, and eventually America. I've never been there. I know it will be an education for me."

"You know I wish you the best. I will be thinking of you often. I want to take this opportunity to thank you for helping a young boy and making his wish come true. He has come far under your tutelage. Now, I will become his assistant, so that he will continue to be as competent as he is now."

CHAPTER 55

Chovinne went to the city a few days later to purchase household items. Returning after a few hours, she saw a coach outside her home. She wondered who it could be. She stopped her carriage, got out with her purchases, and went inside to investigate. This person would be waiting for her in the front parlor, so she went there immediately.

The woman was standing in the parlor waiting for her.

"Bonjour madame, je m'appele Simone."

Chovinne looked at her.

"I'm afraid you have me at a disadvantage. I don't believe we have ever met."

"I have come from Paris. I have met your husband many times. He gave me his address and told me to visit him if ever I was in London."

She was impeccably dressed in the finest clothes money could buy.

"Let's sit down. We will be more comfortable."

"Let me tell you about myself. I'm an actress. I will be appearing in theatres in the city for some time to come. It will be nice to see Andrew again."

"Tell me how the two of you came to know one another," Chovinne said.

"Your husband has many clients of means in Paris. There are many dinner parties. I met him in that manner. He is a genuine gentleman, and he is well liked in our circles. The last time I saw him he told us all he was going to be married. He invited us to the wedding. I was disappointed I couldn't come because I was ill at the time."

"Andrew and I had a wonderful wedding and reception. I met many of his Parisian friends."

"You must be hungry and thirsty?"

"Yes, I am."

"Excuse me, I'll get some tea and tarts for us."

She came back with a tray.

"Chovinne, this is premature to ask, but would it be an inconvenience for you to let me stay for a week in your home? It's so lovely here. I have other accommodations waiting for me in the city, whenever I get there."

Chovinne didn't get an opportunity to respond. They didn't know Andrew was home and standing next to them.

"I see you both finally met. This is quite a surprise, Simone. Have you been here long?"

"A few hours, Chovinne and I have been getting acquainted. Your wife is very gracious."

"She is that and much more."

"Are you on holiday?"

"No, I'm here to act in various theatre productions. I will be here for some time."

They conversed for a long while. Then, Simone reiterated her question to Chovinne.

"Andrew came in, and you didn't get the opportunity to reply to my question."

"Andrew and I would be delighted to have you as our guest. There are bedrooms that aren't being occupied. You're welcome to one of them."

"Thank you both. I am quite tired. Would you show me to my room so that I can get some rest."

"We would be glad to. Follow us."

Chovinne and Andrew returned to the parlor after

showing Simone her room.

"Finally, I can talk to you alone, Chovinne. I couldn't believe it when I saw her here. I'm glad she came. She's a good friend and a good client."

"Tell me more about your friend, Andrew."

"I'm sure you've guessed her avocation by now."

"I have, but everyone has a story to tell."

"Yes, but hers isn't that different."

"She's a courtesan, the demi-monde known as la garde. Simone, along with others like her, loves to scandalize society. Whenever a courtesan decides to ensnare the husband or lover of someone, it will happen. She sells her favors for material benefits, money, respectability, and marriage. They consider it essential to be seen. Simone's high visibility on the Champs Elysees and the Bois de Boulogne guarantee that. Her ambition is marriage to someone who is wealthy, and, in that way, she can continue to live the life to which she has become accustomed."

*

The next day, Chovinne found Simone reading in the front parlor. Chovinne thought this was an opportune time to speak to her concerning William.

"Simone, I have something important to ask you. I ordinarily wouldn't, but this concerns a good friend of mine."

"I know a charming young man, an aspiring actor. He is acting now, but somehow his ability isn't being recognized. I was hoping that you would help him with his career. It would mean so much to him. You are acquainted with many accomplished artists who could give him an audition, if they chose."

"No, they are busy, and they don't want to be bothered. They find aspiring actors a nuisance."

"I'm sure if you introduced him to your powerful thespian friends, and they witnessed his talent on stage, all of you would be highly impressed."

"I won't change my mind."

"That is your last word, then? You won't help at all?"

"Yes, it is."

Since there wasn't anything more to say, and she couldn't convince her, Chovinne got up and left the room.

*

The next morning Chovinne was in the kitchen preparing her breakfast when she heard Simone's shrieks from her bedroom. She ran up the stairs to investigate.

"What's wrong?" she asked.

Simone was standing motionless in front of her vanity.

She turned and faced Chovinne.

Chovinne took a step backward when she saw her and made an inaudible gasp. Simone's left eye was missing.

"I dropped my artificial eye and now it's cracked and chipped. I didn't bring any extras with me, and now I can't possibly show myself in this condition. There is no time to have more made in so short a time limit. I have commitments for stage performances. I will have to cancel them."

"You don't have to do that. I can help you, if you help me."

"You're serious, you can help me, how?"

"I am acquainted with a doll's eye maker in the city. My afternoon is free. I could go to the city and speak to him on your behalf. When I explain your situation to him, I'm sure he would help you even though he is a very busy man."

"First things first, have you changed your mind? Are you going to help my friend?"

"I have no choice. You have the upper hand."

"I won't go if you have that attitude. It's a very small favor that I've asked for, and if you still don't want to help me, then don't do it!"

Simone glared at her as she sat there contemplating

everything Chovinne had said. Then, just as suddenly, her demeanor changed.

"You are correct. I have been extremely pig-headed. I will do as you have asked. Even more, I will bring him on stage to perform with me. In that way, my friends and I will see for ourselves if he has the necessary talent."

"I can't ask for more than that. I will contact William and he and I will go together for his audition. When you tell me the day and time, we will be there."

Chovinne contacted the doll's eye maker. He consented to help her.

*

The next day, they were sitting in his office, which contained many cabinets and drawers, that housed artificial eyes.

Chovinne watched as Simone's eye was measured for exact size. Soon, she was fitted with the perfect size and the right color. He also had extras in stock for her. Everything went smoothly, and they returned to the estate.

Chovinne wasn't convinced Simone would truly help her. She would have to take matters into her own hands and help William herself.

It was a mere few days before the celebration she and Andrew had planned. Today, she would take as long as necessary to find William in the city to tell him about the celebration she and Andrew were having. He was to be an integral part of the entertainment provided for her guests. He didn't have much money, so she would provide him with enough money to buy everything and anything he considered he must have–costumes, props–for any role from Shakespeare's plays he would choose to perform. She would send a coach for him at his address. Also, she would tell him secrecy was important. He wasn't to be seen by anyone on the estate until someone went to get him in one of the cottages.

Among Andrew's friends were thespians. She was hoping perhaps one of them would see and appreciate a marvelous fellow thespian and give him an opportunity to act with the most accomplished actors of his time.

CHAPTER 56

Everything was in readiness for their first celebration. The caterers had arrived early, had taken care of all the details, and would be there for the duration. All she and Andrew had to do was to wait for their guests.

Chovinne had seen the coach arrive with William inside. She went out to give him last minute information that he needed to know.

The guests arrived. Andrew's friends were very amicable, and she felt comfortable in their presence. The conversation was effortless, relaxed, and congenial.

As the evening progressed, Chovinne announced to her guests that she had planned some entertainment for them.

"Ladies and gentlemen, may I have your attention please? You all know that the renowned magician, George The Extraordinary, who was hurt some months ago is now sufficiently recuperated to once more astound his audiences with his magic. He has been convalescing here with us and has graciously consented to give us a preview of some of the acts that he will be performing on a London stage in the near future. You won't have to wait until then. A small stage has been erected for this purpose here in my parlor. The stage curtains will be manually opened and closed as needed."

"Ladies and gentlemen, George is behind those curtains waiting to amaze you with magic acts, along with his assistant, Trevor."

The curtains opened. The magic acts were flawless in their presentation. Chovinne was so proud of Trevor. He handled himself with great aplomb for his age.

The guests stood up and gave them loud applause.

When they finally sat down, Chovinne addressed them again.

"Ladies and gentlemen, there is yet someone else waiting to entertain you. William, will you come in now."

Chovinne wasn't the least bit surprised when, true to form, William walked into the front parlor with a flourish, full of poise and confidence. Shyness was not part of the fabric of his makeup. He gave Chovinne a huge smile and stood next to her. He was wearing a close fitting dark doublet with long sleeves, thick with gold braid, breaches and hose. He had purchased the best clothes, and he looked every inch the proper young Hamlet, Prince of Denmark.

The guests looked at each other and then at him, perplexed.

Chovinne spoke to them.

"William is an aspiring thespian who I think is quite remarkable. I have brought him here for each one of you to make that judgment for yourselves, after you see his performance."

She turned to William and whispered, "Dazzle them William!"

The curtain behind him opened to reveal the makeshift stage and the props that had been placed there.

He delivered line after line from selected Hamlet soliloquies. Chovinne looked around her and saw that her guests were absolutely captivated by his eloquence and intensity. The undeniable inner torment of the young prince was powerfully expressed.

The guests showed their appreciation for his talent by giving him a standing ovation.

Each of Chovinne's guests, except for Simone, personally congratulated William on his stellar performance.

Simone walked over to Chovinne.

"I have to congratulate you. You have outsmarted me. I wasn't serious when I said I'd help your friend. I only said that so you'd help me."

"I had a suspicion that it was just a ruse. You were too adamant about not helping me to have so abruptly changed your mind as you did. It didn't ring true. I knew I would have to help William, myself."

"I want you out of my home within the hour. A coach will be ready to take you to your accommodations in the city."

*

"Chovinne, your friends liked my portrayal of Hamlet so much that they have asked me to appear with them, seasoned actors, on stage, tomorrow, in Hamlet. They have guaranteed that I will have permanent work. I know all of Shakespeare's works, and it won't be difficult at all."

"You planned all this exposure for me. I'm so grateful that you continued to think of me."

"I've been busy, but I didn't forget you. This opportunity came our way because of Andrew. These thespians are his clients and friends."

"It was taking much too long for you to be noticed. I seized this opportunity and hoped they would see and hear the obvious, and they did."

"I will now be able to leave the squalor, that has been my life, behind me. Acting, and the money that I will make, will allow me to do that. Tomorrow, and the many other tomorrows to come, will be so exciting for me. It's always been a thrill for me to be on stage."

"Your efforts on my behalf have made all this possible for me."

"William, you now have what you've always dreamed of."

"How can I repay you?"

"Seeing you this happy is more than enough. You deserve it."

CHAPTER 57

Ben had been gone for a long time. All Chovinne knew was that he was traversing the vast heartland of colonial America. It must have been difficult for him to post a letter to her. She surmised that was the reason she hadn't heard from him.

Chovinne needed some items that had been left at the townhouse in the city and decided to go get them. While there she went to various stores to purchase staples that she needed.

Finished, she put everything in her coach. While she was momentarily turned around, she was grabbed from behind, a knife was put to her throat. She felt the cold, sharp blade against her skin.

Unexpectedly, the man screamed and the knife fell to the ground at her feet. She didn't know what was happening. She turned around and saw the man's arm hanging limply by his side. She was sure his wrist and elbow had been broken. In her haste to see her assailant, she hadn't noticed the other man. She was amazed to see that, of all people, it was Ben!

"Ben, thank goodness you were in the vicinity. I cold have been seriously hurt or even killed."

"When did you get back?" she asked.

"This very morning, there were some things I had to buy.

That's why I was here. I was going to visit you afterwards."

"Where is the man who attacked me?" she asked.

"He ran away. I was more interested in your welfare, than in chasing him."

"Well, I was going home. Come with me."

When she got home, she and Ben went directly to the front parlor. One of the woman brought them food and tea.

Chovinne was the first to speak.

"Many things have happened since you've been gone. Two members of my family, who were coach drivers, were robbed and thrown to the rats in the sewer. Subina has married and is living in New York. Andrew and I are now married. A few weeks ago my coaching service was destroyed by arsonists. Three additional members of my family were murdered in the blaze. I can't stay here anymore."

Ben looked at her.

"You can always go to America."

"I've been seriously thinking about it. I've broached the subject with Andrew. He'll go with me, if that's what I want."

"If that is what you want, I will bring you and all your family and possessions on my ships."

"Where do you want to live?"

"I have extended family in New York. That is where I will establish roots."

"Then, that is where I will take you."

"Will you be prepared to leave in one month?" Ben asked.

"Yes, Andrew has clients in France, New York, Boston and here."

"Chovinne, while I was away, I purchased a retreatist estate on Staten Island. It's beautiful there. The land is broken up into hills, valleys and lush meadows. You and your family can live there for as long as you find it necessary."

"Ben, this estate has been a very special place. I realize that I, along with my family, will never have a future here. I will put an advertisement in the newspaper that my home is for sale."

"I will pack my possessions, say goodbye to my friends, and leave everything familiar for a country about which I have no real knowledge except for what I have read."

"You won't regret it. The country is beautiful and full of opportunities."

"This is a huge step and will be a fresh start for us all. I plan to do my best, and to put forth a great effort for our well being."

The final link to the teacup prophecies was now understood. The ship denoted the monumental change that would alter her life. She would be establishing residence in America.

CHAPTER 58

The decision had been made. Since it was a beautiful day, Chovinne took this as a good omen to go to the cemetery for a final farewell. Leaving her father's remains behind, and not being able to visit his grave as often as she now did, would be very trying for her. The band between them would never be broken even though there would be a great distance separating them.

She knelt down in front of the crucifix, Abbot Paul had made for him. Her voice broke as she began to speak.

"Papa, this will be the last time I will be able to be here. I don't want to leave you, but I don't have a choice. The malevolence toward us has escalated to the point of no return. The recent arson and murders against us prove that. I'm following the advice you gave me that the welfare of gypsy families are first and foremost and should always be of the utmost importance. I've never forgotten that, and it is why I'm leading them in this direction. I have made plans to go to America to live out the rest of my life with the families. Not a day will pass that I won't be thinking of you. I will love you forever Papa."

She left him and walked the short distance from the cemetery to the Abbey. She went directly to the Scriptorium. Abbott Paul was always there at this particular time of day. She walked inside and found him translating old manuscripts that were already in various stages of deterioration. He was so absorbed in his work that she had to call out his name to get his attention.

"My Little One, how wonderful it is to see you! Please sit down here next to me."

They spoke about common interests for awhile.

"Abbot Paul, I have something that's important and difficult to tell you. There is no gentle way to reveal what I have to say. I've made a decision to start a new life elsewhere, because of the recent difficulties inflicted upon us. New York is where I and the families will be living in the future. I know this is totally unexpected."

"Yes, it is very unexpected. This is a sad day. I find this news very distressing. However, if there is anyone who can empathize with your situation, I can. I have seen for myself the diminution of your heritage. I don't want to see you go, but I recognize that you must. You and your family are very dear to me. It will be a great void in my life."

"We can still keep in touch by writing to one another regularly," she said.

"Yes, we can do that, without fail."

She stood up and so did he. They hugged and didn't say anymore. There just weren't any words to convey the depth of their feelings.

She left him with tears in her eyes.

Abbot Paul went back to his manuscripts. He just sat there staring into the distance. There would be no more translations of manuscripts this day, as he, also, wiped tears from his eyes.

CHAPTER 59

Returning home, she found Ben reading in the front parlor. She told him where she had been and how hard it had been to say goodbye.

While they were talking, Trevor walked into the parlor thinking Chovinne was alone.

"Chovinne, do you think you would have time tomorrow to be my assistant? He saw Ben there.

"I'm sorry, I didn't know you had company. I'll leave and come back later."

"Chovinne, I can't believe my eyes. That boy is the one who tried to pick my pocket the day I met you. What is he doing here with you?"

"He came to me looking for work. We had an agreement that if he stole he would have to leave. He hasn't stolen anything. He is such a joy to know. I'm so glad I gave him a chance. I now consider him part of my family."

"Trevor, would you come here please? I want you to meet someone. This is Ben, a friend of mine."

"I thought I recognized him from when I was a pickpocket."

"That is behind us now," Ben said, "Chovinne has been telling me nice things about you. I'm glad to meet you."

"I am also," Trevor said.

"Are you the owner of the ships that will take us to

America?"

"Yes, I am the one who will bring you there."

"Can Chovinne and I be on your ship?"

"I would have it no other way."

"I can't wait for this to happen. I have to leave now, I have chores to do."

"Ben, he looks upon this as a great adventure, which it is. He's been talking about this ever since I told him we were leaving. He's already talking about what kind of adventures he'll have in America."

CHAPTER 60

Trevor was outside screaming for Chovinne to help him. She ran outside not knowing what the uproar was about. Trevor was hysterical.

"Chovinne, hurry to the stable. He's hurting my horse and I can't stop him!"

She couldn't believe what she was hearing. Who would be doing such a thing? She soon found out when she entered the stable. Following the loss of the gypsies, she had needed to employ hired hands to replace them.

One of them was striking Trevor's horse on the legs with a large stick. Chovinne looked around her for something to knock it out of his hands. She saw several riding crops next to the doorway. She grabbed one and walked toward him. His back was turned away from her. She waited for the opportune moment; she lifted her arm and, with one well-placed blow, sent the large stick out of his hands onto the floor.

A torrent of curses spilled from his mouth.

By that time, many of the family had congregated in the stable and were standing behind her.

"Close your filthy mouth, there are children here," she said.

The gypsy men wanted vengeance. They walked toward him making menacing gestures.

"Stop," Chovinne said, "there will be no more violence here!"

Addressing the hired hand, she said, "Leave my property at once!"

She turned to Trevor who was extremely nervous over the fate of his horse.

"Don't worry. I'll send someone for the veteranarian. Meanwhile, we know what to do for the swelling, and we'll take care of it. I believe we stopped that man before too much harm was done."

The veteranarian arrived and, after a thorough examination, confirmed that he had contusions. He told Chovinne to continue what she was doing to care for him and that he would be fine.

They were all relieved. It was very good news for them to hear.

CHAPTER 61

Chovinne lay in bed, her eyes wide open. She had been apprehensive since the altercation with a hired hand she'd had a few days earlier. She was afraid there would be some sort of retaliation against her. She got up out of bed and looked out her bedroom window. It was a moonlit night making it possible for her to see the grounds. There wasn't anything amiss that she could detect. Suddenly, the horses in the stable began to whinnie. Something was dreadfully wrong from the sounds they made. They were truly frightened. She was in the stable in a heartbeat, but it was too late. Reliant lay on the stable floor; blood oozed from his neck where a knife had been plunged inside to kill him. She knelt down beside him and placed her hand over the gaping wound in a futile effort to stop the bleeding. He was very close to death. She patted his head to let him know he wasn't alone during his last moments. She would stay with him. He opened his eyes to look at her, and then breathed his last breath. A companion and friend for many years lay lifeless before her. She stayed with him through the long night.

The sun rose and its bright rays filtered through the stable window. She finally noticed and got to her feet. The family needed to know what had happened. On shaky legs, she started walking to the house.

Dudras had awakened earlier than the others and was

coming out of the house. He saw her walking towards him.

She hadn't noticed him, but he certainly had seen her. She was a terrible sight to behold, as she walked towards the house. Her arms and legs were caked in blood. Her nightgown clung to her body.

He ran up to her.

"Chovinne, what has happened?"

"Reliant is dead. I know the hired hand killed him. It just keeps getting worse and worse. It's my fault for hiring strangers to care for the animals."

"Chovinne it's cold, you're shivering. Let's go inside where it's warm. We can talk more there."

They went inside and sat at the kitchen table. Dudras brought her some tea, but she didn't touch it.

"Dudras, this is such a shock. My horse is dead! This atrocity was personal. I stopped the hired hand from continuing to strike Trevor's horse, and he unleashed his evilness on my horse in retaliation. Now, I have to bear this tragic loss. When you can, will you collect some of his blood and put it in a charm for me? That way he'll always be with me."

Suddenly, she got up.

"Look at me. I have to bathe his blood from my body!"

A gypsy woman, who had been waiting for her, walked up and told Chovinne they had already prepared a hip bath for her.

When she had finished bathing, she went downstairs into the front parlor. That is where Dudras found her. He told her that they were ready to bury her horse.

Chovinne went outside and stood next to the stable to watch as her beloved horse's remains were interred. She couldn't leave this place soon enough.

CHAPTER 62

Chovinne and Trevor found it hard to walk on the ship's deck. The motion and the wet spray made it difficult for them to navigate. She and Trevor laughed as they struggled and held on to each other for firm footing.

"Chovinne, do you think I could climb the rigging?"

"You'll have to ask Ben."

The words were barely out of her mouth when, from behind her, she heard Ben say he would take him up.

Trevor's face lit up. He was thrilled by what he perceived as a great adventure on a clipper.

On the way up, Ben explained to Trevor the proper way to grasp the rigging and the correct placement of his feet. When he reached the top, he waved excitedly to Chovinne watching from below. Ben maintained a firm grip on him. His age and enthusiasm were getting the best of him, and he wasn't as cautious as he should have been. He didn't realize the very real danger of being hurt or dying from injuries sustained from falling from so high a perch. Ben knew it was essential to have a talk about safety with Trevor.

A few days later, Chovinne and Trevor experienced their first bout with heavy weather. The ship was rolling and pitching badly. A fearful lunge threw them clear out of their berths. Books, dishes, small furniture and other items had all become airborne. She and Trevor were somewhat stunned by the impact of their bodies hitting the floor. They both sat up slowly. Checking to see that no bones had been broken, they stood up.

"The weather is really bad; it looks like we'll have to stay in our cabin until the storm blows over. It's safer for us in here."

"What an adventure!" Trevor said.

Chovinne took a moment to look at the situation through his eyes. Every day brought something different to contend with. What was considered a burden for adults was often fun for children.

"Trevor, find any unbroken dishes that we can use, while I spread this tablecloth upon the floor for us."

Trevor brought her what he found.

"Would you please set the table for us, Trevor."

While he did that, she gathered up the food they would eat and set it down on the tablecloth.

"We won't have anything warm to eat or drink today, and perhaps not tomorrow or the next day, if the storms persist."

"Chovinne, this is just like a picnic, only inside. Isn't this fun?"

"Yes it is, Trevor, fun and different."

There was a knock on the cabin door.

"Come in," Chovinne said.

The door opened and Ben stepped inside.

"I can see the two of you are fine. I would have been here sooner but, at times like these, I'm needed elsewhere."

"We understand, come and join us. We are having a picnic," said Chovinne.

"I see that."

Ben sat on the floor with them.

"This is really nice. Being here with my two favorite people, who could ask for more?"

They all talked for a really long time. Trevor was correct. A picnic on board a ship was a lot of fun.

"I really hate to leave you both, but it's time for my watch. We should be in New York in a few days from today. I'll check often to see how you both are faring."

After Ben left, Chovinne addressed her sleeping problem.

"Trevor, I've made a decision to sleep on my bedding on the floor. I'm not too enthusiastic about being catapulted to the floor again."

"I'll do the same as you."

CHAPTER 63

The weather had, at times, been turbulent, but Ben and the family made it safely to New York. Ben's ships took Chovinne, her family, and all their belongings to America's Gateway, Castle Garden, the first receiving station and immigrant landing depot in America.

Inspectors, there, took their names from the ships manifest and began a barrage of questions to each one. They wanted to know their name, age, sex, marital status, occupation, literacy, nationality, last residence, their final destination, how much money they had, if a relative was meeting them, whether they had been in America before, whether they had been in prison, in an almshouse, and whether they were deformed or crippled. Caravans, livestock, wagons and other necessities were scrutinized.

Ben stepped in and told the inspectors they would all be employed on his large estate. The gypsies would manage it for him. Satisfied with the answers, they were quickly processed.

Out of earshot, Ben turned to Chovinne, "We've made it through this first hurdle. It can be difficult if inspectors think that something is questionable."

Chovinne, Ben, and the rest of the family walked toward the ships.

"Chovinne, you'll be amazed at how stunningly beautiful

this island sanctuary is. It can be a virtual hideaway, while yet maintaining accessibility by ferry to the other islands."

"I'm really anxious to see it, Ben."

They all boarded their respective ships. Thirty minutes later they anchored. Chovinne and her family disembarked for the final time onto a new continent, a new home, and a new life.

Chovinne looked around her. It was even more than she expected. It was an ocean infringed land with a strong tidal reach. She couldn't wait to see more.

"Are the caravans and wagons ready to go inland, Dudras?"

"Yes, we're ready. Everything has been loaded and secured."

The caravans and wagons proceeded slowly with Ben leading the way. Chovinne could see the land was diversified. The farms they passed were generously sized. Cattle grazed on lush meadow grass. The orchards would yield their fruit in the fall.

"We're almost there, Chovinne. We are on an upward gradient because the estate sits on top of a hill. Trees are strategically dispersed on the estate giving you all the privacy anyone would want."

Just as Ben stopped speaking, Chovinne saw the estate.

"Ben, how did you do this? It is almost exactly like the estate I left behind."

"When I saw it, I loved it. I knew it had potential. I had a crew of men working in shifts to get it ready for us. The thatched roof came from reeds abundant here in the marshes."

"What can I say? The estate is so similar. You must have loved my estate very much to almost duplicate it."

"I did love your estate, but that's not the reason I did it. There is yet another reason. He reached inside a pocket and removed a folded document and placed it in Chovinne's hands."

Chovinne hurriedly unfolded it to see what it was all about.

A sense of utter peace came over her as she read the contents. All her fears for herself and her family's future were gone. It was a deed that specified that this estate was theirs. They now had permanent roots on American soil.

"I'm thoroughly surprised and completely overwhelmed. Thank you so very much for this beautiful estate."

"Chovinne, you gave me a wonderful new life and changed my whole world. Now, I'm doing the same for you. I'm giving you one now. When you told me that you wanted a new life in America, I made the decision to give you this estate. Earlier, when I visited New York, I lingered on this beautiful island and bought this home and property before someone else did. You needed a home, so what could be better than for me to give you this gift that comes from my heart."

"Ben, so much has happened and we have come so far since we first met. The chain of events that has happened to each one of us has bound us together for an enduring lifetime friendship."

Trevor ran up to them interrupting their conversation.

"Chovinne, I can't wait any longer. We have to investigate this island."

Chovinne and Ben looked at him and smiled.

"Ben, will you come with us?"

"I'll be glad to. It will be really fun for me to show you both your new home."

"Ben, we can only explore on horseback. This island is too large for walking, and it would take too long."

"I have yet another surprise for you. I took riding lessons and I am now a certified horseman."

"How did you do this, and when?"

"I wanted to learn to ride and the horsemen that had been

hired for the frontier expedition taught me. They really put me through my paces. Even if I say so myself, I am quite proficient!"

"Congratulations, let's go saddle up and you can show me all your new-found talents."

Soon, they were all ready to explore their new surroundings. It was difficult to get astride a different horse. Reliant was never far way from her thoughts and he never would be. Perhaps someday, there would be another special horse for her again.

"Ben, there is so much to see that we won't be able to do it all today."

"Chovinne, your estate and all the others were once forest land that was cleared for cultivation. This island supports many species of wildlife. Some very large predators are among them and live in the forests."

"Like what, Ben?"

"I've been told that there are black bears, bobcats, and mountain lions. The smaller predators are foxes and wolves. They are not any less dangerous, though. I have to tell you, this makes me anxious. Chovinne, if you have to venture close to the forests, bring your gun with you for protection. A gunshot will no doubt make them think twice about any attacks."

He turned to Trevor who had been listening closely to all Ben had said.

"Trevor, I don't want you going about alone. This isn't England. These predators mean business, and they will kill you if they feel threatened. You must always use your head and not take any unnecessary chances. You must take precautions to stay safe everywhere. You must promise Chovinne and me that you won't go anywhere by yourself. Can you do that for us, will you give us your word? We don't want to lose you."

"I do promise. I will listen to you."

"After my parents died, I was lost and so alone with no one who cared until Chovinne and the rest of the family, and you, took me in. I now have the largest family ever to turn to if, and whenever, I need to do that. I feel so important."

"You are important and Chovinne and I are relieved to hear that. Knowing that we can trust you has put our minds at ease."

They were all quiet after processing everything that had been said. They gradually ventured even farther inland.

"Look Ben, on that pond over there, so many swans, ducks, geese and other birds."

"There are many more ponds like this one on the island. Also, you will see other wildlife like beavers, minks, deer, and turkeys. From what I've seen so far, there will always be new discoveries for you here."

Chovinne was taking in every detail of her surroundings. As they rode up to a hillside of lush vegetation, her eyes didn't miss the subtle nuance of a light trampling of the vegetation. This was happening on her property, and she would find out what was attracting so much foot traffic on her private land. Just who were these trespassers?

She pointed out her observations to Ben and Trevor. The horses came to a standstill.

"What do you want to do about this, Chovinne?" Ben asked.

"I have to find out why this is happening."

Trevor piped in, saying he loved the mystery and couldn't wait to help her solve it.

"When do you want to start, Chovinne?" Ben asked.

"Right now is a good time. We'll tie our horses here and follow the path down to the water's edge."

They all scrambled down the path. When they reached the bottom, they had to be extra careful on the slippery rocks. They looked around and couldn't see anything amiss.

"Ben, Trevor, I want to look behind the high brush next to

the hillside. There must be an important reason for this path; more than meets the eye. Let's begin there. The branches seem to be growing awkwardly next to the hillside. We'll all go to investigate that disjointed vegetation. Let's see if the branches can be removed."

Each of them grabbed one and pulled it away. They realized that the branches had been placed there to hide something. Upon further inspection, they saw it was the natural entrance to a cave.

"This is the reason people come here," she said, "Let's go inside and see what's there."

They were about to go inside when Trevor stumbled, as he stepped over a large branch. Chovinne and Ben helped him up. To their amazement, they saw that he had tripped over a lantern. The lantern had to have been dragged along by a branch when they were clearing them away.

"Trevor, this lantern you found will help us immensely."

Ben lit it and they went inside. He moved the lantern from side to side and up and down to better view the interior.

"Chovinne, Trevor, look to your right, and you'll see neatly stacked faggots on the cave floor."

Ben lifted the lantern even higher for a clearer, broader view.

"Look, the cave has a charred interior from all the meals that have been cooked in here. I see something else, but we'll have to go closer to see what it is. It's too dark to see it from here."

They walked over.

"Well, well, well. Look at these rowboats. I now have the answer to what this is all about. This is part of the underground railroad."

"What is that Ben?" Trevor asked.

"It's a secret journey Negroes take from bondage to freedom. For decades there has been a steady stream of runaway slaves. Safe havens have sprung up in many places to help and to hide them."

"What kind of havens?"

"They, temporarily, found and still find shelter in swamps, tunnels, barns, attics, secret rooms, churches, and caves."

"Like the one we found?"

"Just like it, give or take some differences."

"That's exciting, Ben, Trevor. My land is part of the Underground Railroad. My land has become a safe haven for runaways. The Railroad uses the same terminology as regular railroads. They have agents, stations, station masters, passengers, conductors, and terminals."

"How do you know about all of this?" Trevor asked.

"I read Uncle Tom's Cabin in London just before we left. Free states offered slaves a permanent refuge until the passage of the Fugitive Slave Act. The difference between then and now is that slaves can be kidnapped and brought back to their owners. The rowboats we found in the cave are used to take the slaves to waiting schooners where ship captains bring them to Canada via coastline routes."

CHAPTER 64

When they returned to the estate, Chovinne told Ben her feelings concerning Sabina.

"Ben, I know there is much more I have to see on this island, but I must go to Manhattan to see Subina. I miss her terribly. I cannot wait another day without seeing her again. Since you know your way around the city, I'm asking you to take me to her shop and home."

"I am at your beck and call. What time do you want to leave?"

"Within the next hour. Is that a good time for you?"

"Absolutely."

The horse and carriage were readied and they left to board the ferryboat that would shuttle them from Staten to Manhattan.

A ferry was waiting for them when they got down to the waterfront.

"Chovinne, I have yet another surprise for you. This ferryboat is yours and your family's to use whenever you have a need for it. I have hired a retired captain and a crew of men that I knew from London to maintain it. They will be at your disposal whenever you need them. I have found that other ferryboat captains have questionable reputations. I didn't want to entrust your welfare to them, so that's why I took these extreme measures to ensure your safety. I have yet another ferryboat at your disposal in Manhattan."

Soon the ferry docked. They hired a carriage to take them to Subina's.

"I see what you meant when you wrote and told me New York was as congested as London. Seeing this, I would think I was back there, if I didn't know better," she said.

Shortly they arrived in front of Subina's home and business address.

"Chovinne, I'll wait here and let you go in by yourself to get reacquainted with your cousin. Take all the time you need."

Chovinne got out of the carriage and took a deep breath before she went inside. The shop's interior was absolutely gorgeous. Shops in London weren't even close to being as nice as Subina's shop. The burgundy velvet drapes, velvet covered chairs, and velvet linings in the display cases cast an elegant aura, but even more than that an inviting atmosphere.

She looked at the clothing. Edward had truly done his best and sent her only the most beautiful up-to-date fashions for her shop.

It was early and there were only a few customers browsing. Chovinne was so excited to see Subina she could hardly contain herself.

She looked around the shop and, finally, saw her at the back of the store placing dresses and other clothing on racks for display. Her back was still to her as she approached her.

"Madam, I need help, could you show me some of your dresses?" she asked.

"I'd be delighted to help you," she said, as she turned around."

The clothing fell from her hands to the floor.

"Chovinne, how wonderful to see you. I can hardly believe my eyes. You're here, you're really here."

They hugged one another very tightly.

"You can't imagine how much I've missed all of you, but most especially you,.."

"How long have you been here?" Subina asked.

"Only a short time."

"How long can you stay?"

"I'm staying here forever."

"What do you mean forever?"

Her eyes were wide with disbelief and excitement.

Chovinne finally noticed she was pregnant and shaking uncontrollably.

"Subina, let's sit on those chairs over there so that you can rest while we talk."

"That would be good. I'm feeling faint."

Chovinne put her arm around her waist and helped her to a comfortable chair. After they sat down, Chovinne asked if she felt better.

"Yes, I'm afraid it was a bit too much for me. I'm having a very difficult time controlling my emotions."

"Take some deep breaths, that will help."

"Tell me more Chovinne, I have to know everything. I'm so incredibly happy. My family is here. Tell me everything, everything. I must know."

Chovinne did just that, beginning with the murders and the fire, wanting to start a new life in America, and, lastly, Ben's gift of an estate for the family on Staten Island.

"I want you to know that Ben has provided us with two ferryboats. One is here in Manhattan, the other on Staten for all of us, whenever we need to use them for transportation."

They talked and talked. Chovinne noticed Subina was getting noticeably tired.

"Subina, I'm afraid all this excitement has worn you down. Where is your bedroom? I'll help you there."

"All we need to do is to open the door behind you. The shop and my home are connected. It's very convenient."

Chovinne helped her to bed.

"Subina, I want you to rest. It's important for you and the baby. When will your husband be home?"

"Momentarily."

"I'll wait until he gets here."

Subina's husband arrived and was also incredulous when he heard the news.

Chovinne stayed for a short time longer before she had to leave. As she was leaving, she told Sabina that she would ask some of the women to come and help her. There was too much work for her to do alone.

"Thank you Chovinne. I am more tired then I thought. I appreciate the help you are giving me."

Chovinne hugged her once more, then left the shop.

"Ben, I appreciate that you waited for me so long. We had so much to talk about."

"It wasn't a problem. Everyone here is very friendly. People passing on the street stopped to talk to me. The time passed quickly."

They returned home.

CHAPTER 65

The next day, Chovinne, Ben and Trevor continued their exploration of the island. She was surprised to see so many small-scale industries. There were tanneries, mills, distillers, blacksmith shops and cooperages. Baskets were an absolute necessity to have. A substantial cottage basket making industry on the island took its raw material from the abundance of reeds from the swamps and wetlands. Accessibility to the ocean waters facilitated sea fishing and cultivation of marine life which was extremely bountiful. Boat building and shipping provided a very lucrative living for the inhabitants engaged in those trades.

They had covered much of the island.

"Have we seen everything there is to see?" Chovinne asked.

"There's one more place left. We'll go there now."

On her way there, she made observations of the landmarks in order to remember the route. Wherever Ben was taking her, it was hauntingly similar to the route she used to access the Abbey, whenever she visited Abbott Paul. It was a dirt lane with large trees on either side obscuring whatever it was that was just beyond them. When they got to the end of the lane and came to a clearing, Chovinne looked into the distance, put her hand on her heart in astonishment, and blinked her eyes several times to reassure herself that what she was seeing was real. There before her in all its significant grandeur stood a monastery. It looked abandoned but still in wonderful condition. The decision to leave had to have been recent.

"I knew it was here," Ben said, "I deliberately brought you here last."

"I've asked those in authority here if they would like to see it occupied again. They said they would. They're also willing to sell the property."

"Wouldn't it be very suitable for Abbott Paul?"

"You read my mind. It would be perfect for him," she said, "I'll write him straightaway when I get home."

"Did you ask if you could go inside?"

"Yes I did, and they gave me their permission."

"Let's all go inside to investigate this beautiful building."

Ben unlocked the door. Together they stepped into a grand foyer. Oak floors led up to the carved main oak staircase. There were stained-glass windows and art decorated the walls.

The monastery had three levels. They climbed the staircase and found at least thirty rooms on the second and third levels. These had been personal quarters. There was also a chapel and scriptorium.

After seeing everything, they returned to the main floor.

"Chovinne, I was told there are lower levels. Do you want to see them today?" Ben asked.

"I can wait. I want to go back to write my letter to Abbott Paul."

They left and returned to the estate.

Chovinne immediately went to her writing desk, took out some white paper, dipped her pen into the inkwell, and began writing.

Dear, Dear Abbot Paul,

This letter I'm writing to you is one of the most special I've ever written. My new home is on Staten Island in New York. Ben gave me and my family the estate where I'm living as a gift. It is truly an idyllic locale.

What is the most remarkable and unanticipated discovery is that there is an abandoned monastery here on the island just waiting for you, if you'll come here and make it your home. It is completely habitable. I've seen it and it's beautiful inside. The grounds are also well-kept.

I miss you terribly. I think of you all the time. Would you consider coming here to live? Being reunited with you once more would make my life perfect.

I know it's a lot to ask of you to leave everything familiar in your life. I believe you won't regret it.

Ben told me to tell you his ships will bring you here. You'll have nothing to worry about.

I will post this letter today. I do hope that you will say yes.

Take care.

I love you.
Chovine

CHAPTER 66

"Chovinne, I want talk to you about something very important to me," Ben said.

"What is it Ben? This sounds serious."

"It is. I want you and Trevor and any gypsy who is interested, to learn and master the techniques of the martial arts. In my travels, I've seen the proclivity toward lawlessness in this new land. Also, I saw what happened to you in London, and it really frightened me. You could have easily defended yourself, if you had known the techniques of self-defense, and that is what I plan to teach you and the others. The training will be intensive in its implementation of all the necessary movements to protect yourselves. Once you know them, your reaction will be instinctive and you'll be able to incapacitate those people who mean to harm you. This knowledge can be used to really hurt them and will give you the necessary time to flee. A word of caution is important. This is an art and is not to be taken capriciously. These techniques should only be used when totally necessary."

"I can't wait to learn. I, too, was totally frightened."

"Good, we'll start tomorrow," Ben said.

CHAPTER 67

"Chovinne, I'm home," shouted Andrew.

Her name resounded throughout the house.

"Oh, my goodness, that's Andrew," thought Chovinne. She ran from the kitchen to the front door.

"What a wonderful surprise! It's been too long for us to be apart. When did you get here."

"It's a very long story. I'll tell you every detail later. I traveled elsewhere before coming home. I had important business to attend to that couldn't wait."

"Did you accomplish what you wanted to do?" she asked.

"Yes I did. I was very determined to get this surprise for you and it's outside."

"Let's go outside right this minute. I have no idea what it could be and I'm really curious."

Together, they went outside.

"Andrew, I don't see anything different out here."

No sooner had she uttered these words when she saw a man walking toward them. Next to him was a thoroughbred yearling. He came closer and closer to her.

"I believe this young fellow belongs to you," he said, as he handed her the reins.

Chovinne couldn't have been more surprised.

"Andrew, where did you go to get him?"

"A client of mine purchases thoroughbreds. He travels to

Kentucky to do that. I asked to go along with him because of his expertise. I told him about your loss. He told me that he would find you one of the very best horses that was available."

She stepped back from the yearling to get a better look at him. She liked what she saw. He had a small, refined, chiseled head, a long lean neck and sloping shoulders giving him a long free stride. He had a deep chest and body, a strong back, muscular hindquarters and hard legs. He was undeniably special; she could sense it. Like all his ancestral bloodlines, he would have heart, courage and stamina.

Andrew interrupted her thoughts.

"Chovinne, I managed to persuade his best friend, his groom, to come here with me to share with you all of the pertinent information and important details concerning your new horse."

"I really love that you did this for me. It certainly will make it easier to get acquainted with him."

"He will stay as long as you want him to stay."

She looked at the groom and extended her hand to him.

"I'm very glad that you came. I look forward to working closely with you. Thank you."

*

Chovinne and Andrew were relaxing at the kitchen table, enjoying a soothing cup of tea after a day filled with excitement.

"Andrew, Subina is expecting a baby in a few weeks. I went to see her soon after I arrived. It was absolutely wonderful to see her again. Her dress shop is also doing very well. I'm so happy that everything is going so favorably for her."

"I have something else to tell you that will really surprise you. When Ben, Trevor and I explored the property, we stumbled upon a cave at the water's edge. It's an underground railroad for slaves fleeing from the southern states."

She proceeded to tell Andrew everything she had learned about it.

"The slaves have to cross this property to freedom. Much like us, it's their only way to a new life."

"Andrew, I have yet something else of importance to tell you. Ben is teaching us the martial arts of self-defense. He wants us to be able to defend ourselves in threatening situations. This knowledge will give us the confidence we need to defend ourselves against anyone with the intent to harm us."

"I'm glad to hear that. They won't be anticipating any retaliation from you, and the surprise element alone will be disarming. It will make them think twice about continuing the attack."

"It's late, we need to get some rest. Tomorrow will be another full day with much to do. I can't wait to work with my yearling. Thank you again for such a wonderful gift."

"I'm really glad to know that you like him. I wanted you to have your very own special horse again."

CHAPTER 68

The greatly anticipated letter from Abbott Paul finally arrived. Chovinne hoped it was the good news she wanted so much to hear. She couldn't endure the suspense one seond longer. Chovinne quickly tore it open and began reading.

My Dearest Little One,

My answer to your invitation to live on the same island with you and your family is an overwhelming yes! yes! yes! The emptiness in my life has been dreadful. There wasn't any joy at all for me, just a great loneliness that wouldn't go away. Now I can tell you that it no longer exists. I am counting the days until I can join you there.

Please give my very best to everyone.

Until I see you again, My Little One,

Abbott Paul

She was exhilarated by his response. Abbott Paul and the monks were very dear to her. Having them living in close proximity couldn't be more ideal.

CHAPTER 69

Chovinne had spent a good part of the day visiting Subina. It was always so good to just sit and talk with her. All too soon, it was midafternoon and she had to leave her to return home. As she stepped outside, she was distracted by some very loud shouting coming from down the street. Always very inquisitive, she had to find what the fuss was all about. As she approached, she saw that the lawn in front of a hotel was filled to capacity with men and women. So many that, to the side, men were standing in their wagons to get a better view. The front porch of the hotel was filled to capacity with elderly men sitting on chairs that had been provided for them. Everyone was listening with rapt attention to the gentleman Negro speaker standing on the porch's highest step. Very tall in stature, this man's physical presence was commanding. Chovinne listened to the fiery passion, eloquence and erudition of this very animated man as he tirelessly denounced slavery. In his anger and wrath, he wanted to educate his listeners to the very real atrocities of bondage, and to inspire them to act against the deprecation of his people. As Chovinne listened, she became aware that each word uttered by him was specifically selected to arouse public opinion to action.

Suddenly, she realized it was getting late and she wouldn't be able to stay any longer. She quickly turned around to leave, and in so doing, knocked to the ground all the packages that a Negro man behind her had been holding.

"I'm sorry, I'll pick them up for you."

"That isn't necessary, madam."

"I insist. It's the least that I can do."

She retrieved the packages and placed them in his outstretched arms. He stared at her with his dark, piercing eyes.

"I hope I didn't damage anything in any of them. My name is Chovinne. If anything is amiss, I will gladly reimburse your loss."

She told him where she lived and gave her address.

He watched her leave. It was the first time, in a very long time, that anyone had treated him as a person worthy of attention and consideration.

Chovinne didn't realize that she had just met one of the most ruthless, notorious pirates of her time.

*

Returning home, she found everyone everyone had congregated in the kitchen.

"Everyone, I have so much to tell you about my afternoon. I stopped to listen to an abolitionist speaker before coming home. This man, among other abolitionists like himself, are very brave people. The core of their cause is freedom. He told a crowd that they make businessman here in the North, who need markets to prosper, very nervous when they speak. They fear secession and a civil war if this issue is allowed too much notoriety. We were told to be on guard for our safety while there, because mobs frequently disrupt many of their gatherings. He informed us that he and the others will remain undaunted. They will still persist in their quest and will not be deterred from their goals."

Chovinne had read her tarot cards recently; they predicted an extremely turbulent time to come. She read in the papers about many very disturbing events. She believed the country would eventually be involved in a civil war.

"I have to find Ben. Do any of you know where he is?" she asked.

"He and Trevor went riding a few hours ago."

"I'll go outside. Perhaps they have returned by now."

She didn't have to look far, since she saw they were coming to the house.

"Did the two of you have a nice afternoon?"

"We certainly did. I showed Trevor some places he hadn't seen yet."

Ben abruptly changed the subject.

"Chovinne, I'm leaving for London tomorrow. When I return, Abbott Paul and the monks will be with me."

"Ben, bring my father home too. I want him here with me. Can you do that?" Chovinne asked.

"I promise you, he'll be on my clipper."

"Ben, that makes me so happy. I don't want him left there all alone."

The next morning Chovinne and Ben said their goodbyes. She watched as his ship sailed away. She knew that waiting for him to return with his precious cargo would be the longest wait of her life.

CHAPTER 70

That same night, Andrew told Chovinne that he too would be leaving the next day for Boston. He would travel the Post Road by coach to get there.

The next day she saw him off. She visited with Subina, then returned home. When she got there, Trevor was waiting excitedly for her. He ran up to her.

"Chovinne, Chovinne I have found something amazing to show you. I saddled a horse for you so that we can leave right now."

"What is this all about?"

"It's a pigeon loft in an abandoned barn on your property. I know this because the birds are flying outside the loft just like the ones you brought me to see in England."

Chovinne took a minute to let this news register in her mind.

"This sounds very intriguing. I wonder who's keeping pigeons there and for what purpose. I'm very anxious to go see what this is all about. Let's be on our way."

The farther they rode into the countryside the more the terrain began to look familiar.

"Right here, it's right here that we turn off the road," Trevor said.

They rode a bit farther on the green turf.

"We're almost there, but we first have to go around these

large trees and high brush. Here we are."

Chovinne looked at the barn. It was in good condition. The glass in the windows was intact. Although the wood had weathered, there weren't any broken pieces on its exterior. Why it hadn't been used and was abandoned was anyone's guess.

"Did you go inside, Trevor?"

"I didn't think it was safe to go inside. I gave my word to you and Ben that I would be careful and would think twice before doing something."

"I'm very glad you did that. There is safety in numbers."

"Let's go inside to investigate this."

Once there, Chovinne stopped and glanced around her to get her bearings. Everything suddenly became crystal clear. It wasn't a coincidence that the loft wasn't very far from the cave. Pigeons are released in the early morning hours. When Trevor saw them, it was midmorning. By then, they had already returned. Some had chosen to go inside; others decided to fly around the loft a bit longer. Since Trevor had last seen them, they, also, had gone inside the barn.

"Trevor, let's go inside, and I'll tell you what I suspect this is all about."

"I can't wait to know, let's go."

Once inside, Chovinne had hardly begun speaking when both she and Trevor were distracted by a creaking sound.

In unison, Chovinne and Trevor looked toward the barn door when they heard it slammed shut. Two Negro men came into the barn. Seeing Chovinne and Trevor there, they walked menacingly toward them. The intense look on their faces was interpreted by both Chovinne and Trevor that they meant to do them harm; a woman and a young man were nothing to fear.

Chovinne and Trevor were prepared. They were confident in their ability to defend themselves. They didn't freeze because that would have immobilized them. Ben had impressed upon them both that the attacker is most vulnerable at the moment of attack. Each man held up a hand to strike them. The hand attacks were met by an incapacitating sharp blow at the bend in the elbow causing them extreme local pain and numbness. Chovinne and Trevor then moved swiftly so as not to be in the range for a second hand strike or kicks from these men. The element of surprise had been so painful and unexpected that no reprisals materialized against them. The men realized that these two people knew defense strategies they had never before seen. They knew that they had lost their presumed advantage over a woman and a young man who had taken command of the situation.

"Don't move!" Chovinne told them.

"Trevor, would you get those empty crates next to the wall for us to sit on. We're going to be here for a while."

Trevor retrieved them and placed them far enough on opposite sides so they would be able to face each other.

"Sit down," Chovinne said.

"I want answers. Who are you? Where do you come from? Why are you trespassing on my property and using this barn for your pigeons?"

There was silence.

"I'm waiting," she said.

"We are free Negroes who work the oyster beds. We are using your property as a station on the Underground Railroad. The pigeons are used to relay information to people who are helping Negroes who want freedom. We wanted to scare you away."

"Well, that won't ever happen."

"I know the pigeons you have are used for communication. I've seen lofts in England similarly used. I'm aware of your clandestine activities concerning the Railroad. I was exploring the grounds and stumbled upon the cave where you assist Negroes fleeing to freedom, and where you provide food and shelter for them."

"Yes, it's true. We do use it for that purpose. I'm afraid that it will be difficult for us now that you have found it."

"You are wrong. You have nothing to fear from us. I understand the importance of what you do. I, and my family, won't do anything to put any of you in harm's way. Go on with your lives as before."

"You can leave now, but be assured that I, and my family, will keep watchful eyes over our property to thwart any potential problems for us as well as for you. I also want you to come to my home tomorrow. I'll be waiting there."

On her way home, Chovinne was so very, very grateful to Ben for having taught her, and Trevor, techniques of self-defense. The outcome would have been very different for them had they not known how to defend themselves.

CHAPTER 71

Following the altercation in the barn, Chovinne hurriedly called a family meeting to inform everyone about what was occurring on the estate. She stressed to them that utmost secrecy from all of them was paramount to ensure safety for the plantation fugitives from slave hunters who sought, at all costs, to take them back.

Anticipation hung heavily in the air. The family was gathered in the parlor awaiting the arrival of the two Negroes associated with the Underground Railroad. They were very interested in what they had to say to them.

They heard the knock on the door. Chovinne opened it and asked them inside.

"Each of us assembled here has been waiting to hear more about this endeavor for liberty for your people."

She led them to chairs and asked them to please sit down.

"Don't be anxious. I assure you that you don't have enemies here."

"One of you may begin whenever you are ready."

He took an obvious deep breath and began speaking to them. He looked directly into their eyes.

"I know you now have some knowledge of the Underground Railroad. The pigeons in the loft are used to communicate with other agents, conductors, etc. I am one agent among many, many others on the Railroad. The cave is

315

but one terminal among a multitude. We take great risks delivering these passengers. We help them escape any way they can. We use wagons and buggies to conceal them. There are many stowaways that we help onto various vessels that navigate the waterways."

Chovinne interjected, "We found the cave while exploring my, and my family's, property. We were quite stunned to find out the property was being used for this purpose."

"It's a very important terminus to Canada and other states."

"There is more. I'm sure all of you have seen quilts in plain view on the island. The quilt codes mean nothing to white people. The only exceptions are those on the Railroad. It has been crafted by us to communicate information and escape tactics. All these quilts contain hidden messages. The types of quilt and the arrangements on them tell the story we need to know; whether or not it is safe to proceed with our plans."

"As I'm speaking to you, slave hunters are prowling around the city of Manhattan. We have conductors and station keepers there, who are always prepared to receive the fugitives at any time, day or night. We harbor them in special Underground Railroad storerooms, homes, several churches, and even livery stables. The interim protectors make arrangements to conceal them. Then, when the time is right, these people arrange conveyance elsewhere. These fugitives come to us very fearful and destitute. It's very expensive to provide food and clothing for them, as well as the necessary money for their journey. Only through the charitable donations of businessmen and professional others, can these clandestine activities continue. We provide two horse teams and drivers from livery stables to take them to another depot and, finally, to freedom."

"You undoubtedly saw the skiffs in the cave. This is the method we to use take them where they need to go."

"I've told you everything that occurs here and our part in it. Now you can understand why I wanted to stop you and the young boy, even through force, in the loft. There is much at stake."

"It would have had a much different ending if we hadn't been able to defend ourselves," Chovinne said.

"I'm very thankful that it was resolved without violence."

CHAPTER 72

Early the next day, Chovinne went to visit Subina. She was expecting her and had a hearty breakfast and a pot of tea waiting for them both to enjoy. They had barely sat down when Chovinne began to tell Subina about the events that were unfolding almost daily on the estate. Subina listened with rapt attention, her eyes wide with astonishment.

"What are you going to do about all that?" she asked.

"Allow it to continue as before. I won't deny these fugitives their freedom. They deserve a chance."

All too soon, it was time for Subina to open her shop for the day's business.

"I'll see you again in a few days," Chovinne said.

Stepping outside, Chovinne decided to take advantage of the beautiful day by shopping for the few incidentals she needed. She was just about to enter a shop when she heard her name called. She was surprised by this, because she didn't know anyone in the city except Subina and her family and other gypsies.

A man was running fast down the street coming ever closer to her. When Chovinne saw who it was, she was totally unprepared.

"William, William what a wonderful surprise!"

"What are you doing here?" she asked.

They wrote regularly, but he had never mentioned he was

coming to New York.

He had to catch his breath.

"As you know, I wrote you that I had formed my own acting troupe. Imagine my surprise, when after a London show, a representative agent of a person who owned a theatre in New York asked me if I would be interested in performing there. Furthermore, I would be paid handsomely to entertain American theatre attendees."

"What a wonderful opportunity to come my way! I've missed you very much. You wrote how much you loved New York. I decided to come here to see it for myself. I, and my acting troupe, are registered here at the Metropolitan. We have a six-month engagement here. It's at Niblo's, the most magnificent one in the city."

"You have your dream, William. No one can for ask more than that."

"I'll never forget who gave it to me."

"Yes, I helped you, but it's your talent that has propelled you to such tremendous achievements."

They spoke for a long time. She hadn't noticed how much later it was. When she did, she asked William to walk with her to where the ferries were, so she could show him which ferry to take when his schedule allowed him time to visit her.

"Ben gave the family two of them for our own personal use. I'll inform the operators that you can use them any time. I hope to see you soon. I can't wait to show you my home."

CHAPTER 73

A month later, Chovinne was eating breakfast when she heard a knock on the door. Upon opening it she saw a man was standing there. He asked if her name was Chovinne. She answered that it was. He proceeded to hand her a white slip of paper, telling her he was a courier, and that the note was from a friend.

"I was told to wait for a response," he said.

She hurriedly opened it.

> *Hello again,*
>
> *Chovinne, I've been very, very busy. I haven't had the time to visit like I said I would. I would like to show you the theatre where I'm performing. Would you come to see me tomorrow? I would really love that.*
>
> *William*

"Tell him yes," she said without hesitation.

Chovinne was familiar with London's Pleasure Gardens. Niblo's, on Broadway, was also a major pleasure garden attraction in New York. It featured a grand theatre. She was going to see it for the first time. William wanted to show her where he performed, and she was excited about that. He had come so far; she was thrilled for him.

*

The next day Chovinne arrived at the theater. It was huge and impressive. It had beautiful colored lights on the outside. The name, Niblo's, in broad letters, was printed in the center of the theatre marquis.

She gave the doorman her name and told him that she was there because of an invitation from William. He escorted her to the main theatre to a seat in the center of the first row, directly in front of the stage. It was all so formal, nothing to which she was accustomed. She was told to have a seat and that William would soon be joining her.

Suddenly, the theatre's gaslights were dimmed and the curtain went up on the stage. There, standing before her in his theatrical regalia, was William.

"Surprise, Chovinne," he said smiling from ear to ear. "This is a special encore performance for you only. Your favorite Shakespearean tragedy, Hamlet, will be performed by my cast and me. Enjoy!"

How utterly wonderful she thought. She felt like she was in another dimension. It was difficult to absorb it all. She was so elated that he would take the time to do this for her. She was mesmerized. The performances were so fine. She was completely moved and involved, much as the actors were.

Time passed quickly and, all too soon, the epic performance was over. Chovinne didn't want it to end, nor did she want to leave.

William came down the stage steps and walked over to her.

"I hope you enjoyed the performance as much as I enjoyed presenting it to you."

" I did so much. You were magnificent as always. Thank you for doing this for me. I feel special."

"You are so special to me. I resolved a long time ago, that if it was ever possible for me to perform Hamlet solely for you, I would seize the opportunity to do so in a heartbeat."

"This is, undoubtedly, one of my most perfect days ever. Thank you again, William."

"The pleasure was all mine," he said, as he sat down next to her. They chatted for a long time.

CHAPTER 74

"Chovinne, Chovinne where are you?" Trevor called.

Chovinne could tell by the tone of his voice that he was excited about something.

"I'm here, in the kitchen." She was having a cup of tea.

He ran up to her.

"Chovinne, look at this!"

He placed the newspaper he had purchased, in the city, directly into her hands.

"Read this article."

She wondered what was so important to him. She began to read the article. It advertised the fact that the people of New York should take advantage of the once in a lifetime opportunity to witness a thrilling, unforgettable horse show that was scheduled to appear at Niblo's in a few days. She looked up at him when she finished.

"Can we go, can we go?"

"I don't see why not. It would be interesting to see this man's accomplishments for ourselves."

Distant memories surfaced in her mind. Before leaving London, she had read about a remarkable horse tamer whose prowess with aggressive horses was phenomenal. He did this without cruelty. He didn't use whips or switches, beatings or bloodletting to weaken the animals. This man maintained that horses used all their senses to reconcile themselves to any object or situation that didn't hurt them. Once habituated to sight, sound, smell, and stimuli of man, it would respond accordingly to him. He was quite a celebrity. She had read that he was showered with gifts from Queen Victoria, the King of Sweden, Czar Alexander of St. Petersburg, French Emperor Louis Napoleon, German scientist Baron Alexander von Humboldt, and the Arabs in the Middle East. In England, he entertained audiences at the Crystal Palace.

*

Trevor woke up before anyone else. He wasn't going to miss this day for anything. He loved horses as much as Chovinne did, and this horse show was the epitome of thrilling importance to him.

Chovinne came into the kitchen and saw him having breakfast.

"I didn't know you were already up."

"I made breakfast for me and for you. I couldn't sleep thinking about what we'll see today. Do you think it will be the greatest horse show ever?"

"I do. There isn't any negative press about this man or his work. I'm as ready and excited as you are. Let's go, then. We have a big day ahead of us."

On the ferry ride, Trevor asked Chovinne about Niblo's.

"You'll be surprised to see just how spectacular it is. It's so grand. I won't describe it to you. You'll have to see it for yourself."

CHAPTER 75

Trevor was very impressed by the theatre's vastness and its absolute grandness.

"This place is huge and beautiful"

"I knew that you would love it," Chovinne said.

"Look at all the people that have come here."

"You'd never know there is a war raging and engulfing the country," she said.

"This man has toured major cities such as Cincinnati, Philadelphia, Chicago, Boston, and is now here in New York."

"This isn't a formal occasion, Trevor. Let's hurry to get to the very first row. I can see there are some seats still unoccupied next to the stage."

They didn't have long to wait. The curtains opened and the participants were in their places. The horse show began. The horse tamer demonstrated, on stage, all the techniques he used to confront a horse with new stimuli. He first used a strap to hold the horse still. Once immobilized, he was able to hypnotize the animal. Animal hypnosis concentrated on the technique of gradually applying positive stimulation like patting and stroking the horse to calm him, to remove the fear that man is a source of pain. That result, though, was not what she was seeing on stage, but something altogether different. This was simultaneously noticed by both Chovinne and Trevor.

"There is something wrong." Trevor said.

"I know," said Chovinne, "I'll have to help before it's too late."

The horse tamer was down on one knee in obvious pain, clutching his abdomen and unable to continue. This was a dangerous situation because he hadn't completed his acclimation of the horse. The horse's ears had started twitching, a sign of worse things to come, if his fright was not immediately contained. Chovinne sprang to her feet and rushed onstage.

The horse tamer yelled to her, "You can't be up here. It's too dangerous. Get off this stage immediately."

"I can handle this. I don't have time to waste arguing with you," Chovinne said.

She did what always worked. She walked slowly and deliberately towards the horse, directly looking into his eyes, hypnotizing him, and conveying that she wasn't a threat and wouldn't hurt him. As always, her well modulated voice and measured gestures were meant to not alarm him any further. Her kindness and caring was understood and accepted as the stress left his body. He stood there quietly and passively.

The owner of the theatre appeared to announce that the remainder of the show would be cancelled. It would be rescheduled with advance notice provided, so that those in attendance could attend free of charge.

*

A few days later, Chovinne answered the knock on her door. When she opened it, she instantly recognized the person standing there.

"Do you know who I am?" he asked.

"Yes I do."

"I'm so glad to meet the gracious woman who didn't hesitate to assist me during a very dangerous situation."

"You needed help. I'm glad I was able to do that for you,"

said Chovinne.

"It was very fortuitous for me that you were in the audience. I've always worried about the worst-case scenario in this line of work. What I didn't think about was that the problem would be me."

"What happened to you?"

"I suddenly felt very ill with severe stomach pain. It went through me like a knife, and I couldn't move. The doctors that examined me gave me many tests and determined that I had a colossal case of food poisoning."

"I'm glad you came through all of that without any complications."

"I've been dying to know. How did you find me?" Chovinne asked.

"I had difficulty finding out who you were. I asked everyone at the theatre. Finally, the doorman gave me the information, after I described what you looked like. He remembered you and your name. Then, he directed me to find and speak to an actor named William who worked in the same theater. Believe me, William was very reluctant to help until he was sure my intentions were real and honest."

"I have to ask the big question. How did it come about that you can do whispering?" he asked.

"It is a gift. I have the ability to render horses into wonderful, docile creatures with very likable personalities."

"Your talent totally amazes me. I will never forget you. You saved my life and the lives of countless people in the audience. One never knows what the outcome would have been, but it certainly would have been devastating. I will be touring more states. If you ever want to see my show again, I have, in my possession, tickets for free admission for you and everyone in your extended family.

CHAPTER 76

Although she kept herself busy, the days and weeks were passing too slowly for Chovinne. Abbott Paul and Ben were constantly on her mind. She hoped that they were safe crossing the Atlantic, and that nothing disastrous would happen to them.

Every day, she spent hours down at the waterfront waiting and looking into the distance to see if she could spot the clippers coming home. Today wasn't any different. Chovinne had waited for hours, only to be disappointed again. Slowly, she stood up to leave, glancing one final time for the day. She squinted her eyes to get a better look. This time, her eyes saw sails in the distance. The clippers were coming home; the waiting was over! A whoop of exuberance escaped from her lips. Jumping up and down, she couldn't contain her extreme joy. The ships came closer and closer to the waterfront. She was ecstatic. She didn't need to worry anymore about them. They were all safe.

As they landed, Chovinne stood patiently waiting for Ben and his crew to attend to their last tasks before they disembarked.

The first person off the ship was Abbott Paul. A huge smile was on his face as he briskly walked towards her.

"I've waited so long to see you again, My Little One," he said as he hugged her.

"I've missed you so much. There are no words that can convey how wonderful it is that you are here with me now to stay."

There were tears in their eyes.

"Life was miserable for me also. Each day I awoke knowing I wouldn't see you and the family anymore, and that made my life an unbearable, predictable routine."

"That deadly separation is over for us now. You are here. That's what's important. Together, we'll make the best of what we have offered to us here. We'll help each other as always. She then turned her attention to the other monks, hugging all of her dear friends, one by one.

Last, but not least, was Ben.

"I'm so happy Ben. I'm ready to burst." Chovinne said, as he walked towards her.

"I know. I can see that you are," Ben said, hugging her.

Before anything else could be discussed, she had one very important question to ask him.

"Ben, is Papa with you?"

"Yes, he's here."

She gave a huge sigh of relief.

"How did you clear customs with Papa's coffin in the hold?"

"There are methods."

He didn't elaborate which meant he wouldn't share the details with her. She knew that if something were to happen, then she wouldn't be implicated.

While they were talking, the crews on each ship had begun the task of unloading the cargo onto the wagons with the horses ready to pull them to their destination.

The last cargo that was removed was special. Ben was overseeing the workers. Her father's coffin was placed on the last wagon. It had been meticulously cleaned for transport. Chovinne went over to it and placed her hand on the lid. She was flooded with memories.

Ben had walked away to allow her private time with him.

"It's wonderful that we're together again. When I left England, I thought I had left you behind forever. Never did I anticipate that meeting and befriending Ben would have resulted in such far-reaching consequences. Without him, I wouldn't have been able to come here, nor to eventually bring you here to join me."

Ben's generosity has made me, and the family, the recipients of a marvelous estate. Having you and Abbott Paul, along with the other monks, living here in a monastery makes my life complete. You will be interred in their cemetery. I will visit you often and so will the family."

Ben returned and the coffin was anchored to the wagon. Chovinne and Ben rode on horses supplied for them and followed the procession as it made its way to the estate.

All the family members came running out from wherever they happened to be when they saw the procession coming closer to the house. There was much joy and laughter as everyone hugged one another. They had so much to say to each other after the long separation. Some time elapsed before Chovinne announced to everyone that it was time to move on with their plans. Everything was in readiness, and it was just a matter of getting into their wagons to accompany the others on the final phase of their long journey from England.

After a brief time, Abbott Paul saw the new monastery, where he would live.

"It's magnificent, Chovinne."

"I knew you'd like it."

"I can wait to see it. I want your father interred before anything else."

"Thank you," she said.

Everyone followed the wagon, Chovinne, Abbott Paul, and the monks to the cemetery adjacent to the monastery. The family had prepared earlier for this eventuality, and the grave had been dug. Her father was again laid to rest. Abbott Paul recited committal prayers for his friend once more. When the prayers were over, he turned to Chovinne.

"You didn't think I would forget this, did you," as he handed Chovinne the same cross he had given her before.

"I knew you wouldn't forget."

She placed it in the soft earth once again. Chovinne turned to the family.

"Now that Papa is safely interred here, we can all tour the monastery."

It was a huge success. The monks were happily impressed.

"There is more. Is everyone ready to see the island? she asked.

"I can't wait and neither can the others," Abbott Paul said.

"The beauty and diversity are breathtaking. You will love living here. Ben's generosity gave me my second heart's delight."

CHAPTER 77

Subina's baby daughter was born in the pre-dawn hours. Chovinne had spent the day and night by her side. Gypsy midwives had delivered the baby. They bathed her and massaged her with oil to make her strong. They then dressed her and placed amulets and talismen on her clothing. The amber locket would bring her luck, protection, and even more strength.

Chovinne was so excited to welcome Subina's child into the family. Subina was very special and her little daughter would be also. It could be no other way. She hoped this little one would have a better life than the one that, thus far, had eluded them.

One of the women placed the baby in Subina's waiting arms.

"Subina, she's absolutely beautiful."

"I know, she's just perfect!"

Abbott Paul, who had been waiting in another room, came in to baptize the baby. It was essential to do this as soon as possible to protect the baby from evil spirits. Her name had previously been determined. The prayers were said, and little Celestia was now protected by this benevolent ritual. Abbott Paul kissed Celestia and Subina. He then left to attend to personal matters.

"Chovinne, thank you for being here with me, and also

for your's and Andrew's consent to be Celestia's godparents."

"Your so very welcome. I'm thrilled that all of us are together again. You and I will watch over and protect Celestia as she grows. Our love for her will know no bounds."

CHAPTER 78

There was tremendous traffic in the streets. Chovinne knew instinctively that something monumental had happened. She bought a newspaper, *"The Trib,"* from a street seller. What she read was alarming. Emblazoned on the front page, in bold italics, was the news she had been dreading to read, ***The Union is Dissolved***. Fort Sumter, a small island in the middle of Charleston harbor, was fired upon because it was a federal presence on Southern ground. South Carolina had seceded from the union.

Chovinne was very upset about the onset of civil war. Living with uncertainty had always been a way of life. This was different. War would affect an entire populace. The chain of events and unexpected outcomes would be extremely calamitous for everyone. Lives would be disrupted and would never be the same.

In anticipation of war, artists had drawn recruiting posters. Printing presses had duplicated them. They had already been placed throughout Manhattan. She rode around, in a conveyance, looking at them. Written on most of them, in bold letters, was the message, **"To Arms, To Arms, Now or Never Patriots Fall In**." Patriotic imagery included eagles with their wings spread to their fullest. George Washington posters incited patriotic fervor. Other famous patriots, as well, were included to entice men to enlist and fight for their country.

The city became a melee of men who were enlisting. They found the notion of war thrilling and glorious. Designated buildings and saloons became volunteer centers. Chovinne witnessed parades and speeches extolling the virtues of war. She saw regiments practicing under tents, preparing to go into the fields to fight soon.

*

After many months, the abyss of being in the throes of war showed on the faces of the people Chovinne encountered on the city streets. A pall of intense anxiety affected everyone. Fear and dread had taken up residence in their hearts. Smiling was something these people had done in the past. The daily onslaught of reporting the war's progress did nothing to alleviate their concerns.

Diversions were necessary to maintain some semblance of normalcy in their lives. Religion was important and going to church to pray for the soldiers and for an end to the war helped them to cope. People attended the theatres and concerts. When the weather permitted, they saw circus shows, played cricket and baseball games.

The Civil War continued to rage unabated. Daily newspaper headlines gave it extensive coverage. Today, Chovinne decided she would make it a point go to the photographer's studio on the corner of Broadway and Fulton streets to look at Matthew Brady's photographic images of the war.

Once inside the studio, she realized that she wasn't as prepared as she thought she was. She took a deep breath. The truth and full reality of the brutality was starkly naked before her eyes. The tortured, grotesque faces of the men who died or were seriously wounded in battle were captured forever in infamy. The enormity of their suffering etched itself in her mind, never to be forgotten.

CHAPTER 79

It was very busy in Subina's clothing store. She, and the gypsy ladies, hadn't expected so many shoppers. Chovinne pitched in by taking temporary responsibility caring for little Celestia. She loved the time she spent with her. She was growing fast, and each time she saw her there was always some new milestone she had recently reached.

Someone came into the store and walked towards her. She couldn't believe her eyes. It was Andrew! It had been months since she had last seen him.

"Andrew, how wonderful that you are here," she said as they embraced.

"I couldn't stay away any longer, so I got on a coach and came home. All these months of building up the clientele. I can say that our stock portfolio is doing very, very well. I have left the investments in the capable hands of someone that I trust. He knows exactly what I expect him to do should anything unforeseen happen."

*

Chovinne was now more familiar with the Metropolitan Hotel. Today, she went there accompanied by Andrew. Inside, she asked the desk clerk for the room numbers of Andrew's thespian friends. She was told that they had rented a large room to facilitate knowledge about one another's schedules.

Walking down the hall to their room, Charlene and Andrew commented on how nice it would be to see them again. They knocked on the door. It took a few minutes before it was opened.

"Hello friends!" Andrew and Chovinne said in unison. When the occupant saw who they were, he shouted the news to the others. They came running over too. It became very noisy with everyone talking at once. Finally, they all went inside to continue catching up on what everyone was presently pursuing.

Chovinne took the opportunity to discreetly leave the room for William's room. She wanted to inform him that the thespians he had met at her home, and who had helped to further his career, were also registered there. She knocked on William's door. It took a few minutes for him to open it.

"Chovinne, what a wonderful surprise to see my very best friend at my door. Come in, come in."

"I have a very special surprise waiting for you."

"Tell me, I'm all ears."

"The thespians who were at my home, to do a special favor for me by judging your acting ability, are registered here also. Their room isn't far from this one. I've just come from there to get you to come visit them. I'm sure they would love to see you again."

"I would like that. Their kindness, as well as yours, allowed me to secure a place for myself in the theatrical world, that I thought would never materialize for me."

"They don't know that you're also registered here. Imagine their surprise when we walk into their room in a few minutes."

"I'm ready, let's go now."

When they arrived, the door to the thespians' room was still open, so they went in.

"Gentlemen, may I have your attention? Look who I have with me," shouted Chovinne.

The thespians walked over to greet them.

"We've kept ourselves informed about your theatrical progression. We weren't at all surprised when we read the rave reviews written about you," they said, "We saw the playbills in the city, and we were planning to catch the play tomorrow."

"I will inform management that you all are to have free admission."

They continued catching up on what was happening in each other's lives. Suddenly, their conversation was interrupted by a feminine voice of someone entering the room.

Chovinne looked in the direction of the voice. She couldn't believe her eyes. It was Simone, of all people!

Her dramatic entrance could rival anything she did on the stage. The woman wallowed in her divaness charm. True to form, she began talking to her thespian acquaintances about her current play. She looked over at Chovinne and William, who had kept their distance. Their faces didn't hide their animosity toward her, and that fact wasn't missed by her entourage either.

Nevertheless, she walked over to them. I've been told that you will be having a party at your home, Chovinne. I can't wait to go," said Simone.

"You aren't invited," Chovinne said, "How dare you think that your past behavior will ever be accepted, or that I will ever condone it? You aren't to be trusted. That's a mistake I made once and will never repeat."

"Can't you forget about it, Chovinne?"

"No, I helped you. I brought you to a doll's eyemaker to have him make an eye for you. You stayed at my home and accepted my hospitality. The only thing I asked of you was to speak on William's behalf to your friends. A simple request, but you wouldn't help."

William's eyes, as well as those of the other men, were

wide with disbelief. They had never noticed the false eye, because it looked so real.

Her friends were also angry at what they had just heard about her.

"Are you happy now? she asked.

"Coming here, you brought it upon yourself, and, no, I'm not happy. Life has consequences. You had to know we wouldn't take this lightly. You chose not to help us; now, we have chosen to exclude you from our lives," replied Chovinne.

CHAPTER 80

Chovinne was concerned about extended family in Charleston. The war was escalating and the blockade was preventing them from getting the provisions they desperately needed to survive. The city lay in ruins. Many homes and streets were deserted. Warehouses that dotted the riverbanks were vacant. Decay was all around. It had become unrecognizable. This situation needed her immediate attention.

Chovinne knew who she could depend upon to help her. She went down to the oyster bars and asked the men there if they would relay a very important message to the men she had met from the Underground Railroad. They had come to her home to speak with her about their involvement in it. She told them she would be, at home, waiting for them. She had donated money for their cause many times.

They arrived a few hours later. She informed them about the situation her family found themselves in Charleston. She told them that she needed their expertise as Underground Railroad agents to help her locate her family at the last address they sent her. She also wanted to contact Ben, who was a privateer in the area, to take them to Canada.

"Are you willing to help Dudras and me get to Charleston?"

"Yes, of course," they said without hesitation.

"Thank you. I'm so glad you will help me. I know that it couldn't happen without you, and the other agents, who know all the best routes to travel on, plus those to avoid, to enable us to get there the best and fastest way possible. Time is of the essence."

"Tell me, what is the best way to start our search and rescue operation?" she asked.

"We'll begin by boarding a train here in New York. It will get us as far as we can go and that is Maryland. I've been told that the rails have been blown up there, and we'll have to find different accommodations. These have already been secured as I speak."

The next day all three boarded the train. As it rumbled along further and further south, Chovinne saw scene after scene of macabre male casualties that were strewn on the ground very close to the tracks. She wished she had stared straight ahead instead of looking out the window. As if those weren't bad enough, she saw a sunken trench, also close to the tracks, replete with dead bodies that were askew.

Negroes were trudging slowly along the fields carrying what were, in reality, the only meager possessions they called their own. Their tired faces were tense with fear. There was only today for them. Tomorrow would just bring more of the same helplessness.

Surviving battlefield soldiers with no agenda before them sat on the roadsides, in the fields, and outside tents stunned into a catatonic state.

Her thoughts were interrupted.

"This is where it ends for us," the underground conductor told them.

They disembarked from the train. Once outside, he pointed to a train trestle in the distance that was in ruins.

"We'll have to walk beyond those ruins to our next mode of transportation. There is a horse-drawn wagon and driver waiting for us there," he said.

The countryside was eerily quiet. A tremendous battle had been waged here. It was quietly understood that this was sacred ground. Nothing was moving; it was devoid of all sound. As they walked further along, they came upon a dead man lying alone on the ground. Chovinne noticed that he had a tintype in his hand. She bent down to pick it up. It was a picture of himself, his wife, and two beautiful, small children. The last memory he brought with him was of them. Chovinne placed it inside a bag with her belongings. Later on, when she had the time, she hoped to find this man's family and return the tintype to them.

Continuing their journey, they crossed a few small bridges. The countryside that lay before them was now changed. There were more trees and fewer open fields. It was a devastated landscape. There had once been a small hamlet here, but now it was gone. Remnants of torched churches, homes, and businesses had turned it into a somber, gray-ashed wasteland.

Finally, they arrived at the place where the horse, wagon, and driver were waiting for them. They hurriedly placed their possessions in the wagon and climbed inside.

"How far are we going?" she asked the conductor.

"About three miles."

"What happens after that?"

"When we get there you will see a church. We will be fed by the members of the congregation. When we've eaten and rested, we'll be on our way to another destination. Another horse, wagon, and driver will be ready to help get us to our destination. We will travel over some pontoon bridges. I was told not to worry, that they are very dependable. We'll be watchful anyway because you never know."

Road conditions were very rough. The conductor wisely stayed away from the more traveled roads, keeping a low profile. As they traveled on, they kept their wits about them for any suspicious activity that might surface. The most worrisome part of every day was wondering if they would find a decent place to spend the night. The conductor knew where to make camp, but nothing was guaranteed. There were many displaced people and the probability of someone finding them who did not have the best intentions toward them was very real. The conductor knew about a secreted area and brought them to it. Sleep was immediate for her companions, but not for Chovinne. Her life as a wanderer had made her senses acute. She knew how vulnerable they were, and she wouldn't let her guard down. She slept fitfully.

In the wee hours of the morning, she heard a noise that sounded like a twig being broken. Now wide awake, she knew that either an animal or a person was out there. Cautiously, she went to investigate. Chovinne came face-to-face with a man who simultaneously spotted her. He came rushing towards her. Chovinne wasn't the least bit frightened. Everything Ben had taught her about self-defense was clearly in her mind. She met the first blow with one of her own. As he got to his feet to deliver more, each one was met with her knowledge of self-defense. He wouldn't stop; he meant to inflict serious injuries or death. Chovinne realized she would have to deliver a fatal blow and she did.

When it was over, she saw Dudras looking at her, a slight smile on his face. His arms were folded across his chest. He had watched everything unfold. The man had met his match. For the conductor, it was an awe inspiring surprise. He couldn't believe his eyes. He wanted to know more about it. He had faced her in the barn but hadn't known all of her capabilities.

The morning had begun badly enough, but, now, looking at the sky, she saw threatening black clouds. They had been fortunate thus far. They hadn't had to cope with pouring rain. Today would be different.

"Even though the weather looks bad, we can't really stay

here. We don't have the luxury of time," Chovinne said, "We'll use the canvas in the wagon to shield ourselves from the rain and keep dry. The driver has his own canvas attire for protection so that won't be a problem. Let's be on our way. I'm more than anxious to get to Charleston."

As they wound their way down the road, the rainfall became progressively worse and worse.

"We'll have to find a place soon," she said.

Their faces peered from beneath the canvas looking for something, anything, hoping that there was a place that would provide them with a shielded retreat to wait out the storm.

"What's that up ahead?" asked Dudras.

"It looks like a reinforced fortification. I hope it's deserted, so that we can use it".

They approached with caution. Looking around them, they hadn't seen anything outside. It could be a different story inside. Getting out of the wagon, they stealthily approached.

"This place would be an ideal temporary retreat," Chovinne said.

Looking at it more closely, she told Dudras and the conductor that she had seen pictures of fortifications exactly like these at Brady's studio. Since she was unfamiliar with this type of structure, having never seen one before, she had asked the tour guide to explain it to her.

He explained that men at war had dug and entrenched themselves inside this type of fortification. They realized how beneficial it was to protect themselves from iron and lead. He pointed to the opening that was buttressed with logs. Next to and over the opening were gabions, cylinders of wicker filled with earth and/or stones, also used to fortify the structure. Sandbags filled with earth over that provided even more protection.

"We might as well try our luck and go see what's inside

for ourselves. Although it's overcast, I believe there is enough light to allow us to see a bit of the interior," Chovinne said.

Together, they went inside. As their eyes adjusted to the semi-darkness, they saw cots, blankets, some clothing, canteens, and cans of food.

"Look to your right," Chovinne said, "I believe there are some lanterns over there and some matches. What good luck for us!"

They walked over and each picked one up and lit it. The added light gave a clearer view of the interior. The cot had blankets on it that were dirty and torn in many places. There were cans of food rations, but not many. Broken wagon wheels, waiting to be fixed by a wheelwright, had been placed close to the exit.

Chovinne was tired, but couldn't bring herself to sleep on a soiled cot. She looked around her and saw some straw. This she could use to sleep on. She had done this before when she had spent the night in the stable tending to a sick animal. There was enough straw to make a comfortable temporary bed. She examined the entrance once more to assure herself that it was well fortified. Chovinne slept soundly through the night.

She, along with the others, awoke early the next morning. They all packed their possessions quickly because time was of the essence. The conductor told them there would be a nice breakfast waiting for them a few miles away. In a short time, they were in a farmhouse eating a hearty breakfast. Chovinne was astounded at the Underground Railroad's organized communication skills. The planning was expertly executed. They were told that more underground operatives would supply them with necessary provisions all the way to Charleston and more if needed.

"Look over there. There is a crowd of people. Something is going on. Let's investigate," said Chovinne.

A vendor was selling newspapers from his cart. She hadn't read a newspaper since she had left home. The predominant news was coverage of the war. Who won and who lost strategic battles, the high mortality rate for both sides, and conjecture about what would happen next. She also read other articles of interest.

They pressed on. Chovinne was getting tired. It took a long time to travel, she was aware of that. It seemed endless, because she was very worried about whether or not she would find her family, and, if she did, what condition they would be in. Just then her thoughts were interrupted.

"Chovinne, there in front of us is Charleston. We've finally arrived," the conductor said.

"At last, I hope the family is safe and well, wherever they are," she said.

Suddenly, out of nowhere, a man was standing next to them.

"Chovinne, this is another of our agents who will take us, in a skiff waiting for us to board, directly to Ben's clipper."

Chovinne was excited now. She was eager to see Ben again. He was the best. She was the luckiest person to have met him and was fortunate that they had become very best friends.

She, Dudras, and the conductors climbed into the skiff. They made it without incident to Ben's clipper. He was waiting for them and helped them aboard.

"Ben, it's been too long since I've seen you," she said.

"Me too, waiting for you to get here has been hard."

"I have to ask you right now. Do you have any information for me about the family?"

"I do, but I'll do better than that. I'll show you."

Her family members came out of a concealed area to surprise her.

Standing on the deck with everyone around him, Ben told everyone what his plans were for them.

"We leave in the morning for Canada. The Underground Railroad agents will see to it that you are safely taken care of. When that is done and you are situated, the rest of us will leave for New York."

The final part of her journey was a whirlwind compared to the beginning. She had to catch her breath. Her extended family was now safe in Canada. She, Dudras, and the conductors were home too.

"Chovinne, I can't stay. I have to return right away. I have a job to do."

"I wish you didn't have to go so soon. I've hardly had any time she to spend with you."

She sadly watched him sail away.

*

The following day, Chovinne was at Subina's home to give her the latest news about all that had transpired on her trip.

Subina's eyes were wide with disbelief when Chovinne told her about everything she had seen. The devastation of humanity and the incalculable suffering had affected everyone in some manner.

CHAPTER 81

The war was finally winding down. People who lived each day in the throes of a terrible abyss of melancholy could now see a glimmer of hope at the end of a very dark tunnel.

Chovinne was going to the city to learn more about what was happening from the newspapers.

"Trevor, I'm going to Subina's. Would you like to come with me?" Chovinne asked.

"I always love going anywhere with you. Most of the time it's an adventure for me."

"We'll make a day and night of it. We'll shop a little, have a nice lunch and dinner, then go to the theatre. We'll spend the night at Subina's house. She knows about it and she's expecting us. Pack an overnight bag to bring with you."

The ferry brought them to the city. There they shopped and ate and shopped some more. Walking on the sidewalk with Trevor, Chovinne suddenly, for no apparent reason, felt compelled to look across the street. She couldn't believe what she saw. Coming out of a restaurant were Simone and Linuet. They hadn't seen her and were crossing the street towards her and Trevor. Chovinne couldn't avoid them. She stood stock still, looked directly at them, and waited for them to speak.

"It has been a long time since I've seen you," Linuet said.

"Never seeing you again would have been better. What

are you doing here?" Chovinne asked.

"It isn't any of your business, but I'll tell you. I'm a Confederate soldier. I have business here."

"I have met this lovely lady by chance, and we have become friends," he said.

Simone smiled at his remarks, thinking she was a fortunate person to have met him. Chovinne was amazed at how these two vile people had met each other.

Through all this, Trevor remained unnoticed in the background. He had spotted a paper sticking out of Linuet's pocket. When people who passed them accidentally jostled them, he immediately grabbed the paper from Linuet's pocket and placed it in his own.

When Linuet and Simone left, he gave it to Chovinne.

"I took this from his pocket because of what he said. I thought it would be important."

She looked at it and was aghast at what she saw. It was a mapped plan by the Confederates to burn New York. The buildings were labeled by location, and the time to set them ablaze that would be most effective. To her amazement, the date for all this to happen was today. Her hair stood on end. She was frightened beyond belief, because she also saw Subina's home and store were also labeled. Linuet was going after Subina because of her tremendous success and her friendship with Chovinne. His business here was to put into effect a Confederate attack, to oversee that nothing went wrong. The most targeted were the hotels, theatres, and the docks along with Barnum's Museum.

She suddenly became aware of pandemonium in the streets. Alarms rang out from everywhere. She saw dark smoke and red flames coming out of windows. It was complete mayhem. The police had been dispatched but couldn't keep the crowds under control. The tolling of the fire bells didn't let up. It was imperative that she get to Subina's before Linuet did. There was chaos everywhere.

People were crazed with fear. It took Chovinne and Trevor an hour just to make their way to Subina's house. When they arrived, she tried to open the door, but it was locked.

"Subina, it's me Chovinne, open the door."

There was no answer.

"This is crazy Trevor, something is very wrong. Linuet must be inside."

Suddenly from behind her, she heard a voice.

"Chovinne, I'm here to help you," he said.

She turned. There behind her was a black man with numerous weapons on his person. Behind him were forty or so men dressed exactly the same way.

"Do you remember me?" he asked.

"Yes, of course I do, how is it that you're here?" Chovinne asked.

"I was here in the city when all this commotion began. I know that you come here often. I decided to come here to help you if you needed it, and you do."

"Yes, I really, really do. My cousin, her little daughter and husband live here."

"Men disperse, place yourselves around this home and on the roof. If anyone comes close, move them back. Use all the force necessary to get it done."

The pirates knew what to do. It wasn't their first fight, nor would it be their last. They had noted everything about the house while walking toward it. Windows for entrance and doors for exits. An intentional fire here would be quickly extinguished. There were rain barrels around the house, and public wells along the street. Some men moved quickly to surround the house. Others opened the windows very quietly and went inside.

"I won't let anyone harm any of you, although I know that you are more than capable of defending yourself. Let's go inside. He had an ax in his hand. The door was smashed in mere seconds, the ax easily broke the lock and the door was down.

Throwing caution aside, Chovinne rushed inside. She saw Linuet with Celestia in his arms. She was crying and trying to get away from him. He held her tightly, scaring her to death.

Subina and her husband were nowhere to be seen.

Simone was standing next to Linuet, a maniacal smile on her face. Having been ostracized by her friends and Chovinne, she had latched on to Linuet. She was enjoying this calamitous situation.

"Why did you come here Linuet?" Chovinne asked.

"Sending me away like you did, away from my wife and children made me very angry. You took everything I had. I know how close you are to Subina and her little girl, and I'm going to take her with me away from you. You will never find her again."

The pirate standing next to Chovinne was prepared for any eventuality. It was a very tense situation. The man was seriously demented.

"Chovinne, I, and my men won't let you do that. Give the child to Chovinne right now. You are surrounded. You don't have a chance of getting out of here unless you surrender the child."

He pulled out a dirk.

"If you try to stop me, I will kill her," shouted Linuet.

He raised his arm to stab Celestia. A pirate, who had been standing behind him all the while, grabbed his arm and twisted it. The dirk fell to the floor. Chovinne grabbed Celestia, who was screaming from fright. Linuet's attempt to kidnap Celestia was foiled. Now, the only thing on his mind was how to escape. He looked around him and bolted for the front door. A shot rang out and Linuet fell to the floor mortally wounded. The pirate she had met had shot him.

They then looked for Simone, but she had fled during the melee.

Chovinne spoke, "You all heard what he told me, that I had created his problems. I won't expound on that; suffice it to say I didn't. He would never accept responsibility for his actions."

A pirate had found Subina and her husband. They were unhurt and very thankful that their daughter was also fine.

The focus now turned to the turmoil in the streets outside their house. The noise was deafening. The mobs were very vocal. They were out to do damage wherever they went. Chovinne was glad the pirates were protecting them all. Eventually there was a lull.

Chovinne took the opportunity to ask him what was on her mind.

"You know, I don't even know your name," she said.

"It's Robert."

"Robert, I have to ask you about your comment earlier. You said you knew I was more than capable of defending myself. How do you know that?"

"I have sought refuge on Staten for many years. I know the ins and outs of the island very well. I know where I can hide and never be seen by anyone. I see what happens everywhere. I saw you taking lessons in self defense."

"The person you saw teaching us is a very dear friend of mine," she said.

"Why didn't you come to visit me?" Chovinne asked.

"I didn't want to intrude."

"It wouldn't have been an intrusion."

She turned her attention to everyone assembled there.

"Listen everyone, I want to thank you all for helping us today. I would like all of you to come to my home for an outdoor party. I want all of you to be our friends. I have wonderful friends I want you to meet as well."

*

It was a few days before Chovinne and Trevor felt that it was safe enough to leave Subina's home. Robert provided them with men to be with them at all times until the furor subsided.

When she returned home, Andrew was there waiting for her.

"My god, Chovinne, I have never been so worried about you. I thought I would lose my mind. Getting here was very difficult. The city was burning. It was chaotic. Just getting to the ferry was a monumental task. To make matters worse, when I got here, the family informed me that you had gone to the city with Trevor for a nice fun day, ending with a night's stay at Subina's. There wasn't anything I could do except wait to see what materialized. Thankfully, everything turned out for the best but the waiting was endless," he said.

"The day you chose couldn't have been worse. The fact that you made it home at all is a miracle. Let's sit down and have some tea. I'll tell you about everything that happened. It took Trevor and me forever to get to Subina's. It was a hair-raising experience. Luckily, and unknown to us, a pirate that I had met, and his men, followed us to Subina's. If it hadn't been for the pirates who helped us, I know the outcome would have been totally different. Linuet wanted to abduct Celestia. The pirate I knew, Robert, gave him an ultimatum to let her go. He didn't and was shot dead by him. It's over now, life will get better."

"I am giving a get acquainted party in a few days. You will meet everyone then."

CHAPTER 82

Eventually the war ended, and gradually the pace of life slowed down. Chovinne's life was better; she was not as worried. She devoted more time to happy pursuits. Chovinne often visited Abbott Paul and the monks. Visits to her father's gravesite were more frequent. She saw Subina and little Celestia often. Trevor was always a joy. William decided to live in New York and visited frequently. Ben was asked to make his home with her, and he said he'd be delighted to live there.

The beautiful estate and surrounding countryside gave her complete contentment. She would enjoy it while she could. She was a realist and knew that life was full of surprises, good and bad. Now, all she had to do was wait for the other shoe to drop. It always did.

The End

ABOUT THE AUTHOR

Rejeanne Coupal has degrees in sociology and counseling. She has taught sociology at the college level and has also operated a private counseling practice. This novel merges two of her main interests, history and sociology. One does not exist without the other. Seeing how individuals cope with the set of circumstances they have been given has always been fascinating to the author.

AUTHOR'S NOTE TO READERS

To preserve the richness and uniqueness of life on the city streets of London in the mid-nineteenth century, I elected to use the terminology and descriptions present in Mayhew's London (Mayhew, Henry. *Mayhew's London – Being Selections from London Labour and London Poor*. London: Spring Books, 1851). Such terms as Fancy Ware dealer, Cheap Fish Sellers, and Buy-a-broom girl capture the realism of the day.